A Charm of Powerful Trouble

A Harry Reese Mystery

The Harry Reese Mysteries

Always a Cold Deck

Humbug on the Hudson (short story)

Crossings

Kalorama Shakedown

A Charm of Powerful Trouble

Emmie Reese Mystery Short Stories

The Birth of M.E. Meegs

Hidden Booty

Psi no more...

*For a glossary of period terms, biographies of the
characters, and a complete chronology, please visit:*

streetcarmysteries.com

A Charm of
Powerful Trouble

Robert Bruce Stewart

Street Car Mysteries

Florence, Mass.

ISBN 978-1-938710-12-4

Street Car Mysteries

streetcarmysteries.com

*To lovers who've been separated
by circumstances*

You'll find a map, glossary, and list of characters at our Web site:

streetcarmysteries.com/charm

1

I've spent a good deal of time puzzling over just how to recount the strange events of that autumn back in 1902. The difficulty's not solely with the mystery itself—though I doubt many have encountered one as tortuous—but also with the outlandish way I came to be involved. It might help to keep in mind Mr. Burns' cautionary words about the best-laid schemes of mice and men oft going awry. But even more essential is an acquaintance with my wife, that chasm of logic familiarly known as Emmie. If you haven't had that unique pleasure, the experience can be distilled to this: in Emmie's presence all laws of physics, and metaphysics (including the aphorisms of Scottish bards), are prone to mutation. So when *her* carefully laid scheme went awry, she got none of the grief and pain anticipated by the poet, but the murder she had craved all along.

When Emmie's cousin Charlie was married earlier that year in Buffalo, we had missed the wedding. In truth, we'd been asked to miss the wedding. Though not without reason. There's no denying that our own betrothal had proven a bit of a cataclysm for Charlie's fiancée, Catherine. It's a rather long story, but you might sympathize with poor Catherine on learning that the celebratory spirit of our wedding supper ended abruptly when Emmie named her father as the murderer of Charlie's. We quietly left town the next day.

That was two years before the present account, and apparently any lingering ill will had dissipated sufficiently that the couple accepted Emmie's invitation to visit us. As was her habit, she'd told me nothing about the matter until the evening before their arrival.

"Harry, I received a letter from Cousin Charlie."

"Oh? How are he and Catherine getting along?"

"Fine."

"And his mother?"

"Aunt Nell's fine as well."

"Any news?"

"Only that he'll be arriving tomorrow morning."

I set down the newspaper and looked over at her. She continued typing throughout the conversation, never glancing at me.

"In town on business?"

"No, I invited them to spend Labor Day with us."

"Them?"

"Him and Catherine, and of course Aunt Nell."

"Emmie, I haven't had much work lately. How do you expect us to entertain them?"

"We've the money in the savings account."

"Drained. As are both of yours."

"Two of mine.... 'Both' is only used when the number is definite. And how do you know that?"

"I found your secret cache in the flour bin."

"One of my secret caches. And what were you doing in the flour bin?"

"Doing an inventory. To make it easier for the fellows auctioning our goods after the inevitable bankruptcy. How many bank accounts have you in toto?"

"Remember, before we married, I told you how my father had taught me to spread my money among at least four banks?"

"Yes, but of course that was a lie...."

"Only that I had four accounts. But it wasn't a lie in regard to my father. It was due to this forethought that he came through the panic of '93 unscathed, and was subsequently able to acquire sole interest in his business. His former partner hadn't been as prudent and was forced to liquidate."

"What you mean is, he took advantage of his partner's bad luck to buy him out at a time of depressed prices. It's ironic that his disloyalty led to his working himself to death."

"My father didn't work himself to death."

"That's what both you and your mother told me."

"*Drank* himself to death, dear. I assumed you saw through the euphemism. Of course, being a liquor wholesaler, it amounted to much the same thing."

No one likes finding out his wife has an indefinite number of secret bank accounts. Nonetheless, when Emmie handed me three hundred dollars later that evening, my feeling was one of relief. She told me it was to be used solely in my capacity as host and that whatever remained after the visit should be returned to her. As it happened, all the theatre outings, expensive meals, and traveling about over the next several days ensured there was little likelihood I'd have anything left beyond spare change.

It was the evening of Tuesday, the 2nd of September, that Emmie told us she had a surprise in store. After a morning of sight-seeing, we'd spent the afternoon at Sheepshead Bay—losing sheaves of ready cash on the horses by covering the wagers of our guests but graciously declining any share of their winnings—and then gone to a Manhattan Beach hotel for an early dinner. So Emmie's news that her surprise would necessitate a late-evening trip across the bridge to Manhattan—our place being just above Prospect Park in Brooklyn—wasn't greeted with much enthusiasm. But, as we all knew, resisting Emmie's plans requires more energy than executing them.

We arrived at Park Row about quarter past ten. It had started misting sometime earlier and the damp streets had an eerie cast, with each lamp radiating its own little atmosphere. The perfect night for an expedition to Emmie-land.

She led us to an electric wagonette bearing the sign "Visit the Celestial Kingdom—Only $5," and there introduced us to Mr. Yuan. He was a dapper, well-dressed Oriental fellow about my age. And there was nothing exotic about his salesman-like manner.

By now it was rather obvious what was afoot. We were going slumming, a popular New York pastime since time immemorial. And though most visitors came expecting it as their due, it seemed an odd choice of Emmie's for this Buffalo branch of the family. Especially given the fragile state of Catherine's nerves.

We were given a reminder of just how delicate they were when that evening's *Brooklyn Eagle* headlined an article about ongoing naval exercises "Montauk Attacked by Naval Enemy." The news that Long Island was under siege caused Cousin Catherine a great deal of distress. She grew pale, then recited something of Tennyson's about the blood-red blossom of war. (I only know it was Tennyson's because she took the time to tell us, immediately before swooning.)

As Charlie and I were helping the ladies board the wagon, a fellow rushed up and pushed his way past poor Catherine. Then, as if suddenly remembering his manners, he apologized. From then on he was downright convivial—joining our conversation, calling us by name, and quickly making us as weary of his company as we were of each other's.

He was an ordinary-looking fellow, of medium height, clean-shaven, and no older than forty. But the outfit he was wearing bordered on the clownish. His jacket combined bright yellow and red checks woven into a sort of parody of a tartan. His trousers were similarly colorful, but of a jarringly different pattern.

It was while assessing the interloper's wardrobe that I caught sight of a tough-looking egg watching us from just across the street. I had the feeling I knew his craggy face. He seemed to likewise recognize me and we exchanged perfunctory nods.

Mr. Yuan—Jimmy, he told us to call him—collected five dollars per head and announced that we were about to embark on our tour of Chinatown.

"You shall see just how the Celestials live! Both the good... and the bad...."

He spoke English like a native—better, really. And he put a healthy amount of drama into it. His depiction of life in Chinatown sounded not dissimilar to that of a cheap magazine I had read as a boy. It wasn't long after we'd left Park Row that I realized we were headed to the southwest, exactly opposite the direction of Chinatown. Not surprisingly, the out-of-towners failed to notice. As did Emmie. Of course, her grasp of geography was so tenuous it still confused her that from Brooklyn one traveled west to reach the East River.

We'd headed down one of the dark streets near the North River and then into an alley. The wagon finally stopped beside an old warehouse which I expect fronted onto West Street, the thoroughfare that ran along the waterfront. As we approached, two Chinese fellows who'd been napping on crates sprang to their feet. One picked up a lantern and the other said something in Chinese to Jimmy.

"Oh, no!" he announced in mock distress. "These men refuse to allow us to enter, unless you pay them one dollar each."

"But we've already paid you for the five of us," Emmie told him.

"Oh, this is an unexpected expense," he assured her. "These men are merciless ruffians. We are in their power."

From all appearances, they looked to be novice ruffians who would have gladly bestowed whatever mercies they had available if allowed to get back to their naps. But the late-comer to the tour was anxious to proceed and generously covered the cost for us all. Jimmy then led us inside and up some rickety stairs to a door marked with several brightly painted characters.

"Behold! The Joss House!"

It was a large room, carefully lit so your attention focused on a wooden figure seated on a sort of throne. There was a fellow sitting beside it and arrayed on the floor before him a number of candles and a jar of sticks. Beyond that little scene, everything was in darkness, as if we were in a theatre.

"Who would like to make a prayer to the joss? He will grant your wish... tell you your future...."

"How much?" I asked.

"Special price tonight, one dollar."

Aunt Nell, who seemed to be warming to the show, made an offering. She was given a lighted candle and a bunch of sticks.

"You must light the incense and place it in the bowl before the joss," Jimmy explained. "Then you make a prayer."

"I wish to know what the future holds in store," she told him.

Jimmy leaned down and took a small wooden slat from a jar before the joss. It had a single Chinese character on it, but apparently an especially articulate one.

"Oh, your future is very good, most auspicious. You will be very happy. But first you must go on a great adventure."

The old joss knew how to please his supplicants, and Aunt Nell was thoroughly imbued with enthusiasm for the superstitious nonsense. Which it was, of course, even if later it did prove somewhat prescient.

Next, Emmie took a turn. She followed the same routine and Jimmy let her pull out her own wooden slat. She handed it to him and he puzzled over it for a good while. Then he consulted with the other fellow in Chinese. He seemed equally mystified. In time, they came to some sort of agreement and Jimmy turned back to Emmie.

"Be prepared for the unexpected," he told her.

This was a little like warning the iceberg about its impending rendezvous with the steamship. When the latter was plunging to the murky depths, the former would be drifting away unscathed and unconcerned.

Jimmy moved us on to the far end of the room and there opened another colorfully decorated door.

"Behold! The Fan Tan Parlor!"

We entered another little theatre. In the center of the room, a single electric light hung over a gaming table that was manned by one of the fellows who'd extorted us at the entrance. He poured out a large pile of buttons and immediately covered them with a bowl. Then Jimmy attempted to explain the game.

"It's very simple, really. Each player bets on a number from one through four, based on what he supposes the remainder will be when the total number of buttons is divided by four. Unless there is no remainder, in which case the winning number is four."

Any game of chance loses its allure when reduced to a mathematical formula, but most at least offer an engaging diversion in the course of the fleecing. It took a good deal more salesmanship on Jimmy's part before he roused any interest in the game. Luckily, he was a bottomless pit of flimflam.

I wasn't sure how one cheated at fan tan, but took it as a given there was a way when Emmie was first to place a bet. Aunt Nell, still aglow from her encounter with the joss, was next to bite, and then the newcomer and Jimmy took the last two numbers. They played a round and Aunt Nell won—surprising herself and, apparently, Jimmy. He seemed to admonish the sleepy fellow handling the buttons.

They had another go and this time Emmie caught the dealer clumsily palming a button. Harsh words were exchanged. Jimmy protested his innocence, but the others were unconvinced. In an exaggerated display of pique he upset the table, sending buttons flying and the bowl crashing to the floor, which, in turn, sent Cousin Catherine flying into the arms of her husband.

"Perhaps we can go now?" Charlie asked.

"No, no. The best part is still to come!" Jimmy assured him. His pride may have been wounded at the gaming table, but the thick hide of the huckster heals quickly.

As he spoke, another fellow came into the room and joined our party. He stood back too far in the dark to see his features, but from his dress I took him to be another tourist. Jimmy greeted him in English, took his five dollars, and then led us through another door. This one unpainted.

The room beyond was lit subtly for effect, and yet well enough that a subscriber to *Harper's Weekly* would recognize at once he had entered an opium den. Several men lay languidly in rough bunks sucking on long pipes. And just beyond, the requisite partially clad white woman wallowed in her depravity.

"Behold! The Opium Den!" Jimmy announced rather belatedly. "A place of sin, and intrigue...."

There didn't seem to be much of either going on at the moment. And while I wasn't sure what opium smelled like, I did recognize the odor of cheap tobacco. The colorfully dressed member of our party had wandered over to the wallowing woman and said something. She whispered a response. Then one of the Chinamen jumped from a bunk, shouted something in Chinese, shot the interloper, and dropped through a trapdoor at the far end of the room.

The woman screamed, then cried out, "My poor husband, shot dead in his vain attempt to rescue me. Oh, what evil have I wrought?"

Catherine likewise screamed, and promptly lost what little of her composure remained.

"I had better take her home," Charlie said. "You should come too, Mother."

Aunt Nell declined, insisting she was still keen on seeing the remainder of the show. Charlie gathered up the quivering Catherine and they departed post-haste.

I had no doubt that the shooting was staged and considered it confirmed when I recognized the scantily clad woman as my cousin Carlotta, partly from her facial features and partly from her distinctive voice, but primarily from her utter lack of talent. Though she has many positive qualities that endear her to her kin, there's no denying she's a third-rate vaudevillian who normally knew enough to steer clear of any part that demanded more than her feeble gifts could deliver.

Emmie had gone over to examine the corpse. "My god, he's really dead!"

I muttered an "Oh, dear," and then greeted Carlotta.

"Hello, Harry. What did you think?"

"Oh, very persuasive. If I hadn't recognized you, I'd have rushed after the fiend who did in your late husband."

"You always were gallant, Harry. Even as a little boy."

It's simple enough to jot down something Carlotta said, yet impossible to convey how she said it. Her voice has a tendency to change pitch mid-word. The two short sentences above involved such a variety of tones that you'd have thought they were delivered by a choral quartette—each voice allocated certain syllables, but none entrusted with three together. A more accurate rendition would be: "YOU always **were** galLANT, Harry. EVen **as a** LITTLE boy." Keeping in mind that Carlotta's **low** notes are delivered in a contralto, her normal ones in a soprano, and her HIGH notes in an ear-piercing attack that invariably frightens children. Since it would be difficult for everyone concerned were I to render all her dialogue as accurately, I'll limit myself to occasional reminders.

"He really is dead, Harry," Emmie insisted.

"Oh, dear," I repeated.

Aunt Nell went over and dipped her fingers in what looked to be ketchup pooled on the corpse's chest. "It's still warm," she said.

Then Carlotta took a dip. This time her scream was thoroughly convincing. "Oh my gawd, Jimmy. He's really dead!"

Curious now, I verified it for myself. Then Emmie leaned down, gave me a peck on the cheek, and whispered, "Happy anniversary, Harry."

2

Even as accustomed as I was to living under Emmie's regime, I was momentarily nonplussed at finding myself kneeling over a dead man in a faux opium den, with my half-naked cousin standing beside me and my wife whispering joyful tidings in my ear. But I soon recovered, and, trying to be helpful, suggested Jimmy send his driver out to fetch the police.

"I'll find a policeman," he replied. "He must pick up the midnight tour. That's always the most popular. And this will be a very compelling show—a dead body, the police... a magnificent show!"

The second he and the driver went off, the other Chinamen vanished like phantoms in the night. The only ones now in the room were myself, Carlotta, Aunt Nell, and Emmie—plus the dead man, whose pockets she was exploring.

"Do you think that's a good idea?" I asked. "It might be best to wait for the police."

"Perhaps," she said. "But I am after all the one who paid to have him shot."

"You paid to have him shot?" Aunt Nell asked.

"Well, not him specifically."

Aunt Nell looked at me for an explanation.

"Welcome to Emmie-land."

"I can't find anything with his name," its chief inhabitant announced. "But he's carrying quite a bit of money. Three hundred and thirty dollars."

"Well, make sure you leave it there," I told her. "Society at large generally frowns on the mugging of corpses."

Carlotta, who'd been sincerely shaken since the discovery that the man had indeed been shot, informed us he was an actor named Ernie Joy.

"I thought the victim was going to be played by one of the Chinamen," Emmie said.

"Yeah, me too. I don't know why Ernie was here."

"Do you know him?"

"Sure, I know him. He's a big act. You must've seen him."

"How is it exactly you paid to have the man shot, Emmie?" I asked.

"Well, it was for you, Harry. Remember on our anniversary I told you your present would be a surprise to come later?"

"I assumed you'd just forgotten to buy something."

"Oh, no. I wanted to get you something exciting. I hate to say it, Harry, but you've become rather listless lately."

"Have I?"

"Yes, you have. And in thinking about it I realized you're always least listless when we've gotten involved with some crime, preferably a murder. So I've spent the last several weeks trying to get you interested in various murders that came up in the newspaper. But you were always indifferent. Even the case of the man found shot dead in a locked room, with no gun to be found."

"Emmie, the killer shot him and left the room, locking the door after himself. And the dead man's son had threatened to kill him four times in the prior week. There was no mystery about it. But how's any of that explain your connection to the shooting of Mr. Joy?"

"Well, last week I ran into Carlotta. She told me how

she'd been performing for Mr. Yuan's tours. Then it dawned on me—instead of finding a corpse to interest you, I could arrange to have one laid at your feet. So I spoke with Mr. Yuan and, for a price, he was more than happy to comply."

"Where'd you get the gun?" I asked.

"From Carlotta. It was just a prop gun. Someone must have switched it with a real gun."

"And the intended victim?"

"That fellow who joined the tour in the fan tan room. He was really Mr. Yuan's driver."

"And the killer?"

"A Chinese farmer. All the opium addicts are played by farmers, I'm not sure why."

"THEY work **cheap**, THAT'S why," Carlotta added.

"Perhaps we should look for the gun," I suggested.

We made a thorough search of the room, but found nothing. The obvious conclusion was that the killer had taken the gun with him.

"So where's the prop gun?" I asked.

Carlotta began feeling around her bunk.

"I can't find it. I put the gun near the edge here. Lou—he's the one who plays the killer—takes it from there, shoots, and then he's supposed to drop it."

"Why doesn't he just carry the gun away?"

"Because I need it for my act. It doesn't leave my sight."

"Did Lou take the gun from your bunk tonight?"

"Sure."

"So you must have put a real gun where the prop gun was supposed to be."

"Where would I get a real gun?"

Carlotta went into a little room off to the side that

she used to change. When she'd finished, I searched the room just in case the prop gun had gotten left in there. It hadn't. About a minute later, Jimmy returned with a beat cop and showed him the corpse.

"If this is another prank of yours, you'll be on the next boat back to China."

"Singapore," Jimmy corrected. "It's no prank this time."

The cop looked us over suspiciously and then knelt down by the late Ernie Joy.

"Looks like you got a real one. I'll go call it in."

When he'd left, I asked Jimmy what he'd meant about pranks.

"When Mrs. Reese came up with the marvelous idea to include a murder, I thought it would seem more authentic to have a policeman appear soon after the shot was fired. Regrettably, Officer Conroy didn't appreciate the opportunity I was presenting him."

"Have you been having a murder for each tour?" Emmie asked indignantly.

"Sure, why not?" Carlotta answered.

"I was paying an extra fifty dollars for mine!" Emmie said.

"Yes," Jimmy agreed. "But see, you have a real murder. It's much better."

"He's right, Emmie," Carlotta added. "Yours was a lot more believable. Jimmy's driver would just fall like a sack of potatoes. Say, Harry, what did you think of my scream? I know the first one wasn't any good. But that last one was a real pip, wasn't it?"

"Oh, yes. Blood curdling."

"I need to remember it. A good property scream comes in handy."

There'd been a marked change in Carlotta's speech over the past couple years. Deterioration, her mother would call it—a strict woman who took matters of grammar, and most everything else, rather seriously. I remember having to forgo cake one afternoon after misusing a gerund. Until she entered show business, Carlotta had spoken impeccable English. But five years in theatrical boarding houses had taken a toll.

"I expect a full refund, Mr. Yuan," Emmie insisted. "In the meantime, perhaps we should agree on a story for the police. After all, the truth might give the appearance that we were involved in the murder."

"Not Aunt Nell and myself," I pointed out. "We'd better stick to the truth. I think that will be fantastic enough without any of your embellishing."

"I wasn't thinking of embellishing, but simplifying."

This was an absurd notion. Emmie is genetically incapable of simplifying anything. If she comes home from the butcher without the intended pork roast, her explanation will require ten minutes and encompass a dozen characters. And an innocuous incident involving one of the neighbors sounds like grand opera by the time she's done with it.

I asked Jimmy if he'd taken pains to set up legally.

"I pay Officer Conroy five dollars every Saturday."

"Very generous. What about his captain?"

"I don't know his captain."

"Something tells me you'll be meeting him in the near future. I hope you have your bankroll with you."

"We'll need to keep Ernie Joy's identity a secret," Emmie announced.

"Why's that?"

"Well, for one thing it will look very bad for Carlotta.

A man she knows stands in the wrong spot and is shot by a gun she provided. And that, in turn, would reflect badly on Mr. Yuan, as manager of the show."

"Yes, better the police not know about that," Yuan agreed.

"All right," I said. "But they'll figure out who he was in a day or so."

A minute later, Officer Conroy returned with a sergeant named Eckel. He was a typical precinct sergeant, a big, middle-aged fellow with the old-style policeman's moustache. He began questioning Jimmy in that sharp way precinct sergeants do when they come across some criminal enterprise operating in their dominion without their having profited from it.

"Who gave you a permit to operate an entertainment here?" he asked Yuan.

"Permit? This is no entertainment, Sergeant. I merely provide a glimpse of Chinatown life for educational purposes."

"Yeah? Why do it down here on the West Side?"

"You see, no one can operate a proper tour in Chinatown just now. On account of the tong war."

"What tong war?"

"The Chop Sing Tong tried to steal sight-seers from the Hip Sing Tong."

"They're fighting over the tourist trade?" I asked.

"Yes. A very brutal court battle. First the Hip Sings sued the Chop Sings, then of course the Chop Sings counter-sued."

"So you thought you'd set up here in the second precinct and corner the market?" Eckel asked.

"Sergeant," Emmie interjected. "Aren't you the least bit interested in the dead man?"

"Who are you?"

"She's my wife," I said.

"And who are you?"

"Harry Reese. We were on the 10:30 tour. It seems part of Yuan's show involved staging a murder. Tonight, instead of firing blanks, the gun fired a real bullet."

It was then that Sergeant Eckel noticed Carlotta. "Who's the baggage?"

"I'm a professional," she told him.

"I don't doubt it." Then he turned back to Jimmy. "Who fired the gun?"

"Lou Ling," Yuan replied.

"Where's he now?"

"Part of the act is that he makes his escape through a trapdoor," I said.

"He should be back for the midnight tour," Yuan explained.

"What makes you think he'll be back?"

"Oh, this was just an accident."

The sergeant walked over to the trapdoor.

"Where's this lead to?"

"Just out to the alley."

"Conroy, check it out."

The patrolman knelt down and opened the door.

"It's too dark to see anything," he said apprehensively.

Eckel gave him a kick of encouragement. "Get going." Then he walked over to the corpse. "Who's the dead man?"

"Just another fellow on the tour," I told him.

"Part of the act is to shoot a tourist?"

"No," Jimmy said. "Another of my people, Wah Lee, is the one who is supposed to be shot. But he was delayed, and the dead man unfortunately stood in the wrong place."

Just then, Jimmy's driver arrived to say that the midnight tour was waiting downstairs.

"There won't be any more shows tonight," Eckel announced. Then, nodding toward the driver, he asked, "Who's this?"

"This is Wah Lee," Jimmy told him.

"Where was he when the shot was fired?"

Yuan queried Lee in Chinese, then told Eckel, "He stopped to tie his shoe."

"Oh, yeah? Why just then?"

There was now what seemed an extended dialogue between Jimmy and his driver. When it was over, Jimmy turned back to Eckel. "Because it was untied."

"You'll notice, Sergeant," Emmie said, "the men are about the same height. The shooter probably just mistook the dead man for this fellow here."

"Not seeing he wasn't a Chinaman? Or the jacket?"

"He was standing half in shadow. I'm sure this was just an accident."

"That will be for the captain to decide."

A police surgeon arrived and began looking over Joy's body. When he'd finished his examination he came over to the sergeant. "He's dead. Shot once just south of the heart. Couldn't find anything with a name." He directed his men to remove the body and then he handed Eckel Joy's effects, counting out one hundred and fifty dollars.

"But I...," Emmie began to protest, but I gave her a little kick.

Officer Conroy returned. "Leads out to the alley, just like he said. No sign of a gun."

Eckel turned to Jimmy. "All right, here's where we stand. This may just be an accident, and you all innocent. Or it may have been murder, in which case this operation will be closed and all your goods and chattels confiscated. That will be up to the captain to decide in the morning." Then he poked Jimmy in the chest. "You're free to go tonight, but I suggest you make good use of the time. Call on your friends and take up a collection. Be at the Second Precinct at eight sharp. And you be there, or there'll be hell to pay."

With that he left us.

"I think they have you, Mr. Yuan," I said.

"How much do you think I'll need?"

"Oh, quite a bit, I imagine. This isn't the Tenderloin. Opportunities for payoffs are few and far between, and the captain may harbor a certain resentment about it."

"You could hire us to solve the case, Mr. Yuan," Emmie said.

"You?"

"Yes, Harry's a well-known insurance investigator. And I'm his able assistant. Surely you heard of the episode of the missing gold? Just last summer, on the steamship *L'Aquitaine*. Harry found the gold in just five days. Hire us and we'll prove your innocence, and no doubt garner you a good deal of publicity besides."

"But in the morning...."

"Just stall them," Emmie advised. "Then you can get the proper permit in another precinct."

"Yes, perhaps that would be less expensive."

"Perhaps," I agreed. "But certainly more dangerous. That sergeant meant business."

"Don't mind Harry, he's prone to these bouts of caution. Think instead of the free advertising. Your tour will prove more popular than the real Chinatown."

Though Emmie's advice was typically suspect, it seemed to appeal to Jimmy's venal nature. She took his equivocal response as approval.

"As it happens, both Harry and I are free to begin the investigation at once. Where would we find the man who fired the gun?"

"Lou Ling. He works at one of the farms over in Queens. He's a cricket charmer."

"A cricket charmer?" I asked.

"Yes. The best there is, I'm told."

"The crickets give testimonials?"

"How would we find this farm?" Emmie interjected.

"You take the ferry to Hunter's Point. Then catch the Steinway car. After about two miles, you'll come to Astoria, where you'll see the silk mill. It's just down toward the river from there."

"And Lou Ling works there?"

"I believe so. But perhaps it's the other farm, up at Bowery Bay. I don't remember which."

Then he hurried off to tap his friends. An unpleasant task, but a sure way to get an accurate measure of their affection.

3

Finding ourselves alone in the warehouse, the four of us made our way through the poorly lit labyrinth. After several wrong turns, and a long detour through a corridor lined with barrels of what smelled like offal, we eventually arrived at the alley where we'd come in. Jimmy's driver and the electric wagon were nowhere to be seen. And since we weren't likely to find a cab in that neighborhood at one in the morning, we started walking toward Park Row and the all-night cars.

"SAY, HarRY. COULD **you** put **me** UP FOR the **night**?" Carlotta asked. "I've been staying at a friend's place and she's already pretty bothered by me coming in late. And now I can't find the key. If I wake her up again, she'll murder me."

"We're pretty full right now. You'll need to take the maid's room."

"With her in it?"

"No, the position's vacant."

"All right, just so I don't have to clean anything."

Even in her present informal state, with her chestnut mane flopping out of a carelessly pinned knot, it was hard to imagine Carlotta doing any sort of drudgery. She carried her stout buxom frame in an almost laughably regal manner. Which, when combined with her singular voice, provided a sound basis for a career in light comedy.

"Could someone have put a real bullet in the prop gun?" Emmie asked her.

"No, only blanks. You can't be too careful with that crowd."

"How do you think the gun got switched?" I asked.

"Can't say. It was definitely the prop gun when we did the show last night. Then I took it home and it never left my trunk, 'til I brought it tonight."

"Didn't you realize it was the wrong man standing there?"

"It was dark."

"Yes, but it looked to me like he whispered something to you."

"Oh, all right. I knew it was Ernie. But I figured he was just playing the part tonight. Definitely an improvement. Jimmy's driver is no actor."

"Of course, Ernie had the benefit of actually being shot. What did he say to you?"

"He just said, 'What are you doing here, Coochie?'"

"Coochie? Do you coochie, Carlotta?"

"Never mind that. Don't tell me you two don't have pet names."

"Maybe so. But we have the good taste not to reveal them."

We caught a Flatbush Avenue car to Prospect Park and then walked the half block to our building through the deserted plaza. Suddenly, out of the darkness, a rough-looking thug came upon us. I made ready to defend the three ladies, or, at the very least, facilitate the handing over of their valuables. But this was no desperado effecting an ambush. It was my old friend Seaman Thibaut Francher, formerly of the steamship *L'Aquitaine*, and more recently part owner of a Red Hook saloon, La Musardine Miellée. A rat hole sort of place that chiefly provisioned passing French sailors.

Thibaut is not the sort of character you can just drop into the stew with a cursory comment, so you'll need to excuse a short digression. He was a short, squat Frenchman, with a round face and dark, oily hair. He knew no English, so we had communicated through a combination of my rudimentary French and his expertly executed pantomime. His talent at this art was his most notable characteristic. His unquenchable thirst being a close second.

He had been on watch when the gold was stolen aboard *L'Aquitaine*. And I used his notorious incompetence to lure the thieves into relocating the treasure they'd hidden. On the concluding day of our voyage, I uncovered the gold. Then, as they so often have since I married Emmie, things took an unexpected turn. There was a sort of mutiny by the three fellows who'd been helping me—Thibaut being one of the three. Eventually, I negotiated my way out of that predicament and was able to turn over the gold to the authorities—less the three bars the mutineers had won through hard bargaining and compelling threats on my life.

When we landed in New York, I helped them dispose of their loot, and was amply rewarded for it. That was a year before the present account.

Thibaut and Emmie, who spoke French much better than I, had a little conversation.

"Poor Thibaut's been put out by his friends," she announced. "Apparently the business hasn't been going well. I told him he could sleep on the sofa."

Up in the apartment, we found a note from Charlie. He and his wife had left for an early-morning train back to Buffalo. No one was terribly surprised. And even Aunt Nell seemed relieved to be rid of the daughter-in-law she'd taken to calling "the swooner." As an added benefit, their exit alleviated our housing shortage. We could now put Carlotta in the third bedroom and Thibaut in the maid's room. I went with him through the kitchen to show him the way. As soon as he opened the door, a shrill voice screamed from the darkness.

"*Not now, Harry!*"

Thibaut jumped back, and the others soon joined us.

"Who was that?" Aunt Nell asked.

"The damn parrot. It's in the maid's room," I informed her.

I went in and carried out the cage.

"*Ohhhh, Harrr-eeey,*" the bird goaded.

Carlotta giggled. "He pick that up from you, Emmie?"

"One of our guests thought it would be amusing to make people think so."

I put it in a closet and muffled its protests with Emmie's winter coat. Then, at long last, we all went to bed.

For me, the respite was a short one. At eight I was woken by a steady drip of ice water on an exposed knee.

"There had better be a fire, Emmie."

"Oh, there is a fire, Harry. A murder is being neglected. And only we can put things right."

"Have you been reading dime novels again?"

"Are you suggesting I imagined what happened last night?"

"Well, it did have all the markings of one of your imaginings."

"Yes, I suppose it did. It's marvelous, really."

Emmie thought a great deal of her imaginings. In

written form they were amusing enough. But living them was another matter. Over the previous twenty-odd months I'd made dozens of visits to Emmie-land. Some lasted just hours, some days. Given the prize plum of an opening she'd been handed the night before, I expected this stay would be an extended one.

As it happened, my work had gone from slow to dead a month or so before. So I couldn't claim any pressing engagements elsewhere. Besides, it's generally a good idea to keep an eye on Emmie whenever she involves herself in police matters. She frequently becomes impatient in a way policemen find annoying.

I emerged from my bath to find her making some sort of intricate chart on a large pad of paper mounted on an easel.

"Planning our lines of attack?"

"Before we can do that, we need to ascertain the facts. Now, since we have a murder where the dead man and his killer *appear* to be unknown to each other, the first thing we need to do is determine all the various connections among the parties involved."

"Are you sure what we have isn't an accidental killing brought about by the coincidental incompetence of Carlotta and the fellow who has trouble lacing his shoes?"

"You're forgetting the additional coincidences."

"Which are?"

"First, that Ernie Joy, a man who resided in New York, would join a tour of Chinatown, alone, and seemingly on the spur of the moment. And when we were taken to a place nowhere near Chinatown, instead of protesting, he was the one most anxious to proceed. No, Mr. Joy was not out slumming. He had some purpose in mind."

"Well, I admit his behavior was a little odd. What other coincidences do you have in store?"

"Second, Carlotta knew Ernie Joy."

"Yes, but they did seem genuinely surprised to see each other."

"I'm not saying they were complicit in the crime. No doubt they were mere pawns for the mind that engineered the intrigue. Mr. X, we might call him."

"What intrigue?"

"The carefully planned intrigue that brought Ernie Joy, a loaded gun, and a willing shooter to that particular place, at that particular time. What makes it so diabolical is that the killer was an unwitting tool. Yes, there can be no doubt that Mr. X is a criminal genius. And most likely unknown to all the others involved."

"Kind of a Professor Moriarty?"

"Yes, exactly. Our work will not be easy, Harry."

"No, and I have a feeling it won't be very rewarding. The odds of Jimmy Yuan having anything left after that precinct captain bleeds him are extremely long."

"Oh, who cares about money?"

"The landlord seems to have developed an affection for it. Not to mention the butcher, the grocer, the laundry...."

"Would we be any wealthier hanging about here?"

"No, but we'd at least be better rested when opportunity finally arrives."

"Opportunity? We've been handed a golden opportunity. Even if Mr. Yuan pays us nothing, think of the exposure. Remember how right I was about the case of the missing gold on *L'Aquitaine*. It was the publicity that allowed you to set up in business."

"Partly. Mostly it was my share of the booty."

"Oh, I feel certain Mr. X must have wealth far beyond that trifle of gold."

"And you expect him to share it with us?"

"Harry, couldn't you show some imagination for once?"

"I've always thought it best to leave that to you," I admitted. "Were there any more coincidental connections?"

"Yes, there is one more. Your connection to Carlotta."

"And your connection to her by marriage. But there's another you don't know about."

"Don't you think you should tell me?"

"When I was in college I was on the debating team for a period."

"I find that rather hard to believe. What do you know of rhetoric?"

"A lot more since marrying you. My tenure on the team was brief. But I remember meeting Jimmy Yuan on an opposing team. Maybe Syracuse."

"He didn't seem to remember you."

"It may surprise you to learn, Emmie, but among upstate college men, a fellow from China stands out a bit more than a fellow from Utica."

"Singapore. Still, your point is a valid one."

"So now that we have the web of connections, what's next?"

"We only have the visible connections. Now we need to find the invisible. I suggest we first visit Ernie Joy's boarding house."

"How do you know where he was living?"

"From a receipt I found in his pocket."

"I thought you said there was nothing with his name on it."

"Did I?"

A few minutes later, Emmie and I took a car across the bridge and then the L up to 14th Street. Joy had lived at a house just a couple blocks from the station. A girl answered the door and Emmie opened the conversation.

"Hello. I'm Ernie Joy's cousin."

"He ain't here. Didn't come home last night. But you come on in."

She led us to a dining room where a fellow and two women were sitting with coffee.

"This here's Mr. Joy's cousin," she told the middle-aged woman at the head of the table.

"I'm Mrs. de Shine," she said. "I'm afraid Ernie seems to be out."

"I'm Lucinda Ormsbee," Emmie told her. "And this is my husband, Oliver. I take it you haven't heard the news."

"What news is that, dear?"

"Poor Ernie was killed last night. Shot dead," Emmie announced. Then she dabbed her cheeks with a handkerchief in the manner of a tent-show tragedienne.

"Ernie, shot dead?" the younger woman squealed. Mrs. de Shine went over to her.

"Where'd this happen?" the fellow asked.

"At an opium den, I'm afraid," Emmie confessed. The handkerchief made another trip north.

"You two better sit down," our hostess advised. She poured us some coffee.

"An *opium den*?" The fellow seemed disbelieving.

"Well, not a real opium den," I told him. There didn't seem any point in exaggerating the faults of the dead. "A fellow named Jimmy Yuan has been running a make-believe Chinatown at a West Side warehouse. I don't suppose you'd know anything about that?"

"Ernie's been headlining at Proctor's 23rd Street for the last two weeks," he informed us.

"Was he there last night?"

"Sure he was there," the squeaky one said.

"When did he leave the theatre?" Emmie asked.

"Just after his turn."

"What time was that?"

"Just before ten, didn't even bother to change."

"Maybe he was meeting someone," Emmie suggested.

"The White Rats," the girl whispered.

"White Rats?" Emmie asked. "Who are they?"

"Just some friends. That's all," the fellow said. He gave the girl a stern look. "A club for show people."

"Ernie's mother asked me to bring back some of his things," Emmie told Mrs. de Shine.

"All right. I'll take you upstairs."

"It's curious the cops haven't stopped by," the increasingly troublesome fellow interjected.

"Oh, they've a lot on their plate," I assured him.

As we climbed the stairs, Emmie asked about the girl who was so upset.

"That was the future Mrs. Joy. Least that's what she thinks."

"They were engaged?"

"Ernie was a little free with the promises. There's lots of future Mrs. Joys, and more than one current act."

While Mrs. de Shine was opening a door just off the landing, Emmie turned to me and whispered, "Divert her attention, Harry. I'll search Ernie's room for clues."

4

I had no intention of diverting the landlady's attention. Blindly following Emmie's directives is a dangerous habit I'd broken myself of long ago. However, in turning my ear toward her, I missed seeing the plant stand at the head of the stairs and gave it a direct hit with a knee. I managed to steady it, but a pot of geraniums that had called it home went tumbling down into a matching plant stand below. The crash of glass and pottery did indeed draw the attention of our hostess.

"Been there ten years and no one's had trouble getting round it," she said to me.

I went down and began picking up shards. Mrs. de Shine followed and called for her servant.

"Leave it for the slavey," she told me.

"I insist on making good." I took out my wallet.

"While you're at it, you can make good the thirty dollars Ernie owed me."

"I'm afraid all I have is ten with me."

She took it, but didn't offer a receipt.

"I'd have thought his sister would be by."

"She's catching a later train," I said.

"Train? She's right up the street."

"Oh, *that* sister. Well, you know her."

Apparently she did. "Yeah. Worse than her brother, that one."

She gave me a conspiratorial smile and then led me up to a room where Emmie was rifling a bureau.

"What's it you're looking for?" Mrs. de Shine asked.

Emmie promptly picked up a hair brush from the top of the bureau. "This! All his dear mother wanted was a lock of his hair."

"Funny way of goin' about it."

"We'll leave you now, Mrs. de Shine. Thank you so much for fulfilling an old mother's request."

She showed us out and then stared at us as we walked down the street. As soon as she went in, Emmie flung the brush under a stoop.

"That was superbly done, Harry. I didn't expect you to cooperate without an argument."

"Anything to accommodate you, Emmie. Did you find anything?"

"Well, I have the address of his agent. And here's something much more interesting."

She handed me a small slip of paper with a cryptic note:

> W'day. Erbe's
> W.R.

"What do you make of that, Harry?"

"A meeting of the secret society of White Rats at a fellow named Erbe's place on Wednesday?"

"Precisely."

I was well acquainted with how Emmie's mind worked and knew from hard experience that the safest course was to humor her.

Our next stop was the Sheedy Vaudeville Agency, Erwin Sheedy, Prop. It was located in a building of small offices on Broadway. We entered a cramped room filled with a motley assortment of would-be vaudevillians—enthusiastic novices, precocious truants, and a girl in tights whose act incorporated a surly monkey. Behind a desk, a blonde sat giving herself a manicure—and us a practiced look of indifference. Not wanting to be saddled with another moniker like Oliver Ormsbee, I took the initiative.

"I hear you need a replacement for Ernie Joy tonight," I said.

"Ernie? Why, what's wrong with Ernie?"

"Well, let's just say he won't be performing tonight... or tomorrow...."

"Mr. Sheedy will be very upset."

"Yes, but fear not. I have with me the latest sensation. No doubt you've heard of her—Greta Glopnik, fire dancer extraordinaire, just returned from her lengthy European tour."

"*She's* a fire dancer?"

"She might not look up to the task, but in costume, she's transformed."

Emmie dug her right heel into the toes of my left foot.

"What'd you say her name was?"

"Greta Glopnik, formerly Brunella Bopswitch of Kansas City."

She went into an inner office and a moment or two later, a big round fellow stuck his head out.

"What's this nonsense about Ernie?"

"I'm afraid he's indisposed."

"Get in here."

As we did, the girl passing the other way tugged at Emmie's sleeve. "Just between you and me, sister, you need to come up with a better name."

"I need to come up with a better something, certainly."

The door closed behind us. This time, Emmie didn't give me a chance.

"Hello, Mr. Sheedy. I'm Emily Reese and this is my husband, Harry. We've been hired to investigate last night's tragedy."

"Which tragedy, the dancing dogs playing Keith's that turned up foaming at the mouth, or the sharpshooter who ended her act by nailing her husband between the legs at the Orpheum?"

"I was speaking of Ernie Joy's death."

"Death? Don't kid me. I'm not in the mood."

"I assure you, he's very dead."

"That son of a bitch."

"Mr. Sheedy!"

"What?"

"That language."

He turned to me. "Is she on the level?"

"Rarely. But Ernie Joy seemed very dead. And the police surgeon concurred."

"When did this happen?"

"Sometime around midnight."

"Why wasn't it in the papers?"

"Can't say."

"What we'd like to know, Mr. Sheedy, is who would want to kill him?" Emmie asked.

"How should I know? Where was he killed?"

This necessitated recounting the convoluted goings on of the previous evening. And I must say, Mr. Sheedy gave us his rapt attention. I suppose it appealed to his theatrical temperament.

"So was it an accident?" he asked.

"It was made to look that way," Emmie said. "But only a fool would believe that it was. So I return to my question, who would want Ernie Joy dead? You must know something of his associations."

"I'm not his social secretary."

"What about his wife?"

"Which one?"

"How many were there?"

"Two, legally. But he's still paying them—why would they kill him?"

"Why did you say 'legally'?"

"It was a little ploy of Ernie's. He'd take up with some girl and then take her to get married out on Long Island. Some friend of his would perform the ceremony. A week later, he'd dump the girl and let her know what was what."

"And you carried on business with such a man?" Emmie was indignant.

"Well, as long as he kept it out of the papers, I didn't see any harm in it. These were show girls. So what's this I hear about you being a fire dancer?"

"One of the best," I told him.

"My husband is playing horse, Mr. Sheedy. I am an authoress. What can you tell us about the White Rats?"

"The White Rats are dead."

"Ernie Joy is dead," Emmie said. "But we have reason to believe the White Rats are still scurrying about."

"Where'd you hear that?"

"We have our sources. Was Ernie Joy a member?"

"Ernie? He didn't need them."

"I see. Do you know who Erbe is?"

"Erbe who?"

"That, I can't say."

"I don't know any Erbes," he told her. "I got three hours to find a headliner. I don't have any more time for you."

He shooed us out and called in the girl. "Sorry it didn't work out, honey," she told Emmie. "It's that name."

While we headed for home, Emmie gave me her assessment of the situation.

"I think we're on to something, Harry."

"Are we?"

"Did you notice how shaken he became at the mention of the White Rats? He must live in fear of them."

"Looked more like annoyance to me."

"Oh, no. Definitely fear. Just like at the boarding house. I imagine the White Rats are ruthless assassins."

"And Ernie Joy was killed for revealing the secret handshake?"

"More likely, Mr. Joy was working as a secret government agent to expose the ring."

"Is it a sartorial quirk of secret government agents to go about in loud plaids? And if the White Rats killed him, where's that leave Mr. X?"

"Oh, Mr. X is alive and well."

"Well, I'm sure he'll be relieved to hear that. What's the next order of business?"

"We go question our own Mrs. Joy."

"If you're referring to Carlotta, I suggest we stop by a drug store for some cotton before having any lengthy discourse."

She laughed at my suggestion, but when I informed her it was normal procedure among Carlotta's own family, she agreed.

We arrived home to find our guests at the table finishing what looked to have been a very full breakfast. They'd brought the damned parrot back out and Thibaut had taken to teaching it French. He paced back and forth in imitation of the bird, then squawked, "*Ne mords pas si fort, Har-ree!*"

"What did he say?" Aunt Nell asked.

"Don't BITE so **hard**, HarRY!" Carlotta told her.

The three of them shared a laugh, too engrossed to notice our entry.

"Oh, I rarely make that complaint," Emmie divulged.

They spun about. Then all four of them had another laugh. I returned the bird to the closet and this time locked the door. I gave Thibaut a stern look, but he responded with his customary impish smile. It was always difficult to stay angry at Thibaut. Ten minutes after he and his fellow mutineers threatened me with a watery grave, all was forgiven.

In contrition, he offered to prepare omelets for Emmie and me and left for the kitchen humming a ditty.

"Thibaut's an excellent cook, Emmie," Aunt Nell told her. "You should ask him to stay on."

"I'm afraid we couldn't afford to keep him in wine," I said.

She went off to attend to some part of her toilette and Emmie turned her attention to Carlotta.

"I hope it isn't too sensitive a subject, dear, but were you married to Ernie Joy?"

"Who wasn't? But it was only for a month. Last spring."

"We heard he'd developed a habit of tricking young girls into thinking he'd married them," I said.

"Oh, maybe sometimes. I knew what it was about. I ain't no young girl."

"Then why did you go along with it?" Emmie asked.

"Look, there're two kinds of actors. Some aren't much

different from other people. They save their money, go to church on Sunday, maybe even raise a family on the road. Then there are people like Ernie and me. We put all that stuff off 'til later. Now's for having fun. My act broke up and I was out of work, and you can guess what that means. For a month I was Mrs. Joy, while Ernie did the western circuit. And Ernie lived high, when he had it. We both had a good time. When we got back here, it was done."

"You started a new act?"

"I got a legit part in the third company of *Lady of Lyons*. *Loins of the Lady* we called it. They canceled us in Louisville. I had to leg my way back in the chorus of Billy Watson's Burlesquers."

"So you didn't harbor any hard feelings toward Ernie. But what about his other wives?" Emmie asked.

"Who knows? There are some real hot-heads out there."

"We heard about one who shot her husband on stage last night," I mentioned.

"Yeah, I saw in the paper. Good old Desirée. I bet I know where she shot him, too."

"The Orpheum, I believe," Emmie told her.

"The Orpheum. That's a good one, Emmie. I'll have to remember that. When I was with Billy, I had to kick a Philadelphia stagehand in the Orpheum. I bet he's still feeling it."

"What about Ernie's real wives?" I asked. "Do you think he was paying them alimony?"

"When he was flush he'd send them something, but he probably owed them more."

"Was his life insured?"

"He told me he didn't see the point. Why would he want to make himself worth more dead than alive?"

"Sound reasoning," I said. Emmie caught me looking her way.

Before she could offer a retort, Thibaut emerged from the kitchen with our omelets, and then, through gesture alone, inquired solicitously of Carlotta if she wanted another. Carlotta responded likewise, opening her mouth wide and making like a hungry baby bird. Apparently they'd already developed a rapport, and this mode of communication was its foundation. And playful flirtation its only function, as Carlotta spoke French as well as Emmie.

"What can you tell us about the White Rats?" Emmie asked her.

"The White Rats? They're the vaudeville union. They won that big strike last year. You remember."

"What strike?"

"The strike against United Booking. You see, the way it works in vaud, to get into the big time, you have to go through the agents in United Booking. Which is really run by the same people who own the theatres, Keith and Albee, and all them. They had a sweet setup where the act had to pay a fee to United Booking. So instead of paying you $50 a week, they were only paying you $45, cuz they got $5 back."

"So the Rats won?" I asked.

"Yeah, they won that round. They're still trying to get rid of cancellation clauses, and how they can change your tour when you're out on the road. You think you're going from Buffalo to Rochester, but they send you to Boston and you lose a day's work."

"Why's it such a secret then?" Emmie asked.

"Cuz the circuit will blackball anyone caught in it. They learned from the last time."

"Was Ernie a member?"

"Ernie? I doubt it."

"What do you make of this?" Emmie handed her the note she'd found. "It was in Ernie's room."

"Who's Erbe?"

"We were hoping you could tell us that. What about the W.R.?"

"Search me. That what got you thinking Ernie was a White Rat?"

"Yes, partly. Someone at his boarding house mentioned them, too."

"Ernie only had time for two things, vaud and women. The last one I saw him with was a real swell. He didn't even introduce me, crossed the street just to avoid it."

"Another actress?"

"I doubt it, she seemed above work."

Thibaut rejoined us and when we'd all finished eating, both he and Carlotta went off to their respective rooms.

5

The most confounding characteristic of Emmie's notions is their perishability. No sooner does she construct some outlandish scenario than she abandons it. And so it was that afternoon when I attempted to chide her about her theory that the White Rats were a gang of ruthless assassins.

"Assassins? What are you talking about, Harry?"

"Never mind. I must have dreamt it. Who's the suspect of the hour?"

"What about Carlotta?"

"You think she wanted to kill Ernie?"

"Perhaps she was more upset with him than she's let on. She could have quite easily invited him there."

"Yes," I said. "But she was as surprised as the rest of us that he was dead."

"That could just have been a carefully rehearsed pose."

"Only if Carlotta had the talent to pull it off," I pointed out. "I have another theory. What if one of the other Chinamen had some grievance with the fellow who was supposed to have played the victim?"

"The man who stopped to tie his shoe?"

"Yes. Maybe they had their eye on the same girl."

"Or better yet, there was an ancient feud between their families."

"Ancient feud?"

"Yes. Dating back to the fifth century, when a wicked and depraved landowner absconded with the beautiful young wife of the village blacksmith. He took her to his mountaintop retreat, where her cries for help couldn't be heard."

"Then she escaped, running across the moors. At which point he sent his pack of giant canines after her. I noticed *The Hound of the Baskervilles* on your night stand, Emmie."

"It needn't follow that line exactly."

"There is a much simpler explanation. The gun was there as the result of accident."

"How is that possible?" she asked.

"Carlotta may have picked up the wrong gun some-place and not realized it. And Lou Ling probably wouldn't have noticed until he'd fired it."

"But if she hasn't been working, where else would she have been using it?"

I couldn't answer that.

"Harry, suppose someone else knew about Carlotta's job there. Someone who wanted Ernie killed. That person could have switched guns and then sent a message to Ernie summoning him to meet Carlotta."

"Who do you have in mind?"

"Remember Carlotta said she'd been staying with a friend? What if this friend was also someone Ernie had toyed with?"

"As a species, the jilted lover usually prefers some-thing more direct, like a butcher knife to the kidneys. But I suppose that's possible," I admitted.

"It's more than possible."

"By the way, whatever happened to Mr. X?"

"I've put him on the back burner for now."

"Yes, let's keep him on a slow simmer. And in the meantime?"

"We see if we can locate Lou Ling at the Chinese farm in Astoria."

"How will we know him when we do? All I saw was his back, and it was plenty dark."

"It certainly won't be easy. Especially not knowing the language."

Aunt Nell came out and joined us and Emmie told her about our mission to Astoria.

"I think I'd like to come along, too. I've never seen a Chinese farm."

Then a few minutes later Thibaut appeared and poured himself some coffee.

"Thibaut!" Emmie said excitedly.

As she and Aunt Nell helped him clean up the spilt coffee, she conversed with him in French. Her proposal was greeted with enthusiasm.

"Thibaut's consented to accompany us as an interpreter," she announced.

"*Thibaut* knows Chinese?" I asked.

"No, but he's a master of pantomime. That will have to do."

Just as we were preparing to leave, Carlotta appeared in full show-girl regalia.

"Where are you off to?" I asked.

"To **the** SLAVE marKET. **With** Jimmy's PLACE closed **down**, I NEED to **find** a JOB. WISH me LUCK!"

Her final words were delivered as she headed out the door and were instantly answered by the howling of an infant in one of the neighboring apartments. A little later the four of us made our way to a car stop.

The transport network of New York is one of the most efficient in all the world—provided one's objective lies in lower Manhattan. But should you want to get from

Prospect Park, Brooklyn, to Astoria, Queens, you must gird yourself for a long journey of ever-increasing dreariness. The trip involved three car routes and took up a good part of the afternoon. Emmie had Thibaut sit beside her so she could instruct him as to what she had in mind. Meanwhile, Aunt Nell and I took a seat a few rows back.

I suppose it's time I offer a fuller picture of Emmie's aunt. At the time of the story, she must have been in her early to mid-forties. But even sitting as close as I was just then, she looked no more than thirty-five. If anything, younger than when we'd first met two years before. She wore her jet-black hair in a casual but carefully fashioned coiffure. Her attire was similarly stylish, yet never ostentatious. The fragrance she wore seemed hers alone, and she used just barely enough of it. And in conversation she was always charming, no matter what the topic.

I know it sounds as if I'm waxing on a bit here. The infatuation may have been partly due to the fact that she compared so favorably to the Williamsburg riverfront, and her scent to that of the factories that lined it. But I suspect it mainly came down to the fact that in all the qualities I've enumerated, she was so unlike Emmie—who rarely endeavored to please anyone but herself.

"Is it true a man was killed in my room, Harry?"

"Oh, yes. Electrocuted."

"Emmie told me she still wonders if you were behind it. That you may have killed him in a jealous rage."

"I wasn't even in town. The parrot chewed on the light cord, the poor fellow didn't notice, and, well, that was that. Haven't you learned not to pay too much attention to what Emmie says?"

"I don't remember her being quite so...."

"Batty? Oh, she was plenty batty when we met back

in Buffalo. Did she ever tell you how she suspected your late husband had been killed by the owner of a Canal Street concert saloon and his body refrigerated in the Erie Canal?"

"She does have an inventive imagination."

"Yes, and sees little need to draw distinctions between it and reality."

"What about that man who was killed in your apartment being the valet to one of her college classmates?"

"Well, that part was true."

"And didn't you name the parrot Telemachus? And charge him with protecting Emmie's virtue? That sounds like jealousy."

"The parrot's name was Polly when I brought it home. The rest is all Emmie's pipe dream."

"Aren't you ever jealous?"

"My usual state is bewilderment. Besides, what have I to be jealous about?"

"Well, it's not just a question of that. Maybe she needs the affirmation. That would explain her inventing the story of your naming the parrot."

Her theory seemed rather dubious. Emmie had never evinced concern for anyone's affirmation. I just muttered some acknowledgement and nodded. Luckily, we'd arrived at Hunter's Point, where we boarded the Steinway Avenue car. For this, the last leg of the journey, I sat next to Emmie. I thought it might be more fruitful to examine her rather than her psychology.

"Is Thibaut clear on what's required of him?" I asked.

"Well, it was expecting too much to think he'd be able to convey specific questions. But I do think I've come up with a way to make good use of his talents."

"Care to elaborate?"

"Um, no, I don't think I would."

She then pretended to take an interest in the passing scenery, which was difficult given that this part of Queens consisted mainly of grimy factories and squalid tenements. I'm sure Long Island City has its partisans, but if there's an uglier bit of real estate anywhere, I haven't seen it.

"How perfectly quaint," she said, as we passed a dilapidated windmill sitting on a rise above the road.

That's when I knew we were headed for trouble. Emmie's interest in things quaint was incalculably small.

About a mile or two further we disembarked at the Astoria Silk Works, the landmark Jimmy Yuan had mentioned. As we walked down past the mill toward the river, the street evolved into a rural lane. There was a little farm off to the right and another to the left with what I at first thought was an extended grape arbor. But on closer inspection, I saw that this hanging garden bore narrow green fruits that looked something like cucumbers. A fellow in a broad, mushroom-shaped hat was tending the trellis of simple boughs set in a series of arches. He nodded in a friendly way when we approached. Then just kept nodding, no matter how many times we repeated the name Lou Ling.

"Perhaps he's Lou Ling," I said.

So I tried a few other names I thought to be Chinese. He just kept nodding. Then another Chinaman joined us and nodded just as politely.

"I anticipated something of this sort," Emmie said.

She gave instructions to Thibaut and he got down on all fours, rubbed his shins together, and chirped with abandon.

"He's fantastic," Aunt Nell pronounced.

"Lou Ling," Emmie shouted, while pointing to Thibaut.

The Chinamen very quickly caught on, and they too started chirping. That drew the German farmer from across the way, soon followed by his wife and their brood of five children. The show was a good one and we were all thoroughly entertained for a good long while. At least until a fellow elsewhere on the plantation began giving an excited alarm in Chinese. Having just noticed that Emmie had slipped away, I had a pretty good idea what it was about.

The whole lot of us went off in the direction of the commotion. We found Emmie outside what passed for the farmhouse. It looked like the sort of thing young boys build as hideouts—odds and ends of lumber, old boxes, stray bits of tarpaper, etc. A fellow with a hoe was keeping her at bay.

"What did you get yourself into?" I asked.

"I simply wanted to see if there was any evidence of a cricket ranch here."

She reluctantly agreed it was unlikely the fellow wielding the hoe would appreciate her reasoning, and so we made our exit toward Steinway Avenue. I saw a car stopping and suggested we catch it.

"It's going the wrong way," Emmie insisted. "We still have to visit the farm at Bowery Bay."

My motion to return home failed on a vote of three to one, so we took a car up to Steinway. By the time we reached there, it was close to six and the vote in favor of stopping for refreshment was three to one. This time Emmie being the dissenter.

Steinway itself was a small, sparsely populated

neighborhood not far from the piano factory. The choices for dining were limited to two German saloons. We went into the more reputable-looking of them and had an enjoyable meal of lager, dark bread, and three kinds of sausage.

"Emmie, you never told us if you found anything at the farm," Aunt Nell said.

Emmie reached into her bag and placed a dried gourd on the table.

"You thought that gourd significant?" I asked.

"Look at it."

I picked it up and found there was an opening at the narrow end covered by a little grilled lid fashioned from tiny slats of wood.

"It's no doubt a cricket cage," Emmie told us.

"How can you be sure of that?"

"The Chinese treasure crickets, Harry. Any school child knows that."

"Then what's special about this one?"

"Nothing. But I found it at a farm where Lou Ling may be employed."

"If you found the revolver he used, it would be a little more definitive."

"Well, perhaps next time you can participate more actively."

She asked the waiter the way to the second Chinese farm, said to be on the nearby Bowery Bay.

"Willie there can show you." He nodded toward a young fellow at the bar. "He speaks their lingo. Hey, Willie! These people want to visit the Celestials."

Willie came over to the table and we invited him to sit down. He looked to be about seventeen or eighteen and was built like a farm boy.

"Do you honestly speak Chinese?" Emmie asked.

"To get by. I truck their goods over to Chinatown for them. I have a regular route."

"Do you happen to know a man named Lou Ling?"

"The cricket charmer, sure. He's just up the hill."

"Did you see him today?"

"Not that I remember." He picked up Emmie's gourd. "Where'd you get this?"

"The farm behind the silk works."

"That's nothin'. You should see the ones Charlie Lam makes."

"Is he a friend of Lou Ling?"

"He makes the cages. They all catch crickets, but only Lou knows how to catch the females."

"Can you take us to the farm and introduce us?"

"Sure, I guess so."

I went and gathered Thibaut from the bar, where he was performing his cricket in exchange for beer. Once outside, I saw a sign advertising the infamous North Beach Casino—known by its patrons as Erbe's. If the White Rats wanted a meeting place away from the theatres, this would be an excellent choice—well off the beaten path, at the far end of Bowery Bay.

Willie led us up a hill that overlooked the bay. It was nearing sunset now, but the farmers were still at work. Willie exchanged a few sentences with one of them.

"He says Lou never came home last night. He's been doing some job in the city until late. The cops were here this morning looking for him. Why do the cops want him?"

"There was a shooting last night where he works," Emmie told him. "Lou was supposed to shoot another man with a prop gun, only someone substituted a real gun, and another man took the place of the fellow playing the victim."

Willie looked to me for interpretation.

"It seems Lou Ling accidentally shot another man."

"I wouldn't've thought Lou knew which way to point a gun."

"Do you think they might be hiding him here?" Emmie asked. "We want to help him prove he wasn't at fault."

Willie reentered dialogue with the farmer.

"He says no one's seen him. But if they were hiding him, I don't suppose they'd let me in on it. I'll tell you what though, I wouldn't be surprised if Lou is around."

"Why's that?"

"Well, if he lost his night job, I wager he'll be looking for crickets. And Lou says there's no better place in New York to catch the right kind of crickets than Bowery Bay. On account of it being so quiet."

"So, if we lie in wait, we may see him tonight?" Emmie asked.

"Could well be."

"Will you stay with us? We'll need to speak with him."

"I have to get up mighty early in the morning."

Emmie tried coaxing, but it wasn't until she pulled five dollars from her purse that Willie's resolve melted. She then instructed us to find blinds from which we could spring on Lou Ling when he arrived.

"Why don't you ladies take position near the farm here with Willie," I suggested. "I'll take Thibaut and we'll cover the slope below."

"Do crickets prefer slopes?" Emmie asked.

"The right-thinking ones do."

"We should have a signal," she said. "Can you hoot like an owl?"

"Give me a quart of gin and I can hoot like a convention of elks."

She asked the same question of Thibaut in French, and he replied with a convincing demonstration. Then he and I went off. About halfway down the slope I left him in a little stand of sumacs and then went on to a windbreak that lined an old farm field. I made myself a comfortable seat of grass and sat down.

6

Willie was right, there did seem to be an unusual number of crickets about. And as dusk was eclipsed by night, the chorus grew even louder. By then, the darkness was near impenetrable. But further along, I could see lights shining in the few houses that lined the bay, and beyond those, the illuminated entertainments of North Beach—Erbe's casino among them.

I waited a good long time, just to make sure Emmie didn't come around looking for me, and also to give Thibaut a chance to fall asleep. I knew from our days at sea that he was an inattentive lookout. And with his belly full of lager and bratwurst, I felt sure he was already fast asleep. I crept down to the road that ran along the bay.

Suddenly, I heard what sounded like a bull charging down the hillside. Thibaut stumbled out of a thicket and fell at my feet. He had psychic powers when it came to drink, and I should have realized there was little chance of leaving him behind. It wasn't hard to imagine how his falling out with his partners had come about. A fellow with Thibaut's predilections would make a poor partner in any business, but particularly one involving an inventory of liquor.

I helped him up and we started walking. Beside us, a fleet of small yachts bobbed at anchor, and the Ferris wheel that dominated North Beach was already visible ahead. The family attractions were winding down and the cars back to Hunter's Point left full. But at Erbe's casino, near the tip of the point, business was brisk.

Unlike those of France, most casinos at American resorts like North Beach are nothing more than humble dance pavilions. If any gambling were to take place it would be greeted by scandal. Erbe's, however, hewed to the European model. At least in its entertainments. The edifice itself was a good deal more primitive.

New York was rife with betting parlors and pool-rooms, but no place was as open about it as Erbe's. I suppose that was partly because it was so far from the favorite haunts of the morality workers of Manhattan. Erbe, no doubt with the connivance of the local precinct captain, simply took advantage of the neglect.

We arrived in the barroom about ten. If the White Rats were meeting after the shows in Manhattan, they'd have difficulty arriving before eleven. So we naturally stopped at the bar. After quickly dispatching the first round, Thibaut went into his act. The cricket, the owl, and the tiger were all well received, but it was the ape that truly captivated. He leapt up on the bar, whooping and howling, picking nits, etc. Unable to compete, the fellow at the piano began playing accompaniment.

I can't say I was surprised. I'd been exposed to Thibaut's genius on board the steamship *L'Aquitaine*. I remember one episode in particular. Each evening after dinner, I'd bring Thibaut a bottle of wine. That was key to my ruse of keeping him distracted. On this occasion, I found him with a bag of mail he'd taken from the hold. He was opening letters and reading them as a way to while away the hours he spent alone. As soon as I provided him an audience, however, he began performing them. Solely through gesture, he revealed the emotional core of each. There was love requited, love unrequited, love forbidden, love betrayed, and a lost puppy in Marseille. A lot of tears were shed that night.

But let us leave that moving scene and return to the story at hand. With the time now ripe, I went upstairs and began looking around for where the White Rats might be assembled. There was a roulette wheel running and several tables of rouge-et-noir. And off of this main room, smaller ones where fellows were playing poker. I popped into one and then another, and in the third found three fellows not doing much of anything.

"Private party," one told me curtly.

"Excuse me, I was looking for a friend."

"Do you see him?"

"No, but perhaps you know him. Ernie Joy."

The three of them gave me hard looks. Well, two of them did. The third made a little stage laugh. But at least I knew I was in the right room.

"What's your game, fella?"

"I'm looking into Mr. Joy's death."

"For who?"

"Jimmy Yuan, the owner of the establishment where he was shot."

I then had to go into a rather lengthy explanation of Yuan's business and what had happened the night before. Meanwhile, several additional members arrived and it was necessary to begin all over again. The story didn't sound any less ludicrous on the second telling.

"What is it you want to know?"

"Well, Joy's death was either the result of an im-probable set of coincidences or it was intentional. In which case it had to have an intricate plan behind it. And a motive that required the killer to be beyond suspicion. This was no simple murder, whatever it was."

"So what do you want from us?"

"Was Ernie Joy's life endangered by his association with the White Rats?"

"You mean, would the syndicate have him killed to keep him from joining?"

"They'd just blackball him," another fellow interjected.

"Well, if the purpose behind blackballing him was intimidation of others, wouldn't killing him be even more effective?"

"Why Ernie? He hadn't even signed on."

"But he was thinking seriously about it, wasn't he?"

"Maybe. But there're others who've been in since the beginning."

Then one of the late-comers piped up.

"Why the hell are you telling him all this? Who is he? Do any of you know him?"

"Maybe he's on the level, Cliff."

"Maybe. Or maybe he was sent here by the same people who had Ernie shot. If you're on the level, tell us what Ernie was really doing in that warehouse."

"I told you what I know."

"That Ernie went on a midnight tour of a make-believe Chinatown? And you idiots believe that? He's a damn spy. You know what they did with spies at Homestead? Slit their throats and threw them into the Allegheny."

"Monongahela," I corrected.

"What?"

"The great battle at Homestead. It was on the Monongahela, not the Allegheny."

"It's the Ohio that flows through Pittsburgh," another fellow interjected.

"The Ohio flows *out of* Pittsburgh," I corrected. "The

Monongahela and the Allegheny flow *into* the city."

"How the hell does that make any sense?"

"The Monongahela and the Allegheny are tributaries of the Ohio, which originates in Pittsburgh," I explained. Or tried to. I suppose I should have known better than to attempt to give a roomful of vaudevillians a lesson in riverine toponymy. My reward was a half dozen blank expressions and a good deal of derisive snickering.

Then the lights went off and back on, twice.

"What's going on?"

"It's a signal. The cops must be on their way to break up the fun."

"And the first thing they'll do is take everyone's name. We'd better skedaddle."

"You're behind this," the fellow called Cliff unhelpfully suggested. "A simple way to have us identified."

I didn't wait around to test his skills at throat slitting. One of the more limber fellows crawled out a window and I followed. Unfortunately, I'd chosen a rather poor guide. It was a fifteen-foot drop with not much to hang onto. The first fellow had latched onto a drain pipe and was hanging there precariously. But I went straight down.

It was one of those rare occasions when one thinks fondly of the pools of mud and manure you come across in stable yards. I wasn't looking, or smelling, any too good, but the cushion saved me from breaking a leg. I limped behind some shrubs and waited.

Luckily, the cops didn't stay long. They left with the roulette wheel and a handful of fellows who looked to be employees of the casino. I imagined this was a form of dunning—Erbe must have been late with the monthly payment. I found Thibaut inside under a table, sound asleep. I shook him awake and we went off to find Emmie and Aunt Nell.

It must have been close to one by the time we made it back to the farm. Thibaut and I hooted for a good ten minutes, but there were no responses. When we at last arrived home, sometime after four, the apartment was dark. I turned on a light and saw the jacket Aunt Nell had been wearing draped on a chair.

I said good night to Thibaut. Then after a quick wash, I crept into our room with the light off and quietly slid into bed.... It was empty. Turning on the light, I looked about and saw that someone had been through Emmie's things. Then I noticed the satchel she kept hung on the closet door was missing. She'd packed and gone off someplace. And without leaving a note.

I went to Aunt Nell's room and found the door ajar and the light on. She was sound asleep, but sitting up, as if she'd been trying to stay awake. I was all in myself, so I just turned off the light and went back to our own bed.

You're probably wondering why I didn't show a little more concern over Emmie's whereabouts. Well, I'd learned long before that investing in any anxiety on Emmie's behalf brought very meager returns. Granted, in this case a good deal of trouble might have been saved if I had taken some decisive action. But I'm no seer. And, as I said, I was exhausted.

I fell into a deep sleep and didn't wake until I was forced to by Aunt Nell's persistent prodding.

"What time is it?" I asked her.

"Never mind that. Didn't you notice Emmie was gone?"

"Yes, I noticed. But she didn't bother to leave a note."

"I was to explain when you got in, but I'm afraid I

dozed off," she said apologetically. "Where did you go last night?"

"To a meeting of the White Rats."

"You might have let us know. We hooted our hearts out."

"The cricket charmer showed up?"

"Yes. About eleven, a lantern went on inside the shanty. Then three men came out. Willie said they were looking for crickets. But that Lou wasn't among them. Then, a little later, another Chinaman came. This was Lou, Willie told us. He spoke with the others, and took some things from the shack. An older man told him he needed to leave, or the police would catch him. Then gave some more complicated instructions Willie wasn't sure of. But something about a boat. When you didn't respond to our hooting, Emmie insisted we follow Lou."

"Did Willie go with you?"

"No, he said he didn't like spying on his friends like that and he went home. We followed Lou back to the car stop where we had dinner and got on the same car he did, then changed cars when he did. The second car took us over the bridge back to Brooklyn, and at a ferry dock he got off and walked down past a big factory to the river. There were all sorts of boats here and he approached one of the canal boats. He called over to the cabin something we couldn't make out, and a woman emerged. He handed her a piece of paper and she took it into the cabin, then returned and motioned him to come aboard. By then we were very close and Emmie recognized the woman. 'That's Captain Stanton,' she said."

"Who's Captain Stanton?"

"I asked her that and she said it was too long a story. She wanted to board immediately, but I dissuaded her.

She agreed we would come home and fetch you. Then we heard another man approach Captain Stanton's boat. He was a seaman of some sort. He called out for the captain and told her she should be ready to leave at 6 a.m.

"We got back to the apartment about two and waited for you to get home. About half past three, Emmie said she couldn't afford to wait any longer. I suggested we call the police, but she said the police would be of no use. Then she went in and packed a bag. I was to explain to you that she was going to take a berth on Captain Stanton's boat. She told me that the captain did a business transporting Chinamen who've been smuggled in from Canada."

Then she smiled and added, "It's just like King Brady, isn't it?"

"King Brady?"

"The dime-novel hero who seems to be in a perennial battle with the highbinders. My cook, Anna, has me read her every issue."

"A little too much like that. Are you sure you weren't reading one as you fell asleep?"

"It all happened just as I told you, Harry. Emmie could be in grave danger."

"Well, if she is, it's her own fault. Did you see the name of the boat?"

"The *Sophie Arnould.*"

"Do you remember where it was docked?"

"I think so. But it will be gone now."

"Let's hope they were delayed."

After dressing hurriedly we took a cab up to Williamsburg, then walked along the riverfront behind the sugar refineries.

"It was here." She pointed to an empty berth.

I went over to a sloop where some men were loading

barrels of sugar and spoke to the fellow watching—and no doubt in charge.

"Wasn't the *Sophie Arnould* berthed here?" I asked.

"Joining a tow this morning. Behind the *Captain Shandy*."

"Where's that take place?"

"Out on the river here. But they'll be headed up the Hudson by now."

"How long's it take for them to reach Albany?"

"Oh, two days. Give or take."

"I don't suppose they stop anywhere along the way?"

"Not usually. She was loaded full with sugar."

"Going where?"

"Oh, up the canal."

"Buffalo?"

"Could be. She came down with lumber for the piano factory, might be from Tonawanda."

"The Steinway factory?"

"That's right."

I thanked him and we headed off to catch a car for home.

"One thing I forgot to mention, Harry."

"What's that?"

"When Emmie and I left here earlier, we saw two Chinamen who seemed to also be watching the *Sophie Arnould*."

"Did you recognize them from earlier?"

"We didn't see them that well. They rushed off when they realized we were looking their way." Then she added, "Tonawanda is just across the river from Canada, Harry."

"Yes, and the Steinway factory is just a half mile from the farm. If they're smuggling Chinamen, it would be a convenient way of getting them into New York."

"What should we do now?"

"I'm not sure. I guess head up the river and intercept them."

Back at the apartment, I took out a map and determined the mid-point on the Hudson between New York and Albany.

"If we wait in Poughkeepsie, the tow should pass early tomorrow morning," I told Aunt Nell. "All we have to do is take a train up there and hire a boat."

"That sounds simple enough."

And, of course, it did sound simple. But sounding simple and being simple are two entirely different things. That maxim was handily brought home over the course of the next few days, when a series of seemingly reasonable decisions led to a series of unanticipated, even bizarre, results. And all in the absence of Emmie.

We caught a two o'clock train and were in Poughkeepsie by four. After checking into a nearby hotel, we went down to the riverfront and discovered the first kink in our plan. I don't know if you've ever tried to hire a boat in Poughkeepsie, but it's a lot harder than you might imagine. To get a boat of any size, you need to make arrangements well in advance.

"Couldn't we just row a boat out in the river and wait?" Aunt Nell asked.

"The river's pretty wide here, and that's a serious current."

"All we need to do is take up position, then when we see the tow, drift down to it."

She said we, but of course I'd be the one at the oars. We found a fellow willing to rent us a dinghy, and then went back to the hotel for dinner.

7

It probably won't come as much of a surprise that choosing a hotel based solely on its proximity to a working waterfront necessitates a willingness to accept certain shortfalls in other areas. Still, the degree to which the Troy House exploited this willingness seemed excessive. Small rooms don't bother me, and I can live with an occasional lukewarm bath. But I do expect the food on my plate to at least be identifiable. When we had both given up on our meal of shoe leather and vegetable mush, I found a newspaper with a tide chart and suggested we take a bottle of wine up to Aunt Nell's room to refine our plan. In retrospect, it might have been better to forgo the libation.

"If it takes the tow two days to go from New York to Albany," I told her, "it should reach Poughkeepsie on the morning of the second day. So to be safe, we need to get out on the river fairly early, say about six. And we'll need to bring our bags—we have to be ready to board the canal boat if given the chance. Now all I need to do is calculate what the tide and current will be."

While I was doing this, sitting on Aunt Nell's bed with the map spread out beside me, she was looking herself over in the mirror.

"Harry, do you think I'm a good-looking woman?"

"What's that?"

"I asked if you thought I was good-looking."

"Why, yes. You're a very handsome woman, Aunt Nell."

"Would you mind calling me plain Nell? Aunt Nell sounds so matronly."

"No, not at all."

Then she went back to the mirror and I went back to the calculating. The wine did much to help us forget the unpleasant meal and the bottle was soon drained.

"We're in luck," I announced. "The tide will be going out."

"Are there tides on a river?"

"Oh, yes. Rivers like the Hudson. It's a tidal estuary. Between low tide and high tide, the current goes upstream."

"How is it upstream then?"

"Well, I suppose you could say upstream's become downstream, and downstream's become upstream."

"What about the fish?"

"Which fish?"

"There must be fish in the river. How do they know where they're going with the water going one way and then another?"

"I don't think they're too concerned about where exactly they're going."

I'd already come to the conclusion that Emmie had inherited her reasoning abilities from her mother's side and I took this as confirmation.

"What I want to know, Harry, is: do *you* find me attractive?"

She had come over, shoved the map onto the floor, and sat beside me on the bed. Now she was looking me in the eye and waiting for an answer. I just sort of stammered for a minute or so. Partly because she was my wife's aunt, and partly because we were alone in her hotel room sitting on the bed together. But primarily because I did find her attractive. Very attractive. On the train up, Ben Franklin's advice about the advantages of taking an older woman as a lover had come to mind. And as I remembered it, he made some pretty persuasive arguments. I'm not sure why I'm confiding this to you—it has nothing to do with the mystery per se. But I suppose it might offer some help in interpreting Aunt Nell's actions a few days later.

I still hadn't answered her, but I must have been blushing.

"Did I embarrass you, Harry?"

"Well...."

"That's all right. I'll take it as a compliment."

I arranged to have an early breakfast sent up, said good night, and went off to take a cold bath.

At five, I gave a soft knock on the door that connected our rooms. Though only partially dressed, she let me in and then invited the waiter in when he came with our breakfast. He gave me a wink, apparently assuming impropriety. Aunt Nell caught sight of this and came over and embraced me as he was leaving.

"It's so nice to be suspected of something, isn't it, Harry?"

Frankly, I couldn't see the advantage over having gotten away with something and *not* being suspected. But I imagine I'll always be a babe in the woods where these things are concerned.

We checked out and were out on the river according to schedule. My calculations had been correct—there was a fairly swift current going downstream. All we needed to do was drift down until we sighted the steamboat *Captain Shandy*, then board the tow behind it. There were tugs and other boats traveling about, but the river was a half mile wide so it was a simple matter to stay out of their way. While I maneuvered the boat into the center of the river, Aunt Nell scanned the horizon with the field glasses I'd thought to bring.

"What about salmon?" she asked.

"What particularly about them?"

"Well, to them it matters whether they're going upstream or not. Say the tide's coming in and downstream becomes upstream. Why don't they swim back into the ocean?"

I puzzled over that for a bit, but finally came up with an answer that seemed to satisfy her. "Oh, strictly speaking they aren't swimming upstream. They're swimming uphill. Upstream may become downstream, but uphill is still uphill."

We'd been on the water for more than two hours, and even though we were mainly just drifting, maintaining station was taking a toll on my arms. I was looking back, most of the time, and had noticed a canoe maneuvering in much the same way. I was about to mention it when Aunt Nell announced she saw a paddle wheeler approaching.

"Is there a tow behind it?"

"What's a tow look like?"

"A bunch of barges and canal boats tied together."

"I see something like that, but it looks very far behind it."

Ten minutes later, we were within a hundred yards of the steamboat.

"It's the *Captain Toby Shandy*!" she announced.

I turned around and could see the tow 500 feet behind the steamboat. The trick was going to be to stay out of the wake of the paddle wheeler, but close enough to get to the tow when we got even with it. I began rowing in earnest, and as I did, I noticed the canoe doing likewise. It was coming closer. I asked Aunt Nell to look it over with the glasses.

"The two Chinamen!"

"What two Chinamen?"

"Remember, I told you I'd seen them when we left the canal boat at the refinery. They must have followed us."

She handed me the glasses. It sounded a little fantastic to think these fellows had followed us from Brooklyn. But you just don't see a lot of Chinamen in canoes out in the middle of the Hudson.

"Highbinders, no doubt," she said. "They can be very violent. The Bradys have an awful time with them."

"Why would highbinders be after us?"

"Well, Mr. Yuan had inserted himself in a tong war. The tongs are ruthless. At least according to the Bradys."

The steamboat had passed us and it was time to approach the tow. I eased us in position and it seemed a simple matter now. Then I noticed the Celestials coming up fast on our inside, as if to keep us away from the tow.

It was then that they made a crucial error, misjudging the wake of the *Captain Shandy*. They started to tip. One of them leaned hard to compensate, but his timing was off. A moment later they capsized.

"We need to help them, Harry."

"I thought they were ruthless highbinders," I reminded her.

"Ruthless or not, we can't just watch them drown."

"The canoe will float—all they need to do is hang onto it."

"They don't even see it."

She was right. They were in the sort of panic people

go into just before they go down for the third time. I turned about and we pulled the two of them aboard. They collapsed, panting, giving the impression their ruthlessness was in abeyance.

By this time the tow had passed. I tried to catch up to it, but the tide was now headed against us and my arms were like jelly.

"Look, Harry! The *Sophie Arnould*."

"Do you see Emmie?"

"Not on deck. There's a boy there. But no one else. What do we do now, Harry?"

"Look for a promising place to drift ashore, unless we can convince our friends to take a turn at the oars."

There wasn't much chance of that. For the remainder of the voyage Aunt Nell and the senior of the Chinese fellows interrogated each other. She would ask him a question in very slow, deliberate English, then he would respond in a rush of Chinese. Things hadn't progressed beyond that when I spotted a dock on the west bank. There we abandoned the dinghy—I made a mental note to avoid the Poughkeepsie waterfront for the foreseeable future—and approached one of the houses nearby. We learned we were somewhere below Milton and above Marlborough, two towns I'd never heard of. We headed north on foot with the two Chinamen following about a hundred feet behind us.

"Should we turn them in to the police?" Aunt Nell asked.

"For capsizing a canoe?"

"They must be following us for a reason, Harry."

"That may well be. But can you imagine me going up to some country police chief and explaining about how my wife came to be on a canal boat with a Chinese fugitive aboard, all because of a shooting at Jimmy Yuan's faux Chinatown?"

"The Bradys never have a problem convincing the authorities. But I do see your point. What will we do now?"

"What we should have done in the first place. Go to Albany and the entrance to the canal. Sooner or later the *Sophie Arnould* has to pass through there. And it will be a lot easier to catch her negotiating a lock."

By the time we reached Milton we'd lost sight of the Chinamen. After buying tickets for the two o'clock train to Albany, we had lunch at the small hotel.

"I wonder why Lou Ling would seek refuge on the canal boat?" I asked rhetorically.

"Well, remember Emmie told me that Captain Stanton smuggled Chinamen in her boat."

"But is she taking this fellow back to Canada? Seems a lot to go through for an accidental shooting. And how is it that Emmie knew this captain smuggled Chinamen?"

"She didn't say, but seemed very sure of it."

"Kind of ironic."

"How is it ironic?"

"Canals hold an odd attraction for Emmie. You remember what I told you about her theory in regard to her late uncle and your husband?"

"Yes."

"Well, after that we were in Glens Falls and a body turned up in a canal there. Then Emmie solved a case over in England that involved a body in a canal."

"Emmie was in England?"

"Only by reputation—the solving of the mystery occurred via correspondence. Then, later that spring, I had an insurance case that included a woman being poisoned and thrown into a canal."

"How odd."

"Yes. And now Emmie's come to expect a body in a canal as her due. When we were in Washington last December, she almost dispatched a fellow who was drowning in a lock."

"What had he done to her?"

"Well, his chief offense was that he wasn't dead enough. But then they exchanged words. Unfriendly words."

"I'm beginning to realize I don't know Emmie very well at all."

"Does anyone?"

"I would have imagined you did."

"I would have imagined so, too."

We headed over to the depot and joined a small throng waiting for the train. I saw no sign of the Chinamen, but made sure we were the last to board. Just as it started moving, I saw them come out of some bushes at the far end of the train and climb aboard. When we'd sat down, I told Aunt Nell.

"Oh, highbinders are tenacious, Harry."

"Are they?"

"Yes. We'll have to shake them in Albany somehow."

"It might be they aren't following us, but are just trying to reach the same objective."

"To take their revenge on Lou Ling?"

"Revenge for what exactly?"

"Interfering with the tong's tourist trade."

"I think they'd take that up with Jimmy Yuan."

"Or perhaps they're after Emmie."

"Emmie? Why would a tong spend any time thinking about Emmie?"

"The Oriental mind is very devious, Harry."

"Not unlike her own."

"Aren't you at all concerned for her?"

"Probably more than she is, but it doesn't pay to worry too much about Emmie."

"You've really become blasé about the poor girl, Harry."

"Oh, I wouldn't call it blasé."

"I would. You're never the least bit jealous. And now she's being held hostage on a canal boat, chased by ruthless highbinders, and you act as if she just stepped out for a walk in the park."

"Held hostage?"

"Well, whenever the Bradys come across a white woman, she's almost always being held hostage."

"I see. You don't think you might be able to interest your cook in something a little nearer reality? Maybe Dickens would afford an easy transition."

"Don't try to change the subject. We're talking about your attitude toward Emmie."

"Well, I'll make an effort to exhibit more concern."

"Genuine concern, Harry."

I told her I would, but judging from her expression I think she doubted my sincerity.

We reached Albany a little after four and checked into the Ten Eyck Hotel. Then we set forth to find the entrance to the canal. Of course everyone knows the Erie Canal begins at the Hudson in Albany. But not many people know exactly where. Even in Albany.

Eventually we located the entrance about a mile north of the city proper. There was a little point that projected into the river and we found our way to the tip. Here one could see both the river traffic and the approach to the canal.

"We'll need to come out even earlier tomorrow morning," I said. "We should get back to the hotel for dinner."

We'd just been served when I noticed two men being seated nearby. One was the White Rat who'd advocated dispatching me back at Erbe's casino. He was in his late forties, with dark hair and a lean physique. His face was an ordinary one, but he made lively use of his mouth and eyes. I described him to Aunt Nell, whose back was to them, and she suggested we listen in. Most of the conversation was spent griping about life on the road, cheating agents, lazy stagehands, and actresses who guarded their virtue too assiduously. But as dessert arrived, their talk turned to something more interesting.

"I need you to take over my turn tomorrow night, Fred," the rodent said.

"What's up?"

"I know where the woman behind Ernie's killing is. I'm going up there right after the matinee."

"Up where?"

Just then a woman at the next table did a convincing imitation of a hyena and neither of us heard the reply. We sat through the rest of their meal, but they returned to more mundane subjects. Then they left the room.

"Who could they mean but Emmie?" Aunt Nell asked. "She arranged the shooting."

Not wanting to exhibit any lack of proper concern, I conceded it was a possibility.

8

By four-thirty the next morning, we'd made our way to the little peninsula we'd scouted out the day before. It was nothing more than a vacant lot with a wide assortment of weeds poking through the gravelly soil. But off near the point, I spotted a pile of rubble from a collapsed shed. I fashioned a little bench out of some miscellaneous boards and we sat down and took turns scanning the river with the field glasses. The sun hadn't risen, but it was light enough to make out all the tugs and barges.

It was a cool, damp morning and Aunt Nell had nestled pretty close beside me. I heard her teeth chatter, so I gave her my jacket and put my arm around her. Then she laid her head on my shoulder and moved in even closer.

When a fellow finds himself like that, with an attractive woman pressed up beside him, her hand warming itself on his thigh.... Well, by then I wasn't feeling any chill, and I sensed that things were about to take on a life of their own.

I hopped up and built a little fire, hoping to obviate any pretext for intimacy. But as soon as I'd gotten it going, she coaxed me back on the bench and we were right back where we started.

I hopped up again, stoked the fire, and, before temptation made its presence felt, suggested I go see if I could procure some breakfast, as we'd gone out before the hotel kitchen had opened.

"Yes, perhaps that would be a good idea," Nell agreed.

There was no way of knowing what had been going through her own mind a few minutes before, but I had the impression she'd been feeling the same ambivalence. Then again, she may have just been feeling the cold.

It took some serious searching, but in due course I came across a lunch counter about six blocks away. I had the fellow wrap up some sausage and biscuits, then took that along with a pail of coffee back to our lookout. Nell was nowhere to be seen. I was sure I was in the right spot, so I didn't see any alternative but to sit down and hope she had just needed to attend to things and would be back momentarily. I started on the coffee, setting the food aside until her return.

At first. But fifteen minutes later I was feeling a little annoyed. So I got a head start on the sausage. It was very good sausage, so I had no trouble increasing my umbrage to a point that justified finishing it off completely. After that, it was the work of a moment to do likewise with the biscuits. I watched a couple more tugs on the river, but there was no sign of the *Captain Shandy*.

A good half hour had passed since my return and I realized something was amiss. I stood up, ready to take some decisive action—and only then saw the note that had been pinned to the bench. Why I hadn't seen it when I approached I can't say. I suppose I was focused on seeing Nell. Or the food. Or perhaps some combination. It read simply:

Highbinders spying on us. Will lead them off, you keep watch.

I was relieved to learn I'd unintentionally followed her instructions. But why she was convinced these Chinese fellows were ruthless highbinders still seemed puzzling. They looked an awful lot like two of the farmers Willie had held conference with at the farm on Bowery Bay. And what harm could come from her leading a couple of Chinese farmers about Albany?

That was my thinking until about nine. Then I started to imagine quite a variety of ways she *could* come to harm. And then my having to explain to Charlie how I sat enjoying the view of the river while his mother was being kidnapped by white slavers. There was but one choice: try to find Nell and hope we got back in time for the tow.

I set out toward the main part of the city, visited both railroad depots, the capitol, the hotels, etc. Then I thought I'd check back at our lookout on the river one last time. The only ones about were a couple fishermen.

"I don't suppose you've seen a woman here this morning?" I asked.

"Woman? What's yours look like?"

"Good-looking. Fortyish, but not at all matronly."

"Sounds just like my Celia."

"No, it don't," his partner corrected.

"She was good-looking when she left me."

"Bah. Yours have all her teeth?" he asked me.

"Seems to."

"Then she ain't Celia."

"No, I s'pose not," her former mate conceded.

"Any sign of a tow arriving from New York?" I asked. "I'm looking for a canal boat being brought up by the *Captain Shandy*."

"A couple of tows've gone by, didn't see the names."

"Gone by? I thought the canal boats would be left off here."

"Most go up to West Troy, enter the canal there."

"How far is that?"

"Oh, five or six miles."

My whole life I'd been hearing about Clinton's Ditch going from Albany to Buffalo. Never a word about West Troy.

I left a message for Nell with the fishermen, and likewise agreed to deliver one to Celia should I come across her. Then I went back to the hotel and found Nell in the lobby leaving me a note.

"Has the tow arrived?" she asked.

"Well, I can't say for sure. It seems there's another entrance to the canal upriver. We can head up there after lunch. But I was absent a good part of the morning looking for you."

"Then we're in luck, Harry."

"Are we?"

"While I was leading the Chinamen about, I saw the White Rat at the train depot. He was in line at the ticket counter. I got up close and overheard him." She handed me a slip of paper where she'd written, "Weedsport, four o'clock train."

"Weedsport?"

"Yes, and as soon as I heard it, I remembered Emmie told me that Mrs. Stanton's boat often went to some place that begins with a 'W.' It couldn't be a coincidence. We know he's after Emmie."

"Mrs. Stanton smuggles Chinamen from Weedsport?"

"They must cross from Canada to there."

Nell's familiarity with matters geographic rivaled Emmie's.

"Weedsport is in the middle of the state."

"Then why does it call itself a port?"

"Well, it is on the canal. Maybe they thought it sounded better than Weedsville."

"The point is, the White Rat is going there to confront Emmie. So we need to go there as well."

"You don't think Emmie may just be up in West Troy?"

"No. It's obvious he knows something we don't. Perhaps she's gotten off the boat and taken a train to Weedsport. You can't very well stand idly by and let another man have his way with your wife."

I was disinclined to be swept up by the hysteria, but I knew if I equivocated Nell would accuse me of being inadequately concerned. Besides, I wasn't so sure Emmie had ever gotten on that canal boat. I agreed to her proposal, but took the time to send a wire back to the apartment just in case Emmie had never left Brooklyn.

At the depot, I bought tickets for the four o'clock train and we found a place where we could keep an eye out. A little while later I saw the two Chinamen go up to a ticket window. When they left, I snuck up to the same window.

"Say, did those two Chinamen buy tickets?"

"Why not? Chinamen can ride the train."

"Yes, but I was wondering which train."

"Any train they want. You think we run separate trains for them?"

"No, no. I'm just curious to know where those two fellows are going."

"Weedsport."

"Weedsport? Are you sure?"

"Sure I'm sure."

I went back and told Nell.

"Well, now we have confirmation," she said.

"Of what exactly?"

"That Weedsport *is* the objective, of course. The highbinders must have a secret hideout there."

"Have you ever been to Weedsport?"

"No. Have you?"

"Yes, and I can say with some certainty that it would not be the ideal location for a group of Chinamen to site their hideout. Strangers tend to stand out in a town like that."

"Maybe it's in an old abandoned farm house. Use your imagination, Harry."

The very same admonition Emmie utters just before launching us on some misadventure.

We boarded the train and saw the Chinamen do likewise. I promptly fell asleep. When I woke, Nell was gone. But at the far end of the car I saw the White Rat. He was talking to the conductor and they seemed to be looking at me. Then the Rat went off in the other direction. When the conductor passed, I asked him about it.

"He said he was a friend of yours, but didn't want to wake you. Just asked where you were going."

"Did you tell him?"

"Sure. Was it a secret?"

Nell returned not long after and reported that she'd also seen the White Rat.

In Syracuse, we had an hour layover. Nell went off to attend to things and we agreed to meet in the station restaurant ten minutes later. On the platform, I again saw the White Rat. I followed him to a ticket window and then saw him walk out of the depot. I asked the fellow at the window what had transpired.

"He bought a ticket to Weedsport."

"Weedsport?"

"What's wrong with that?"

"Oh, nothing."

I went to the restaurant and found Nell already seated.

"Look, Harry. The White Rat is over in the corner there."

It may seem the level of detail I've provided regarding the machinations at train depots is excessive, but it will help to explain the farce that was slowly unfolding. The true scope of the absurdity wouldn't become apparent until the next afternoon, but I did have my first taste of it. You see, Nell's White Rat was not my White Rat. In fact, it seemed likely he was no rat at all. Just a fellow who from behind happened to look something like the White Rat.

Nell was feeling pretty excited about the whole thing, and even if she did have some misperceptions as to what was cause and what effect, she wasn't wrong in thinking the White Rat was headed to Weedsport. Or that the Chinamen had chosen that destination as well. So there didn't seem any point in spoiling her fun.

We boarded the train and were in Weedsport at quarter past nine. You may have anticipated what happened next. We saw her White Rat, the non-White Rat, stride off toward town. The real White Rat was hiding at the edge of the depot, most likely waiting to follow *us*. And though I saw no sign of the Chinamen, I assumed they were likewise situated. Nell insisted we follow her Rat. He went to the Willard House, where the clerk greeted him as an old friend.

"The fish running, Mr. Johnson?"

"Notice, Harry, he has no fishing gear," Nell whispered. "And the clerk winked at him. He must be in on it, too."

When the non-Rat left for his room, we booked two for ourselves. Throughout the exchange, Nell inspected the clerk with a suspicious eye. She got him so nervous he toppled a bottle of ink. This, of course, confirmed her suspicion that he was indeed in on the ill-defined "it."

After we put our things upstairs, Nell led me outside and whispered in a conspiratorial tone, "We should look for the *Sophie Arnould*, Harry."

"It won't be here for another week, assuming it's coming here. Canal boats are usually propelled by mule."

"Then the White Rat must *know* Emmie's taken a train."

"Yes, no doubt."

We stopped by the Western Union office to see if there was a response to the wire I'd sent to the apartment. There was not. Then we went out for a stroll.

A walk around downtown Weedsport is not a long one, and even on a Saturday evening, diversions are few. But like any town worthy of the name, Weedsport did have a theatre, the Burritt Opera House. And that Saturday evening it offered a program of vaudevillians. Of course, a small venue like this has to settle for third- and fourth-rate acts, the ones just hoping to cover their hotel bill and fare to the next town. So in one sense, it wasn't particularly surprising to see Cissie Lightner listed right at the top on the sandwich sign out front.

"Carlotta!" I exclaimed.

"Where?" Nell asked.

"There. Cissie Lightner is her stage name."

"Cissie Lightner and the Frolicsome Frenchman," Nell read. "Could it be Thibaut?"

"I suppose it could be. It doesn't take much to launch a career in vaudeville."

"This explains everything, Harry."

"Does it?"

"It isn't Emmie the Rat is after, but Carlotta. She was jilted by Ernie Joy, and was there when he was shot. Naturally, the Rat would suspect her of being behind it."

A familiar, but always disturbing, sensation came upon me. It normally appeared on those occasions when Emmie similarly came to a logical conclusion based on a series of her own imaginings. She so twists your own thinking that you feel the same euphoria at her discovery that she does. At least until you start mulling over how she arrived at it.

Still, there's no denying that it was an extraordinary coincidence that Carlotta would be playing Weedsport on this particular night. I suggested we see if we could still catch the end of the show.

"It's just the final act now," the ticket seller told us. "Still be two bits each."

"What's the final act?"

"Dwight Hotchkiss and his dancing pig."

"Is it worth two bits?"

"That's a matter of opinion."

"What's your opinion?"

"Well, it's a darn sight better since he taught the pig to dance."

The question was rendered moot when the audience began filing out. We went around to the stage door and were informed Carlotta had already departed for the hotel. At the desk there, I was told she was in Room 11. Just then, Nell's faux Rat came down the stairs and disappeared out the door.

"We have to follow him, Harry."

"Do we? I thought I'd pay a call on Carlotta."

"Well, go then. I'll follow him."

She was trying to bluff me, make me feel like a mouse. But I called her.

"All right," I agreed. "We can meet up later."

She went off in a huff and I asked the clerk who it was she was following.

"Mr. Johnson—he's a drummer for some sheet music publishers. Passes through once a month or so. Always on a Saturday."

I went upstairs and just as I reached the second floor I saw my White Rat disappear into Room 11. I suppose a *really* gallant fellow would have barged right in and made sure Carlotta wasn't in danger. But my thoughts kept harking back to Erbe's casino, and the Rat's suggestion that my throat was in need of slitting.

Luckily, my mind was agile enough to rationalize my caution into concern for Carlotta. My appearance would be certain to anger him, and when the slitting started, who could say if anyone's throat would be safe?

9

I went to my own room and left the door ajar. About half an hour later, I heard a door open and voices in the hall. It was Carlotta and the Rat. When I heard it close again, I crept down and knocked.

"HarRY! What **are** YOU doing HERE?"

While a baby across the hall wailed, I went in and closed the door.

"You know that fellow you were just talking with?"

"Cliff Ainslie? You know Cliff?"

"Let's just say our paths have crossed. Did he come to Weedsport to see you?"

"He said he didn't even know I was here. But he told me to be careful, that there's a Pink nosing around the Rats. Say, Harry, you're not working for the Pinks again, are you?"

"I never worked for the damn Pinkertons, Carlotta. Why can't you remember that? He just leapt to that conclusion because I was asking the Rats about Ernie Joy."

"He and Ernie were tight. He wants to find out who killed him."

"Did you tell him what happened?"

"Sure."

"Did he believe you?"

"Who knows? It does sound pretty nutty."

"And you haven't heard about our skirmish with the Celestial navy at Poughkeepsie."

"Poughkeepsie?"

"I'll tell you about it later. Where'd Ainslie go off to?"

"To see if he could catch a night train back to Syracuse. He said he needed to see someone there."

"I hope it's no one we know."

"No, a Mrs.... something that begins with a 'T.' He left this."

She handed me a copy of the *New York Tribune* from the previous Wednesday, the day after Ernie Joy was shot. It was folded open to a story about a man named Cyrus Twinem having been murdered in a room at the Cosmopolitan Hotel. His wife said an intruder shot him and made off with a valuable manuscript. It was a long story, but there were three salient facts that warrant recounting. First, Twinem had been a professor at Syracuse University. Second, the intruder wore a red and yellow plaid jacket. And last, the Cosmopolitan Hotel was on Chambers Street, just a few blocks from where Ernie joined Jimmy Yuan's tour. I tore the page from the paper and put it in my pocket.

"It sounds like Ernie had an adventurous night, even before he joined us."

"Ernie didn't shoot anyone. That's crazy, Harry."

"It's hard to believe there are two jackets like that, even in New York."

"The woman's lying. Cliff was sure of it. He says she seduced Ernie, and then made a sap of him."

"How's he know that?"

"He didn't say. But he was sure of it."

"So now he's off to Syracuse to confront her?"

"Yeah. I told him he should go to the police. But you know Cliff."

"Well enough," I confirmed. "I'm sorry we missed your act. Is Thibaut the Frolicsome Frenchman?"

"Yeah, he's a real clown, Harry. They love him."

"Where's he now?"

"Down in the barroom, most likely. Cadging drinks. Is Emmie with you?"

"No, she seems to have taken a cruise on a canal boat. But her Aunt Nell's with me. I should go find her."

"Well, when you do, meet us downstairs."

Nell was waiting for me in the lobby.

"Where'd your prey go off to?" I asked.

"A house on Willow Street. A woman answered the door. He went in and a little later the lights went out."

"That would be the Simmons' residence." The night clerk had been eavesdropping. "About once a month Leo Simmons goes off fishing with Pete Manley. They always leave on Saturday afternoon and get back Sunday evening."

"And Mr. Johnson's visits to town coincidentally coincide with Mr. Simmons' outings?" I asked.

"Yeah. Coincidentally."

"Lucky for him no one's caught on."

"Yeah," he agreed. "Of course, old Pete's a bachelor."

"Wise man."

"Yeah."

He went back to his newspaper and I led Nell out on the veranda.

"I think there's been a little mix-up, Nell."

"How do you mean?"

"Well, Mr. Johnson is not the White Rat. At least not *my* White Rat. Somehow you followed the wrong man at the depot in Albany."

"But you told me you saw him on the train, too."

"I saw my White Rat. A fellow named Cliff Ainslie. Another vaudevillian. Ironically, he came here, too."

"Cliff Ainslie?"

"Yes, do you know the name?"

"I... I guess I must have seen him in Buffalo."

"It seems he was a friend of Ernie Joy's. He just visited with Carlotta a little while ago."

"Is that why he's here?"

"Well, that's where things get confusing. You see, I saw Ainslie the other night at the White Rats' meeting and he seems to have jumped to the conclusion I was a spy for the theatre syndicate. Ironically, he may have come to see why I was coming to Weedsport."

"Did he see me?"

"I can't say, but I think you're safe enough."

"Where is he now?"

"Trying to get back to Syracuse."

She was looking a little unsettled, so I suggested a trip to the barroom for a glass of brandy. We found Thibaut there entertaining the company with his menagerie. A little later Carlotta came in and sat down with us.

"When you saw Mr. Ainslie, did you tell him about me?" Nell asked her.

"No, I didn't go that far down the cast. I had trouble enough remembering things."

"Nell's a little worried," I said.

"Oh, you don't have to worry about Cliff. He just talks rough."

"You didn't mention you were going on the road, Carlotta," I said.

"Well, I needed work bad, with Jimmy's place closed. When I got to the agent's, he said he needed someone for Friday, Saturday, and Sunday matinee. But it had to be at least a double. So I jumped on it, told him I had a sensational new partner. Of course, I didn't really. So when he asked who, I was caught for a second. Then I thought of Thibaut. 'The Frolicsome Frenchman,' I said. Then I described a whole act, just off the cuff."

"And he liked the idea?"

"Sure. Thought it sounded swell. Said he had the perfect spot for us. The way he was talking, I thought we were up for something big. 'Where's the show?' I asked him. 'Weedsport,' he says. 'Three days in Weedsport?' I says. 'You've got something better?' he asks me. Of course he knows I don't. Then he tells me not to be so proud. 'Oh, I'm not proud,' I told him. 'I don't mind doing a show in some jay town and catching the night train out. But to wake up in Weedsport....'"

She just shook her head.

"Well, at least you're the top of the bill," I said.

"Yeah, that's somethin'."

"What is your act?" Nell asked.

"Well, I'm an American girl who's come to Paris to see the sights. I hire a cab to take me around, Thibaut being the cabby. But when we get to the zoo, it's closed. The cabby feels real bad and so he acts out all the animals. Then we go to the wax museum. It's closed too, so now he does Napoleon and Joan of Arc."

"Thibaut does Joan of Arc?"

"Burning at the stake! It's great. Then we do some bits from my old act, the bad-shot sharpshooter, that sort of thing. Thibaut's a big improvement over the last guy I worked with."

She made us promise to come to the next day's matinee and then called Thibaut to the table. He greeted me like a long-lost brother and gave Nell an affectionate kiss. Then he and Carlotta began communicating with a combination of American slang, elementary French, and exaggerated gestures. I tried following this personalized patois for a while, but it was exhausting enough just to observe it. Nell seemed to have come to a similar conclusion and sat staring at her brandy.

"Could I have another, Harry?" she asked.

"Absolutely."

She drank three more in quick succession but they improved her mood only slightly. While Carlotta and Thibaut carried on their animated conference, she leaned toward me.

"Tomorrow we need to take action, Harry."

"Do we? In any particular direction?"

"We need to find out what Mr. Ainslie knows."

I handed her the newspaper story Carlotta had given me.

"Apparently, he was headed to Syracuse to confront Mrs. Twinem. He only came here because he wanted to see what *we* were up to."

"I see." A moment later she excused herself and went up to her room.

By then, a sleepy Thibaut had pushed his chair up against Carlotta's and she more or less enveloped him. They certainly were an odd-looking pair—her being about twice his size, and him always looking as if he'd just hopped off a moving freight train. They were past talking now, leaving me feeling ancillary. I slipped off quietly for bed.

The next morning, I was woken by Nell's knock on my door.

"He's gone, Harry."

"Ainslie?"

"Yes, Ainslie. The coward. He didn't have the nerve to face me."

"Face you?"

"Face us, I mean."

She seemed a little more upset than the situation warranted. For my part, his exit came as welcome news. Confronting throat slitters had never been on my list of priorities. When we met later for breakfast, she was still looking a bit distraught. I tried to cheer her up by suggesting we look for the Chinamen.

"Yes, that will have to do."

"Just how did you expect to persuade Ainslie to stand for being questioned?"

She placed a gun on the table.

"Where'd you get that?"

"It's Carlotta's prop gun. I took it from her trunk last night."

"Better put it away. Look, let's give up on interrogating anyone and just go back to Brooklyn. Emmie's probably home by now."

"We promised to stay for Carlotta's matinee."

"Well, in the meantime, we can just take a nice walk, out along the canal. Maybe turn up the highbinders' secret hideout."

She scoffed at the idea, but did agree to the walk—even arranging for a picnic basket.

It was a grey morning, but the relaxed pace and bucolic setting offered a serene contrast to the frenzy of the previous few days. After an hour we came to Port Byron, another little burg that could easily have been mistaken for Weedsport. We crossed over to the opposite bank for our return, planning to luncheon at a little glen we'd espied on the way out. It was just about noon when we sat down to enjoy our rustic meal of beer and sandwiches. By then the sun had come out and it had turned into a lovely fall day.

We sat on the grass chatting, mostly about Emmie.

Whatever her shortcomings as a wife, there's no denying she provides limitless fodder for conversation. And keeping her in mind helped put the kibosh on any lapses into compromising informality. It was, all in all, a blissful scene.

So you can imagine how unprepared we were when the two Chinamen appeared out of nowhere, both carrying large sticks. And both shouting in a distinctly hostile manner. When we didn't immediately answer, they started waving the sticks about. I asked for the gun and Nell handed it to me. I fired it in the air. That was enough to persuade the Chinamen to drop their sticks.

"What will we do now, Harry?"

"I suppose we'll have to turn them over to some authority."

The idea went against my principles. I'd never been too fond of authority myself. It was fine in theory, but in practice it left a great deal to be desired. Still, when someone comes at you with a large stick, you can't spend time philosophizing about the viability of the anarchist project. We marched them off toward Weedsport.

There we made the acquaintance of Deputy Carson, a big, slow-moving fellow who looked about sixty. He took the gun from me and then had us all sit down in his little office.

"What's the trouble?"

"These fellows seem to feel they have some grievance with us."

"What about?"

"It's a rather involved story," I told him.

"I got time." He put his feet up on his desk. "I always got time for a good story."

Well, he got what he asked for. It consumed most of

an hour, with Nell and me taking turns. And the China-men periodically providing addenda. Unfortunately, the deputy didn't feel our account adequately explained why I had been parading two Chinamen into Weedsport at gunpoint.

"I suppose we ought to hear what these fellows have to say about it. There's a Chinese laundryman down in Auburn. He speaks some English."

He had a wagon hitched up and then the five of us made the long trip down to Auburn and Woo Sing's laundry. Nell and Deputy Carson had a nice conversation along the way, while I sat in the back trading looks with the Chinamen. When we arrived, the deputy explained the situation to Woo Sing. Then there was a long conver-sation between him and the elder of our two companions.

"He say he trying to find his cousin, they all farmers. Say they find him on river, but you get in the way. Sink his boat in river."

"I didn't sink his boat. I rescued them from drown-ing."

"What else did he say?" the deputy asked Woo Sing.

"They say, he make them think cousin up here, so they buy train ticket. But cousin not here. This man trick them. Leave piece of paper, 'Go to Weedsport, four o'clock train.'"

He handed the deputy a piece of paper, who then showed it to us. It was the note Nell had handed me back in Albany.

"You gave them that, Harry?" she asked.

"I didn't give it to them—I must have dropped it and they found it. It seems we all came to Weedsport because an adulterous sheet music drummer had planned an assignation."

"What's Johnson have to do with it?" Deputy Carson asked.

"Nothing, really. Just a vague resemblance to another fellow."

"Well, then, why don't you all just go back to New York?"

"That would suit me fine," I said.

"These men have no more money," Woo Sing explained. "Spent last dollar on ticket to Weedsport. Because of his trick."

"Maybe you could help them get back to New York?" the deputy suggested.

"Why should I pay their fare?"

"It would just make things go a little easier all around. That way I won't have to bring you up for making a false arrest."

"He trick them," Woo Sing repeated.

"You did in a way, Harry," Nell added.

"Oh, all right. But no more waving sticks at us."

10

Deputy Carson drove us back to Weedsport and then on to the depot. He watched as I bought four tickets for the evening train and handed two to the Chinamen. Nell complimented him for his wisdom in the matter, and then asked if he could return the prop gun she had borrowed. He did so, and then charged me three dollars for the rental of the horse and wagon. Why is it the preferred solution to every dilemma ends with me paying costs?

We'd missed Carlotta's act again, but listened raptly over dinner as she described another stage triumph. Then Nell bought some sandwiches to give the Chinamen, her attitude toward the erstwhile highbinders having mellowed a good deal.

Catching a glimpse of her healthy bankroll, I asked to borrow twenty dollars of it.

"All right, Harry. But you really should learn to live within your means."

A little later, Carlotta, Thibaut, Nell, and I boarded the evening train and found a pair of empty seats facing one another. Just before the train left the station, the two Chinamen came on board. By then there weren't many seats left, and when they tried to sit across from two women, they were shooed away.

"We need to make room for them," Nell insisted.

She sent Thibaut to entreat them to join us. They were a little wary, but finally sat down on the seat beside Nell, with Carlotta, Thibaut, and me wedged into the seat opposite. Nell handed them the sandwiches and they were devoured in short order.

"They look as if they haven't eaten in days, Harry."

"I didn't realize it was incumbent on me to provision my pursuers."

"They're only looking for their cousin. Just as you're looking for Emmie."

"And about as effectively."

"Aunt **Nell**'s RIGHT, **Har**ry," Carlotta interjected. "You should be helping each other."

"The blind leading the deaf and dumb? You're forgetting we don't speak the same language."

"I bet Thibaut could talk to them. What do you want to know?"

"Why did Lou Ling run off to the canal boat?"

That simple question took about five minutes to convey to Thibaut. Then he played a form of double charades with the two Chinamen for a good five minutes more. Then another five minutes of patois with Carlotta.

"The cops came to the farm twice the day after the shooting, so his cousin told him to take a boat trip. He says the cops never believe a Chinaman."

"Why that particular boat, the *Sophie Arnould*?"

This went relatively quickly.

"It's the boat that brought him down from Canada. Something about champagne. Do they bring champagne from Canada?"

"Champagne?" I was beginning to realize just how wrong we'd been. "Could it be Lake Champlain?"

The older fellow nodded on hearing it. I turned to Nell.

"And could the town frequented by Mrs. Stanton that began with a 'W' have been Whitehall?"

"Yes! That's it. Where's Whitehall?"

"Whitehall's on the *Champlain* canal. It's a lumber town. The Chinamen she smuggles into New York must be brought down from Canada. She meets them on Lake Champlain, then picks up the lumber for the Steinway Company in Whitehall. The farm on Bowery Bay is just a few blocks from the piano factory, making it an ideal way-station."

"So what do we do now?"

"Go to Whitehall, I suppose. The *Sophie Arnould* must have to spend some time there loading up."

"Sounds like fun. But Thibaut and I have to go on to New York," Carlotta told us. "We have a new turn beginning tomorrow."

At Syracuse there was a twenty-minute layover and Nell got off to stretch her legs. The two Chinamen followed her and then Carlotta moved opposite me.

"You know, Harry, I still don't understand why you and Emmie went chasing after Lou Ling. He wouldn't hurt a fly. What you need to figure out is who switched a real gun for the prop gun."

"When did you last use it?"

"Just the night before. At Jimmy's."

"Then you took it home?"

"Sure, I can't afford to lose it. I need it for my act. When that one went missing, I had to borrow another from the property man at Tony Pastor's."

"And you didn't use it again until you brought it the night Ernie was shot?"

"Why would I?"

"So you put the gun in the bunk there. When was that?"

"I suppose about ten."

"You suppose?"

"I always wait until I've changed and taken my place."

"So just about any of the Chinamen could have switched the gun between then and eleven, when we showed up?"

"Sure. I wasn't watching it every second."

We were pulling out of the depot, but neither Nell nor the Chinamen had returned.

I went off and walked the length of the train looking for Nell. When I returned, the Chinamen were there having an excited exchange with Thibaut. Then Thibaut had an excited exchange with Carlotta, this time forgoing the pantomime act.

"AUNT **Nell's** BEEN kidNAPPED!"

Every child under five years in that car and the next two began sobbing.

"Kidnapped?"

"Yeah. Either that or she was strangled."

"What? Where did this happen?"

"Right on the platform, there in Syracuse. It sounds like Cliff Ainslie."

"The White Rat? Why would he kidnap Nell?"

"To keep you from spying on the Rats!"

"I'm not spying on anyone."

"He thinks you are. He definitely doesn't like you, Harry."

"I can't say I'm too fond of him, either."

"Aren't you going to do something?"

"She probably just missed the train. Or these fellows saw someone keep her from jumping on the moving car and just leapt to the wrong conclusion."

"They seem pretty sure."

"How would Ainslie know she'd be on the platform in Syracuse at 7:30 Sunday evening?"

"Maybe he has one of the other Rats following you."

The idea that Nell had been abducted was farfetched, but not noticeably more than other recent events. And Ainslie did say he was going to Syracuse to see Mrs. Twinem. If he got there Saturday night, it wouldn't be surprising that he was waiting for a train out of town on Sunday evening.

I asked Carlotta to leave word at the depot in Albany for Nell to meet me at the Ten Eyck Hotel, and also to wire me the next morning to let me know if either Nell or Emmie was back at the apartment in Brooklyn. I disembarked in Utica and caught a westbound train back to Syracuse, arriving just after eleven.

I found the office for the station cops and told the sergeant in charge of Nell's possible abduction—leaving out the fact the only witnesses were two Chinamen who spoke no English and that I communicated with them via a French pantomime who knew neither English nor Chinese.

Without much urgency, he took me out to the platform and spoke with a couple of his men. Then he interviewed several of the porters, one of whom thought he might have seen Nell.

"Was there someone with her?" I asked.

"She was talking to someone, but it didn't look friendly. She was crying."

"Did she leave with him?"

"Didn't see. But I saw two Chinamen watching her. You think the white slavers got her?"

When I confirmed that there were two Chinamen involved, the sergeant asked me repeatedly if I was sure I hadn't just dozed off and dreamt the whole thing. He assured me, however, that he'd file a report.

I caught the next train to Albany and arrived there about four that morning. The message Carlotta had left hadn't been picked up by Nell. It was possible that on missing the train in Syracuse, Nell went straight to New York. But that possibility wasn't enough to allow me much sleep. About seven I went down to the desk, then checked back at the depot. Still no sign of Nell.

There didn't seem much point in contacting the Albany police, but I felt some further action was in order. So I wired Detective Sergeant Tibbitts, a New York cop I'd generally gotten along with in the past who happened to owe me a favor. I asked him to send out bulletins on Nell and Cliff Ainslie. By then a wire from Carlotta had arrived. There was no sign of either Emmie or Nell at the apartment. I decided the best I could do was take the morning train up to Whitehall and try to find Emmie.

On arrival, I went off toward the lumber mills that lined the canal and saw a number of boats taking on loads. There was no sign of the *Sophie Arnould*. But I did locate the mill that sent lumber to the Steinway company. Mr. Clapsaddle, the foreman, was just finishing his lunch.

"Have you sent out a shipment in the last two days?" I asked.

"Not to Steinway. Have one ready though."

No sooner had he finished eating than he'd taken a big jaw-full of tobacco. From then on I had to stay on my toes. Either Mr. Clapsaddle had horrible aim or an exceedingly perverse sense of humor.

"Is that to go on the *Sophie Arnould*?"

"That's right. The she-boat, I call her."

"Captain Stanton's?"

"Her and her daughter, and her little boy."

I went and ate a large lunch myself, bought a news-paper, and then sat reading beside the mill. It was a warm afternoon and I had just dozed off when I was woken by the sound of a tug. It was coming from the north, so I was about to turn over and try for another bit of sleep when I noticed a Chinaman standing on deck.

The tug docked a little further on. I hid behind a stack of boards and watched as the canal boat it was towing coasted to the wharf beside the mill. There was a middle-aged woman at the tiller. As soon as it came to shore, a young boy jumped on the bank and began tying it up, with the help of two young women on deck. One of whom was Emmie.

Another Chinaman had emerged from the tug and walked back to the canal boat and just sort of stood guard there. Mrs. Stanton spoke with him.

"I need to send one of the girls into town for sup-plies," she told him.

He clapped his hands and the other Chinese fellow came over. He was given instructions and then he and Emmie went off toward town. I followed, but from well behind. At one point Emmie started drifting away from the fellow. He pulled her back, flashing a rather impres-sive dagger as a warning.

They went into Mrs. Gregor's grocery. After a bit I followed and tried to just hover about unobtrusively, lifting things and setting them back down. Now and then glancing over my shoulder to see what the others were up to.

Unfortunately, my behavior aroused the suspicion of the proprietress, who evidently was a woman of action.

She picked up a broom and jabbed me in the midsection with a fairly substantial blow.

"Jeez," I cried.

"Harry?" Emmie had recognized my expostulation.

The Chinaman pulled her away, and I made sort of a half-hearted lunge at him. My heart, always chivalrous to a fault, started out fully invested in the program, but then my always-more-cautious cerebellum reminded it of the dagger. The lunge was enough, however, to distract the fellow. Emmie exploited the opportunity by walloping him on the head with her usual aplomb. But also with her usual ignorance of even the most basic principles of physics. Her weapon of choice was a sack of flour. It achieved little beyond blanketing the three of us in a powdery snow.

I had no alternative now but to finish the job with a jar of pickled lambs' tongues—a delicacy previously unfamiliar to me, but whose bouquet we were all three destined to know well. The brine splattered every which way and made a very effective paste wherever it encountered the flour coating. But at least the Chinaman was out cold.

Mrs. Gregor, however, had no intention of withdrawing from the fray. Just as I was dispatching the Chinaman, she gave me another blow. This one a jab to the kidneys from behind. I fell to my knees and only narrowly missed the follow-up shot to the head.

"I think we should probably be on our way," Emmie suggested as she helped me to my feet.

"Yes," I muttered. "I'm not sure I want to patronize this establishment after all."

We stumbled out with Mrs. Gregor just behind.

"You can't leave your Chinaman here!"

"I suggest we find a safe place to formulate our strategy," Emmie said.

"I suggest we do it on the run. Mrs. Gregor is drawing attention."

We sprinted in the direction opposite that of the canal, passing through a few blocks of houses, then crossing a large field, and finally collapsed in a copse of trees on the bank of a small brook. We washed ourselves as best we could, but the water seemed less than pure. It was then I noticed the herd of dairy cows a few hundred yards upstream from us.

"What did you get yourself involved in, Emmie?"

"It's rather a fantastic story, Harry."

11

I was well used to Emmie's fantastic stories, but having her describe one as such struck me as novel.

"I take it Lou Ling is on board the *Sophie Arnould*?" I asked.

"He was. But perhaps it would be better if I recount all that has happened since we separated. By the way, Harry, where did you wander off to that evening at the Chinese farm?"

"I went to a meeting of the White Rats. It turns out the meeting place was Erbe's casino in North Beach, at the other end of the bay from the farm."

"When did you learn that?"

"That evening. There was a sign in Steinway for the casino. I would have told you, but Erbe's doesn't welcome women."

"Well, it's just as well, or we would have missed seeing Lou Ling."

"Aunt Nell told me how he came by the farm. And how you followed him to the *Sophie Arnould*. Then you went back and signed on as a crewman?"

"Yes. Captain Stanton was surprised to see me, but she was quite agreeable to my joining her for the voyage."

"How exactly is it you know this lady canal boat captain and smuggler of Chinamen?"

"She provided me certain illustrations for the inaugural issue of *Psi*."

Psi was a literary magazine Emmie had tried to resurrect. I say tried because the inaugural issue was also its last. Why one would consult a canal boat captain for illustrations suitable for a literary magazine was a question I thought best left unexplored for the present. I responded with a simple "I see."

"I made no mention of having seen Lou Ling come aboard, merely told Captain Stanton I wanted the experience. She raised her eyebrows, but said it would work out fine, because the men hiring the boat had stipulated no males could be aboard, only her son, who's just twelve. 'Why is that?' I asked. She said she had her guesses, but wasn't willing to confide them. On the second day, while we were with the tow on the Hudson, she told me about Lou Ling. She said the police were after him and she had agreed to help him slip out of town unnoticed. 'Where to?' I asked. 'Well, someplace he can find his lady crickets.' Remember, Willie told us that was Lou's special expertise."

"Yes. But I thought they catch the crickets for their songs?"

"Yes, that's right."

"Well, the females don't chirp."

"No, but apparently by finding the right female, you can induce the males to chirp very readily. Then they fetch a higher price."

"Do the males ever get what they're after?"

"If they did, they wouldn't chirp as hard afterward."

"So they're just teased?"

"Yes, I'm afraid so. But I need to go on with the story. When we arrived in Troy, we were met by the tug, the one you saw this afternoon. We were taken all the way up to the middle of Lake Champlain. There we stopped and for the first time saw the two Chinamen on the tug. They were brought to the *Sophie Arnould* in a dinghy. It was already dark, and an hour or so later, a sloop approached and tied up to us. Then it transferred its cargo...."

"Chinamen?"

"Oh, no. Nothing so prosaic. Chinese girls! Seven altogether. They were taken to the compartment in the hold used for smuggling, where Lou Ling was still hiding, unbeknownst to the smugglers. That was how he was reunited with Xiang-Mei Chen."

"I think I missed a chapter...."

"You see, as a boy Lou Ling was betrothed to a distant cousin, Xiang-Mei Chen. They were very much in love, but were forced to separate when Lou was told by his father that he must come and work here for a period. He was promised that when he came home Xiang-Mei would be waiting. A marriage ceremony was held, and the next day Lou caught a steamer for Vancouver. But something happened back in their village. There was some sort of upheaval and Xiang-Mei was separated from both their families and ended up in the care of American missionaries. She actually speaks English rather well.

"Then a month or so ago, she heard about a man who was arranging to send girls to America. She hoped she could in this way find Lou Ling, so she pursued the matter without letting the missionaries know. It wasn't until they were on the ship that she realized the circumstances. The other girls had all been sold to the man by their very poor families. They landed in Canada and were carried in a freight car across the continent. Then they were transferred to the sloop that tied up to the *Sophie Arnould*."

"And by sheer coincidence, Lou Ling was on the canal boat waiting?"

"These things do happen, Harry. Happily, Lou Ling

and Xiang-Mei Chen managed to escape last night to Plattsburgh."

"How'd they get away?"

"Mrs. Stanton and I helped them. The Chinamen haven't noticed she's missing yet, but when they do, Mrs. Stanton will be in trouble. That's why we need to act quickly."

"I suppose we could try explaining it to the police."

"Oh, that would just get her in more trouble with the tong. I already have a plan, Harry. I was hoping you'd show up in time. But I expected to see you before now. Where have you been for the last few days?"

"Well, do you remember passing Poughkeepsie? It was early Friday morning."

"You saw us then?"

"We saw the *Sophie Arnould*. Got within fifty yards of her."

"Who's we?"

"Nell and I. We would have boarded, too, but we encountered our own pair of Chinamen."

"From the tong?"

"No, from the farm."

"And they threatened you?"

"Only later. Evidently they had the same objective, but their seamanship was lacking. We had to fish them out of the Hudson. By then, your tow had gotten way ahead of us."

"Why didn't you meet us in Troy?"

"Well, mainly because we were waiting in Albany. And from there we made our way to Weedsport."

"Weedsport?"

"Yes, on the *Erie* Canal. Why didn't you tell Nell which canal you were headed for?"

"What canal were we on?"

"The Champlain."

"I thought that was a lake."

"Never mind. What's your plan for saving Mrs. Stanton from the tong?"

"It's perfectly simple. You'll love it, Harry."

"I think I'll reserve judgment. And it had better not involve me battling those two fellows on the tug."

"That's what's so perfect about my plan. We just outmaneuver them. You see, they've been instructed to ride on the tug. They aren't allowed to ride with the girls. All we need to do is tie up Mrs. Stanton and her children, then free the girls—making it look as if it was done by a rival tong."

"How do we do that?"

"By dressing as Chinamen, of course. Mrs. Stanton and I have worked it all out."

"What if I hadn't shown up?"

"Well, I was sure you'd show up sooner or later. And you did."

"Not with any help from you."

"You always seem to resent it when I help. But let's not harp on past failures. We need to go over our plan."

"Your plan."

"Oh, I'm perfectly willing to accept credit for it," she said. "Here it is. Tonight we don disguises, and somewhere along the canal surreptitiously board the *Sophie Arnould*, tie up the Stantons, free the girls, and then cut the boat loose from the tug. When we drift to shore, we take the girls off."

"And then where?"

"I was hoping you'd be able to answer that. Aren't you from around here?"

"No, not really. Won't it be a little conspicuous traveling the countryside with half a dozen Chinese girls?"

"That's why we'll need a hideout. But first we need to get in position for tonight's raid. Somewhere down the canal."

"When are they supposed to leave?"

"The lumber will be loaded this afternoon, then they'll set off in the evening."

"We could go down to Fort Edward—that's about thirty miles from here."

"Good. They should get there well after dark."

"We can take a train down, maybe get a hotel room so we can wash up."

"Yes. Thank goodness I thought to bring a change of clothes when I left the boat." She picked up the satchel she'd been carrying. "Where's your bag?"

"Back at the lumber mill. I'll go back for it and meet you at the depot."

"All right. But do be careful, Harry."

I snuck back to the lumber yard, but saw at once that I was too late. One fellow was wearing my favorite vest, and Mr. Clapsaddle himself had on my new silk tie. My bag, and what remained of its contents, was lying behind a pile of woodchips. I decided to make do with this and went off to join Emmie at the depot. Neither of us was looking our best. And we both smelled a good deal worse than we looked.

It's difficult to explain how I allow myself to get drawn into Emmie's schemes. In retrospect, I can think of a dozen more reasonable plans, none of which involved a possible confrontation with the fellow harboring the dagger. I guess the main reason I go along is that she can get so disagreeable if I demur. Emmie was a master at stretching a resentment into a three-week funk. Her chief weapon was the cold shoulder, and she used it pitilessly.

Of course, much as I'm loath to admit it, it's also true that she's her most alluring when she's scheming. I'm not sure why exactly. It's not at all intentional on her part. Though I sometimes suspect she's aware of it.

It was only after we'd found a room at the Fort Edward Hotel and bathed that we discussed our financial situation. All the meals, train tickets, hotel rooms, boat rentals, and wires had started to add up. I had only eight dollars left of what I had borrowed from Nell just the day before.

I'd been counting on Emmie having a stash with her. She keeps two sets of books, so there's never much point in my trying to guess her true financial position. Usually when we're in a real pinch, she reveals some hidden reservoir we can tap to tide us over.

"I've just the three dollars Mrs. Stanton gave me for the groceries," she told me. "I had to give all I had to Xiang-Mei. How would they have been able to get to Brooklyn otherwise?"

"They went to Brooklyn?"

"To our apartment, of course. Where else could I send them?"

"It might be a little crowded. Assuming Nell's turned up."

"Turned up from where? Where did you leave her?"

"I didn't leave her, she left me. She got off the train in Syracuse, but didn't get back on in time."

"Didn't you go back for her?"

"Sure, but she wasn't there. So I assumed she caught

the next train to Albany. When she didn't turn up there, I figured she'd just gone back to Brooklyn."

"Or home to Buffalo."

"I doubt that. She seemed to be enjoying our little adventure."

Emmie produced a full change of clothes from her cornucopia-like satchel. And the yardmen had found enough of my wardrobe wanting that I too looked reasonably presentable. Though the aroma of our adventure in Whitehall lingered.

"Now we must procure supplies," Emmie told me.

Her shopping list included two broad-brimmed straw hats and a long length of sackcloth. When we returned to our room, she fashioned capes for us from the sackcloth. They were meant to look like the robes you see Confucius and fellows like that wearing. Next, she let down her hair and started snipping. She left herself one long length down the back, which she quickly braided into a queue. Then she fashioned another using what she had snipped off.

"This is for you, Harry. I can pin it in place. And we can use some of the leftovers for moustaches."

When she was done, we put it all in a bundle and snuck out of the hotel, having agreed we would remit payment at the first opportunity. As surety, we left our brine-infused apparel.

On finding the canal, we strolled along looking for a suitable location from which to launch our ambush. A few miles above town we came to the intersection of the Champlain Canal and the feeder canal from Glens Falls. There we encountered the *Anything But*, a smallish canal boat captained by a man named Mr. Polley. Emmie complimented him on the originality of his boat's name and then entered into conversation with him. He was headed to Albany from Glens Falls and hoped to find a passing tug willing to add his boat to its tow at minimal expense.

We went on our way and a little further on found a place where the canal narrowed, making it an easy matter to board the passing boat. Then inspiration struck.

"I've got it, Emmie."

"Got what?"

"The problem with your plan is that when we cut the *Sophie Arnould* free, the tug will start moving along much more quickly. Its crew will certainly notice the change in drag. But what if we at the same time attach the *Anything But*? It's smaller, but Mrs. Stanton's boat must be running light with one of her holds given over to Chinese girls."

Emmie greeted the idea with enthusiasm. Not because she appreciated the straightforward logic of it, but rather because it added another level of complexity. To her way of thinking, straightforward equated with pedestrian, and logic was of no consequence whatsoever.

We went back to negotiate with the good Captain Polley. Not only was he agreeable, but he paid Emmie four dollars for the tow. I suppose it goes without saying that we neglected to mention the two knife-wielding Chinese gentlemen.

Later that evening, we dined with him in his little cabin. Then about eight o'clock we went off to the spot we'd chosen for our rendezvous and donned our costumes. I pointed out that if things went as planned, there was no reason to dress as Chinamen. But Emmie insisted. I suspect she was simply not willing to admit she'd made a mess of her hair for no purpose.

About eleven, the tug came into sight. I was relieved not to see either of the Chinamen on deck. At least until we saw the fellow with the dagger walking the tow path beside the canal boat.

"You leap in front of him to draw his attention, Harry, and I'll club him from behind."

I reluctantly agreed. Provided I was allowed to choose the club.

12

My leap got off to a bad start when my foot caught on a vine I later identified as poison ivy. But I did have the fellow's attention. And no doubt Emmie could have swiftly carried out her end had the fellow not tripped over me, putting his head out of range of her club. I grabbed hold of him and we rolled about the tow path, each trying to get the better of the other, while Emmie landed random blows on whatever bodily appendage happened to come within reach.

Suddenly he burst free of my grip and ran wildly in what I can only assume he thought was the direction of the tug, but in fact was that of a low-lying limb. He fell to the ground, unconscious.

"I think my last blow disoriented him," Emmie noted with satisfaction.

"That's only fair, given that the first five rendered me senseless."

"You looked so much alike."

"Yes, thank goodness you insisted we come costumed," I reminded her. "If we ever find ourselves really hard up, the three of us could take that act on the vaudeville circuit."

We tied the Chinaman to a tree and then just barely made the leap onto the canal boat. Mrs. Stanton and family were expecting us and quickly freed the young women. Now time was of the essence. Our plan called for the quick transfer of one boat for the other.

As we approached the junction with the Glens Falls

Canal, we could see Mr. Polley on the deck of the *Any-thing But*. Mrs. Stanton's son threw him the tow line and he secured it to his own boat. Then he waved good-bye and was taken off by the tug.

It's true that when day broke our subterfuge was likely to be detected rather quickly. But Emmie and I agreed that if Mr. Polley survived the encounter with the remaining Chinaman, we'd have to make it up to him in some way. Or his widow, if not.

Then, for the second time that evening, inspiration gave me a thump.

"Suppose, Emmie, that the rival tong we represent were to make away with the *Sophie Arnould* itself?"

"Take it off into the woods?"

"No. Go up the feeder canal to Glens Falls. Once we get to Glens Falls, there's an excellent hiding place."

"I hope you're referring to Mr. Cooper's cave."

She meant the cave from *The Last of the Mohicans*, located just below the falls. But the truth is that the cave was something of a tourist destination and would make a very poor hiding place. As Emmie well knew, I was referring to Mrs. Butler's euphemistic boarding house. Briefly, Mrs. Butler was an affable procuress who owed Emmie and me a favor from an episode two years earlier, when she and her lover covered up the accidental killing of a fellow who was terrorizing one of her charges.

"We're not saving them from the frying pan just to toss them into the fire, Harry."

There was no disputing that Mrs. Butler would, like-ly as not, see the girls as potential recruits. Nevertheless, Emmie agreed a trip to Glens Falls was as good a plan as any. And Mrs. Stanton was keen on any scheme that would delay her reckoning with the tong.

As soon as the girls were once again hidden below deck, I went off to locate the man whose team of horses had brought Mr. Polley down the day before. He agreed to tow us up to Glens Falls, though only after his team had rested another couple of hours. Even then, it was anything but a quick escape. There were at least a dozen locks in the first mile, and the fellows working them were of the thorough, methodical sort. It took us six hours to cover the five miles to Glens Falls.

By the time we arrived, Emmie had come around to appreciating that Mrs. Butler's would offer at least temporary sanctuary. But she insisted that she would negotiate with the mistress alone, while I went to see about a conveyance for getting the girls discreetly from the lumber dock to the boarding house. I hired a covered wagon from a nearby stable and then waited outside Mrs. Butler's. A little while later, Emmie appeared.

"You'll never guess at the greeting I received, Harry."

"A friendly one, I hope."

"Oh, most friendly. 'So you left him, my dear,' she said. 'Quite right, if you ask me. He wasn't the man for you.'"

"Mrs. Butler said that?"

"Yes, just before she offered me a position in her shop, as she called it."

"You?"

"Why do you find that so unbelievable, Harry?"

Well, I'd put my foot into it. Emmie was hurt and bitter in equal measure. At least it started out that way. With her, bitter usually gets the upper hand in no time at all. It took a good ten minutes of supplication before we were on speaking terms again. And even then she was pretty cool.

"What did she say about hiding the girls?"

"She agreed to one night—unless she was allowed to make the girls an offer. In which case they could stay as long as they like."

"Well, I may have a solution for tomorrow. But I'll need to send off a wire to Aunt Purlina."

"You never mentioned an Aunt Purlina."

"Great-aunt. She doesn't mix much with the outside world."

"And she has ample accommodation?"

"That's what I need to find out."

"How far away is it?"

"Ten, fifteen miles, just up the Hudson. A place called Corinth."

I sent off a wire to Aunt Purlina and another to Carlotta back in Brooklyn asking if Nell had reappeared. When we returned to the *Sophie Arnould* for the girls, Mrs. Stanton told us she'd found a buyer for her boat.

"You're giving up your business?" Emmie asked. "But I thought you enjoyed it."

"I liked helping out the poor Chinamen. But now they've made me a white slaver."

"What will you do?"

"My brother-in-law's been wanting me to marry him and move to Spokane. I've decided to take him up on it."

She showed us a picture of her future husband. While the bride-to-be was not what you would call comely, there was no question the groom would be getting the better end of the stick.

We bade her and her family farewell, loaded up the girls, and made our way to Mrs. Butler's. A lavish luncheon had been prepared. The proprietress and her lassies, decked out in their finest clothes and jewelry, treated the

Chinese girls like honored guests. The sales pitch was on.

Emmie drew me away. "We have to get them out of here, Harry."

"All right. But if we leave before hearing back from Aunt Purlina, we can't be sure of a favorable reception."

"We need to take that chance. She wouldn't turn us away, would she?"

"It's difficult to say with any certainty."

Immediately after the meal, we loaded up the girls and headed up the road to Corinth. While the girls chattered behind us, Emmie questioned me about Aunt Purlina. I kept my answers vague, but finally her frustration became too much.

"What is it you're not telling me, Harry? Is she mad?"

"Well, that's a matter for debate. But it's not the crux of it. What do you know about the Oneida Community?"

"Utopians. They're still around, aren't they?"

"Yes, they're still around. Did you ever hear of their marriage practices?"

"Didn't they practice free love?"

"Something like that. 'Complex marriage,' they call it. No one woman is tied to any one man, and vice versa. All part of the communistic spirit."

"But they gave that up years ago."

"Some did. Some didn't. The Great Betrayal of 1879, Aunt Purlina calls it. It caused a bit of a schism. Most of the community agreed it was time for a change. But there were a few who found complex marriage too compelling a theosophy to be tossed aside so easily. They set up on a farm outside of Corinth."

"How many of them are there?"

"Last I heard, five. Aunt Purlina, Aunt Lavinia, Aunt Liz, Uncle Hiram, and Uncle Tim."

"But you aren't related to them all?"

"Only by marriage. Apparently, after the schism it became even more complex. But I'm not sure how many are still with us—they were pretty old last I saw them."

"When was that?"

"Seven, eight years ago. When I was at college. I made the mistake of bringing some of the boys up here. Whatever you do, Emmie, don't make light of their arrangements. Aunt Purlina nearly put out Jim Olcott's eye with a poker."

"Just how old are they?"

"Uncle Tim must be seventy, at least. He's the youngest."

"If they're that old, isn't the matter moot?"

"I doubt that's the case. Not as long as at least one of them is ambulatory. They take their religion pretty seriously."

As we drove up to the house, we saw an old fellow splitting wood.

"That's Uncle Tim, Emmie. He's always liked me. I better broach the idea to him first."

As we approached he turned toward us. I could see that he recognized me. But he went right on with his work.

"It's me, Uncle Tim. Harry."

From then on, he wouldn't even look up. Just swung the ax with increasing ferocity. We walked back to the wagon.

"That doesn't bode well, does it, Harry?"

"No. I wonder what's gotten into him?"

"People do lose their reason as they get older."

"Well, let's hope Aunt Purlina hasn't lost hers."

We found her in the kitchen, dressed in black. Fortunately, she seemed genuinely happy to see me. And to meet Emmie. She had us sit down and gave us coffee and cake.

"Your Aunt Liz passed away, Harry."

"I'm sorry. I noticed you were in mourning."

"Oh, that was three years ago. Then your Aunt Lavinia left us the year after that. But that's not what we're mourning now. It's the edict of August 26th. We have thirty days of mourning each year to memorialize the Great Betrayal."

"It must have been quite unsettling for you," Emmie said sympathetically.

"Unsettling is hardly the word, my dear. But it exposed the hypocrites for what they were. The edict was announced on the 26th, effective the 28th. There were two days of unbridled lust, then they went to pretending belief in monogamy. Just like all the others."

"Yes, that's certainly true," Emmie agreed. "An institution more honored in the breach than the observance."

"The Reverend Noyes realized it, of course. In his letter to the Corinthians, he wrote, 'Without love, I am nothing.'"

"How aptly put."

I was relieved Emmie was handling Aunt Purlina so adroitly. Though later that evening I began to suspect she might have been revealing some of her own feelings on the subject.

"What's the matter with Uncle Tim?" I asked. "He wouldn't even say hello when we drove up."

"Well, you had to expect that, Harrison. Taking on a job like that. We're all disappointed in you."

"Which job? Working for insurance companies?"

"Working for the Pinks! Your cousin Carlotta told us all about it, a year or two ago. She came through town doing some show."

"I've never worked for the damn Pinkertons!"

"Harrison!"

"Sorry. I've never worked for the damn Pinks. Carlotta keeps spreading that rumor just to irritate me."

"It's true, Aunt Purlina. Harry has never expressed anything but enmity for the Pinks. Perhaps Carlotta was just being mischievous."

"I suppose that does sound like her. She was a devil as a girl."

"One thing Harry hasn't explained is why the family so despises the Pinks. I know, of course, how contemptible they are. But why does Uncle Tim feel so strongly about it?"

"It's a long story, my dear. Do you remember the Molly Maguires?"

"Oh, yes. Irish nationalists. I'm a McGinnis."

"Yes, that's right. But you're too young to remember the battles in the coal fields of Pennsylvania. It was in the '70s. The miners, always treated like slaves by their miserly employers, were told their wages would be cut. They rebelled, naturally. Tried to organize a union. But the bosses called in the Pinks, and the Pinks and their venomous spies wove a great web of lies and slander. Said the men were bloodthirsty Molly Maguires. They framed them for murders they'd never committed. Then the innocents were arrested by coal company police, and tried by coal company judges. They hanged six men. But our Tim escaped."

"I see. Then it's no wonder. What an ordeal to have lived through."

"Oh, that was just the first. Tim wandered north, and when he heard about us Oneidans, he saw at once our way was the true way. He joined us, on August 19th, 1879. Just one week before the Great Betrayal!"

"Poor Uncle Tim!" Emmie cried. "But he's so lucky to have found kindred spirits."

"Yes, he has learned to accept things as they are now. Provided no one mentions the Pinks. Why don't you go out and explain the matter to Tim, Emily? It might be dangerous for your husband to approach him while he has the ax in his hands. Don't mention your marriage—just tell him you're a McGinnis."

"Yes, all right."

She went out and we watched from the window. At first, Uncle Tim just kept chopping as she talked. But at last, he laid down the ax and listened.

13

It was then that Uncle Hiram made his entrance, leading a half dozen cows up to the barn. The girls—still hidden in the wagon—must have resumed chattering. Uncle Hiram walked up and just stared for a while. As did the cows. Then, curiosity having gotten the better of him, he gingerly approached the back flap and lifted it. His expression reminded me of a child on Christmas morning who runs to the tree and finds exactly what he's been praying for.

The cows, Uncle Tim, and Emmie all joined him and I could see she was trying to explain things. Meanwhile, the two old boys began helping the girls out of the wagon.

"Harrison! What have you done?"

"I was about to broach the subject. It's a rather complicated story. Perhaps it would be better to let Emmie explain."

"Just when the community had settled into perfect harmony."

"Oh, they aren't here as converts."

Luckily, Emmie soon reappeared.

"I was just about to tell Aunt Purlina about how we rescued the girls from unspeakable servitude, Emmie."

"Oh, it's true, Aunt Purlina."

She then told the whole lurid story. Emmie has no problem creating lurid stories from whole cloth, but this one hewed fairly closely to the facts, which were plenty lurid on their own.

"I suppose we have no choice, as Christians, but to

give them refuge. But arrangements must be made."

"Yes, of course," Emmie agreed. "I've already formulated a plan. We run a marriage bureau."

"What do you mean, a marriage bureau?"

"Well, there are thousands of Chinamen here, but very few Chinese women. The tong wished to capitalize on this in their own brutal way. But what if we exploit it to the good of the girls? We make men compete for them. They must prove themselves, both financially and to the satisfaction of the girl in question."

"These men would pay a fee?" Like all Oneidans, Aunt Purlina had a pretty keen business sense.

"Oh, yes. I would think there would be a handsome return for the community."

"One hates to sound mercenary about such matters, but the truth is, things have been difficult for us."

"Oh, it isn't in the least way mercenary," Emmie assured her. "We are saving souls here."

To see Emmie work a person like this always gives me pause. I can't help wondering which of my own resolutions were reached similarly.

Dinner was an amusing clash of cultures, the two old gents showing great deference to the girls and they in turn matching them courtesy for courtesy. It made for an agreeable, if excessively inefficient, table. It took twenty minutes to pass the potatoes from one end to the other.

Early the next morning I borrowed ten dollars from Uncle Hiram, leaving him an I.O.U. in the jar under his workbench that served as his bank. Then Emmie and I said good-bye to the Corinthians, and the girls, and started on the drive back to Glens Falls.

"You know, Harry, if they'd do a little proselytizing they'd have no trouble winning converts."

"You among them?"

"Perhaps. At least I could be sure I'd be appreciated."

"Not by Aunt Purlina."

"No, she seems rather determined to minimize the competition. You don't think she did in Aunt Lavinia and Aunt Liz, do you?"

"They weren't exactly the competition. Remember, I told you things had gotten pretty complex there at the end. One of the two had given up on men entirely. At least that's what Carlotta told me."

"But I wonder how Uncle Hiram and Uncle Tim feel about sharing one older woman."

"Well, there is a positive for them."

"What's that? Familiarity?"

"There's no longer any need to practice male continence. It always struck me as the kink in their divine plan."

"The Oneidans appear to have the ideal system. Much more equitable than the Mormons, certainly."

"I suppose. But it seems to me they both expound the same basic principle."

"A rejection of traditional marriage?"

"No, something a little more rudimentary. Both sects were founded by middle-aged men, and what middle-aged man doesn't find compelling a religion that allows him to have multiple, younger lovers? The only difference is that the Oneidans included middle-aged women in the program. You see, it was a tenet of complex marriage that the older members should teach the young."

"Very generous."

"Yes—no doubt the work was exhausting."

At Glens Falls, we returned the rig and then retrieved a wire from Carlotta at the Western Union office:

No Nell. Lou's wife arrived.

"Where do you think Lou went, Emmie?"

"Perhaps to the farm. You just better hope Aunt Nell did go back to Buffalo, Harry."

"There is something else I should tell you."

"About Aunt Nell?"

"Yes. There is some—just slight—possibility that she was kidnapped by a White Rat named Ainslie."

At this point, Emmie became rather insistent on hearing the details, including how the report came from the Chinamen via Thibaut's pantomime.

"Is that really true, Harry?"

"If I'm going to believe your tale about the two Chinese lovers being randomly reunited on Lake Champlain—only to be forced into flight by the machinations of the evil tug-boat tong—I think it only fair that you believe mine."

"Well, let's pray Aunt Nell is all right. Otherwise, you'll need to tell your tale to Cousin Charlie."

"Yes, I'd prefer to avoid that. He was always rather attached to her."

"*Was*? Why are you using the past tense?"

"Grammatical imprecision."

We had lunch and caught the 2:10 to Albany. It was about then I was able to identify the species of vine I had tripped over while ambushing the Chinaman. My right ankle was covered in welts and the itch soon became a preoccupation.

"We still don't know who had Ernie Joy killed and why, Harry."

"We know who shot him. Did you ask Lou Ling about it?"

"There was no way really to interview him until Xiang-Mei arrived, and then we needed to act quickly with the escape. But he did say he was aware it was a real gun only after he fired it."

"But he picked it up from the usual place?"

"Yes, wedged in at the foot of the bunk Carlotta was in. So she must have put it there."

"There's something else I learned."

I handed her the newspaper story about the murder of Cyrus Twinem. She read it intently.

"The killer Mrs. Twinem describes sounds exactly like Ernie Joy."

"Yes. The excursion to Weedsport wasn't wholly un-productive."

"That's where you came across this?"

"Remember the White Rat I mentioned? Ainslie?"

"The man who kidnapped Aunt Nell?"

"*May* have kidnapped Aunt Nell. He left it in Carlotta's room. She told me he thinks Mrs. Twinem somehow coerced Ernie Joy into helping her."

"They were lovers?"

"Something like that. But both Ainslie and Carlotta seem sure Ernie wouldn't have shot anyone."

"It does sound uncharacteristic that a man who tires of women so easily would risk so much over one. But it certainly complicates things. And the plot was hard enough to follow as it was."

"I didn't even realize there was one. Did Lou tell you what he did with the gun after he left the warehouse?"

"He said he wasn't aware he still had it until he reached the farm, and then he threw it into some bushes."

"Where was he planning to go on the canal boat?"

"An uncle has a laundry in Plattsburgh. And he'd been assured there were plenty of crickets there. But Xiang-Mei seemed anxious to get to New York."

In Albany, we went to the New York Central depot in order to catch the 4:50 express. I saw a familiar face at the ticket window.

"There's Cliff Ainslie, Emmie. Buying a ticket."

"Confront him, Harry!"

"Suppose we find a cop and let him do the confronting. Ainslie thinks I'm a Pinkerton, and his feelings toward Pinkertons aren't unlike Uncle Tim's."

"Hurry, Harry. He's leaving the window."

With that, Emmie ran off towards him. Or tried to. The gait of a woman holding up a skirt with one hand is always a little awkward. And in a crowded train depot, particularly so. Of course, I doubt she really had any intention of pursuing the fellow. Her purpose was to shame me into pursuing him. A favorite technique of women in general and Emmie in particular. I'm generally pretty immune to the treatment, and probably could have resisted it in this instance if it wasn't for the nagging memory that it was on my watch that Nell had been misplaced. I went after him, and as soon as he saw me he took to a run. He led me out of the depot and then down to the river.

He was a good twenty years older than I was, but evidently in excellent health. And annoyingly agile. He did a wide circle, down alleys and up avenues, until eventually returning to the depot. We weren't going much faster than a trot by then, both of us near exhaustion. I tried attracting the attention of a cop, but he was talking to a fetching young girl and rather intent on explaining in minute detail the route to a hotel which I knew to be just across the street.

Ainslie led me out onto one of the platforms, then across tracks to another, then back into the main hall. Finally, he headed down a corridor that seemed to dead-end. He stopped and faced me from about ten feet away and just smiled.

I suppose the Old Sleuth, or Nick Carter, or even Dr. Watson would have seen what was coming next. Unfortunately, none of them were there to offer their insight. The blow came fast and hard.

I woke up about a half hour later, attended by the station doctor.

"You seem to have slipped on the floor and banged your head."

There was a cop in the room, and I started to tell him the whole tale, which of course was a mistake. I had the two of them just about ready to send me to the State Hospital when I gave up and asked them to page Emmie. A few minutes later, she arrived.

"You let him get away from you, Harry?"

"Apparently he had an accomplice."

"Have the police gone after them?"

Well, when I told her no, she insisted on going into the whole tale again. Only she started all the way back at Jimmy Yuan's faux Chinatown.

"When you call the hospital, doc, make it for two," the cop suggested.

It was clear we weren't going to get any help in locating Ainslie, so we had supper in the depot and caught the seven o'clock express back to New York. By now we were broke. And we'd left a long trail of creditors, including Captain Stanton, Uncle Hiram, and the Fort Edward

Hotel—not to mention Aunt Nell, and Captain Polley's widow. On top of that, I was completely exhausted, both physically and mentally.

It isn't my intention to elicit your sympathy. I simply want to explain why it was that I voiced no objection when Emmie suggested she visit the parlor car with her lucky deck. It's true Emmie had once been kicked off a train for cheating at cards. But to her credit, she'd gotten a good deal better at it since then.

I did think of one possible hitch, however. "Will you be allowed to enter a game without any money to wager?"

"What makes you think I haven't any money?"

"You told me so."

"One doesn't include seed money in such calculations, Harry."

"Doesn't one?"

"Certainly not. Does the farmer add his seed corn to his larder?"

"How much seed corn do you have?"

"Enough to enter a serious game of poker. No more than that. You should be thankful I had the foresight to set some aside."

As much as I hated to admit it, she did have a point. I slipped in and out of sleep over the next couple hours, then woke with a start as the conductors announced our approach to New York. I recognized the older fellow going down the aisle. This wasn't particularly odd, given that my work involved a lot of travel on this line. But then it dawned on me. This was the Empire State Express, the very train Emmie had been forbidden to ride again by its chief conductor.

I got up and went back to the parlor car. There were some fellows playing cards, but no sign of Emmie. Then I went through the entire train. She was nowhere on it. By then we'd arrived at Grand Central. I took our things off and searched the platform. It was quickly emptying, but still no sign of Emmie.

You might be thinking, "If she'd been found by her nemesis, the head conductor, she had probably been set off the train somewhere after Albany." And that would certainly explain matters—*if* the Empire State Express made any stops between Albany and New York.

Would a head conductor be cruel enough to throw a woman off a speeding train? That seemed highly improbable. But when I worded the question slightly differently, "Could a woman so annoy a head conductor that he would—no doubt against his better judgment—throw said woman off a speeding train?" I wasn't so sure. And when I replaced "a woman" with "Emmie," I began to worry.

Just then I saw her being helped out of the baggage car by the smiling attendant.

"There you are, Harry. Shall we be on our way? There's no telling where that conductor may be lurking."

We went out to the street and then up to the L.

"He sent you to the baggage car?"

"No, I believe he never saw me. But when I saw *him*, I took refuge there. The fellows were upset that I left them when I was so far ahead, but I told them I heard my baby crying. Then I met Mr. Purdy in the baggage car."

"He didn't object to you entering his sanctum?"

"No, not at all. I let him win a few hands and he was most agreeable."

We arrived home late that evening, just as Carlotta and Thibaut were doing the same.

"Still no sign of Nell?" I asked.

"NO, but **at** least **you** FOUND EmMIE."

In the dining room, we found a note on the table.

My Dears,

Please forgive my behavior, but there are times when one must take the bull by the horns. Mr. Ainslie and I have decided to elope and we were afraid you'd make that difficult. Do forgive me for the knock on the head, Harry. I hope you'll make a quick recovery.

Aunt Nell

"What on earth does that mean?" Emmie asked. "Did she know Ainslie?"

"She only said she'd seen him onstage. But come to think of it, she did become pretty melancholy after she heard the name. Maybe they were lovers back in Buffalo?"

"Ain't that romantic," Carlotta said. "Maybe Thibaut and I should elope."

"You and Thibaut?" Emmie asked.

"A lot's happened since you left, Emmie. Thibaut and I have a great act going. We're working the Theatre Unique, over in Williamsburg. We go on just before the Dainty Paree Burlesquers. It's the prime spot. By the way, what happened to your hair?"

Having kept it as a souvenir, I pulled the braid Emmie had made for me from my pocket. Carlotta looked at me, then at Emmie, then back at me.

"We're working on a knockabout act with a Chinaman we met on a canal boat," I explained.

Before Carlotta had time to query her further, Emmie gave a mannered yawn and said good night. I did likewise and followed her to our room.

14

The next morning I met Xiang-Mei Chen, the girl Lou Ling had been reunited with on Lake Champlain.

"Sooo *very* pleased to meet *you*, Mr. Reese!"

"And I'm pleased to meet you, Xiang-Mei."

She was an exceptionally attractive, shapely woman, on the far side of twenty-five, but probably not over thirty, with a wide smile that seemed perennially on the point of laughter. She spoke English well, but always with an oddly placed emphasis and exaggerated enthusiasm that verged on the comedic. Her wardrobe was a stylish amalgamation of the traditional Chinese and the contemporary American, and she wore it to advantage. From Emmie's account of her having been raised by missionaries, I had pictured a younger, more modest girl. But then, I'd never been to a Chinese mission.

While she helped Emmie prepare breakfast, I phoned Detective Sergeant Tibbitts to let him know he could call off the search for Nell and Ainslie.

"Yeah? Well, the truth is I never got around to it."

"Didn't I say it was urgent?"

"And now you're telling me it was all horse. It's a good thing for you I forgot about it. I did you a favor."

"Very thoughtful."

I said good-bye and was about to hang up when he stopped me.

"Wait a minute. You were there the night that actor got shot, at that sham Chinatown."

"Yes, and Emmie and I've been hired by the producer of the sham to resolve the matter. Is that your case now?"

"More or less. You going to be around this morning?"

"I suppose so. Do you wish to consult us?"

"I could have you dragged over here if you want."

"No, don't go to the trouble. We'll await you here."

I hung up. Then we sat down to breakfast with our guest.

"Is Lou Ling here?" I asked.

"*Noo*, the farmer must go to work *very* early."

"Did you have a difficult time getting here from Plattsburgh?" Emmie asked her.

"Oh, *nooo*. We had a *very* pleasant journey on the *steam* railroad. Quite okay."

"I just spoke to Tibbitts," I told Emmie. "He's coming by in a little while. He may be working our case now."

"What are you going to tell him, Harry?"

"We could just tell him the whole truth. That would certainly set him back some."

"We can't tell him Lou Ling is staying here. They'd arrest him."

"And us, probably. No, we'll just tell him Lou Ling made off to Plattsburgh."

"And Xiang-Mei?"

"The *police* will come here?" Xiang-Mei asked.

"Yes, but don't worry," Emmie assured her.

"We'll just leave Xiang-Mei out of the story. And if he sees her we'll say we hired her as our maid."

"Oh, I will be a *very excellent* maid!"

"I'd be careful what you ask for, Xiang-Mei," I said. "This place hasn't had a good cleaning since July. I dropped a dime on the floor this morning and it stuck."

Half an hour later, Tibbitts showed up. He was a good deal brighter than the average cop, and at least marginally more honest. Though I imagine an audit of his accounts could prove embarrassing. He was about my age, but taller, and blonder, and had the cop's knack for never looking credulous.

He asked us to tell him all that had happened. Emmie did the talking, telling him only the most pertinent facts and almost nothing he probably didn't already know. The sole exception being Lou Ling's flight northward on the canal boat.

Tibbitts listened attentively. But with that little smirk cops like to exhibit when they're feeling skeptical.

"So you think this Lou Ling is hiding at his uncle's up in Plattsburgh?"

"Well, that was his intent," she said. "I can't imagine where else he'd be able to find refuge."

"Yeah. Well, I can have that checked pretty easy."

"Why is it you're taking over the case from Sergeant Eckel?" I asked.

"It looks like this shooting might be linked to one of mine. Did you read about a fellow named Twinem getting killed last week? Same night as yours."

"Yes, we did come across that. You think Ernie Joy was the killer of Twinem?"

"Maybe." He looked thoughtful for a moment. "Well, I'll give you the whole story. We got a report 10:15 that night that there was a shooting at the Cosmopolitan Hotel—that's over at Chambers and West Broadway. The boys go over and find this fellow shot dead in his room and his wife all hysterical. They can't get anything that makes sense out of her, but the clerk says they checked in just that evening, around eight. Then the shot came just after ten. Lots of people heard the shot, but no one realized what room it came from until Mrs. Twinem screamed from her door a few minutes later. Our boys searched the room and couldn't find a gun. No one was seen going in or out of the room, but then no one was watching it.

"In the morning, I got the case and went and talked to the wife. She told me someone came to their room about ten. Her husband was expecting someone and let him in. But then this other fellow drew a gun and shouted, 'Where is it?' 'You'll never get it,' he says back. Then the fellow shot him dead. He searched the room and found a manuscript that Twinem had hidden, put it under his arm and ran down the fire escape."

"And this fellow was wearing the red and yellow plaid jacket?"

"Yeah. Only at the time, I didn't know about the other shooting."

"What was the manuscript?" Emmie asked.

"Twinem taught at a college, up in Syracuse. His book was about one of Shakespeare's plays. The one about the mouse."

"The one about the mouse?" Emmie asked.

"*The Taming of the Shrew*," I said. "I have a copy."

"You have a copy of *The Taming of the Shrew*? When did you start reading Shakespeare?"

"I'm not the cretin you make me out to be, Emmie. I've a lot of Shakespeare under my belt."

"Is that where you keep it?" she smiled.

"This happens to have been a gift. A fellow I went to school with presented it when he heard I'd married. I expect to begin the program any day now."

"Fat chance," she muttered. "Sergeant, doesn't it

seem rather odd that someone would shoot a man just to get hold of a rarefied work of scholarship?"

"Yeah, but wait 'til you hear the rest. The Twinems had been staying at the Victoria, up on 27th Street, then took a room at the Cosmopolitan that evening. A big step down. Not a lot of college professors stay at the Cosmopolitan. But she says it was just so her husband could meet a man about his manuscript. Then, when he gets shot, she goes back to the Victoria."

"Why were they in New York?" I asked.

"She says so her husband could show someone his book. But she doesn't know who. The whole story sounds like bunk. My first theory is that she checked into the Cosmopolitan with her lover, the husband surprised them there, one of them shot the husband, and the lover fled."

"That would explain a great deal," Emmie said. Then she glanced at me.

"Yeah. But I had the clerk brought to the morgue to look at the body. He said he recognized Twinem. And it was Twinem who checked in at the Cosmopolitan."

"Did someone else verify that it was her husband who'd been shot?" I asked.

"Yeah, I thought of that. His brother came over from Jersey. It was Twinem alright. I asked him about the manuscript, too. He's another professor. Teaches chemistry. He said he'd seen it but it was all nonsense." He looked down at his notebook. "Called it '*obscurum per obscurius*.'"

"Obscure by obscure?"

"My wife says it's a rhetorical fallacy. It means trying to explain the obscure with the even more obscure."

"Your wife?" I asked.

He held up his ring finger—as if a wedding band could explain a policeman's wife interpreting Latin phrases for him, or their discussing rhetorical fallacies at the dinner table.

"But what was it about?" Emmie asked.

He looked down at his notebook. "The title is *What Species Kate?*"

"What species?"

"Yeah." He read further: "Sorex araneus *or* Crocidura etrusca: *Would a shrew by any other name screech as shrill?*"

"He was speculating on what species of shrew Shakespeare was referring to," I said. "The common shrew of northern Europe, or the Etruscan shrew endemic to Italy, where the play takes place. My money is on the former. Shakespeare wasn't a man concerned with details. And his grasp of geography was only slightly better than Emmie's."

Tibbitts looked at Emmie.

"Harry is a font of obscurum," she told him. "What a wonderful conundrum you've brought us, Sergeant."

"I haven't come to the best part. Later that next day, she calls me back over to the Victoria. 'There's one thing I forgot to mention, Sergeant. There was a second man, a Chinaman. He did the actual shooting. Then he held the gun on me while the other man took the manuscript.'"

"And you think she's telling the truth?" Emmie asked.

"No, of course I don't think she's telling the truth. She had described the killer to us already and never mentioned he was a Chinaman. She must have read in the paper that Ernie Joy was shot by a Chinaman a little after her husband was shot."

"But why would she change her story?"

"Obviously she wanted to make sure we linked the two shootings. I took her 'round to see Ernie Joy's corpse and she swore it was the man who took the book."

"Did you check on Lou Ling's whereabouts at the time Twinem was shot?" I asked.

"According to the other farmers, they were catching crickets out there on Bowery Bay until about eight. Then he got to Yuan's place about nine-thirty. They might be lying, but the Twinem woman definitely is. Anyway, I still need to find this Lou Ling. And the gun he used. I'm going back out to the farm on Bowery Bay after lunch."

"You've been up there already?"

"Twice. I took that Jimmy Yuan with me to talk to the Chinamen. But I couldn't find out anything. They told me Lou Ling left town last week and insisted they didn't know where he went. You want to go out to the farm with me?"

I agreed to meet him at Hunter's Point at two. Just then there was a knock at the door and Emmie let in our friend Willie, the lad who trucked produce for the Chinese farmers in Queens.

"I picked up the lotus seed paste," he told her.

"Lotus seed paste?"

"Yeah, I was told to pick it up in Chinatown and bring it here."

"Yes, of course. Let's take it into the kitchen."

While she escorted him there, Tibbitts looked at me quizzically.

"It's great on toast," I said.

I let him out, and Emmie returned.

"Apparently Xiang-Mei requested it," she told me. "This explains everything, Harry."

"The lotus seed paste?"

"Don't be a gink. I mean the sergeant's story. Ernie Joy was Mrs. Twinem's lover. Her husband surprised them at the Cosmopolitan with a gun. There was a struggle, he was shot. Ernie fled and joined the tour just to make sure he wasn't followed."

"But it was the husband who checked in."

"For goodness' sakes, Harry. Ernie Joy was an actor. It would have been nothing for him to play the part of the husband."

"I suppose so, provided they were of about the same build. But that was at eight. Wouldn't he have been at the theatre?"

"His turn was in the second half of the show. And remember, the girl at the boarding house told us he left the theatre before ten o'clock."

"So your theory is that Ernie Joy plays the husband, checks into the Cosmopolitan, runs up to the theatre to do his show, then comes back to the hotel. It makes no sense."

"Why?"

"If they were meeting at the Cosmopolitan for a tryst, why would he pretend to be the husband?"

"Well, perhaps they lured the husband there with the intention of killing him."

"Why come up with such a convoluted plan?"

"I don't know yet. But remember how he acted when he joined the tour on Park Row? He jumped on the wagon as if in a panic. And he was especially anxious to get inside the warehouse. For him, the tour was simply a means of escape."

"I suppose that would explain it. But if they had planned the thing together, why did she call Tibbitts back with the story about the Chinaman? Why wouldn't she have left well enough alone?"

"I have a theory about that, too. Vengeance."

"Vengeance?"

"Yes. She hated Lou Ling for having killed her lover. But if it were proven to have been an accident, he wouldn't be punished. So she wanted to saddle him with an indisputable murder."

Given that this was a conversation with Emmie— and looking at it solely in that context—it all sounded reasonable enough. But I interpreted that as a warning. If things took their normal course, I could expect to soon be embroiled in some absurdity du jour, like dressing up as a Celestial to rescue Chinese girls from a canal boat and then secreting them with a sect of wayward Utopians. In an effort to avoid that fate, I probed her argument at its weakest point.

"Are you suggesting that Ernie Joy shot his lover's husband, and then two hours later was shot by pure chance?"

"Not pure chance. Suppose the gun he was shot with was the same gun he used to kill Twinem. He runs from the shooting with the gun in his pocket. At the opium den, he realizes he still has it, and while talking with Carlotta, he hides it in nearly the same spot she usually places her prop gun."

"Then where's the prop gun?"

"Couldn't she have just forgotten it where she was staying? The same way she'd forgotten her keys that night?"

"Well, it seems to be lost now. She had to borrow another for her act," I told her. "Do you think there's any chance of Tibbitts finding Lou at the farm?"

"Maybe I should go on ahead and warn him."

"And see if he'll show you where he threw the gun," I said. "It might be better if Tibbitts doesn't find it. Especially if the two shootings are linked."

"Are you worried Carlotta *did* bring it to Jimmy's?"

"Not really. At least not intentionally. But I wouldn't mind knowing a little more before the police get hold of it."

"All right."

She left, and a half hour later I headed off myself for Hunter's Point.

15

I found Tibbitts waiting with Jimmy Yuan at the Steinway car stop.

"Hello, Jimmy. How's business?" I asked.

"They still won't let me reopen, Mr. Reese. The police can be very disagreeable." Then he remembered Tibbitts standing beside him. "Excuse me for mentioning it, Sergeant."

"That's okay. We want it to be disagreeable."

"Yes, but need it be so expensive?"

Tibbitts just smiled.

"Have you learned anything, Mr. Reese?"

"Well, I'm more fully informed about the intricacies of the canal system upstate. But not much else."

"Then I don't think I can afford your services any longer."

"Did you really have any intention of paying us?"

"Oh, I assure you my intentions are always honorable."

"Yes, no doubt. How's the follow-through?"

"One must be realistic. Only so much blood can come from one turnip."

"And the police are squeezing your turnips pretty thoroughly?"

"Frankly, yes."

"Well, let's not say anything to my wife. She's enjoying herself, and this way I have some idea what she's up to."

"She won't be disappointed to learn there's no recompense?"

"Not horribly. What will disappoint her is if she can't solve the murder."

"But I hired you to prove it was an accident!"

"Hired, but with little likelihood of paying."

"It probably doesn't matter anyhow. The tongs seem ready to settle their lawsuits. The tours of Chinatown will begin again, and my opportunity will have been lost."

On arriving in Steinway, we walked up the hill to the farm. Emmie greeted us.

"I've looked about for Lou Ling," she told us. "But he doesn't seem to be here."

"Why don't you go ask around?" Tibbitts said to Jimmy.

He went off, with Emmie tailing along.

"What's she up to?" Tibbitts asked me.

"Trying to determine what Emmie's up to at any given moment is a mug's game. Sometimes I wonder if she can keep track."

"Let's look around for the gun," Tibbitts suggested. "We can skip the shack. I've been through it twice. I wonder if he just tossed it someplace."

"Probably the East River, or out in the bay there."

"If he had any sense. But nine times out of ten they don't. Especially amateurs. If they don't drop it right away, they forget they have it. Then when they see it, they panic."

We went about checking the big pots they used to store things, then probed the water barrels. I knew, of course, there was little chance of his finding it. First, because the number of places you could hide something on a farm was close to infinite. Second, because Emmie had obviously arrived in time to warn Lou Ling to take the gun off and hide it somewhere else. But I had made the mistake of thinking I was privy to Emmie's plans.

She and Jimmy approached us.

"They still insist they haven't seen Lou Ling since the shooting, Sergeant," he said. "I don't think there was much point in our coming out here."

"No, probably not." Tibbitts was looking squarely at Emmie.

Though we didn't know Sergeant Tibbitts particularly well, his acquaintance with Emmie was sufficient to provide him some idea about how her mind worked.

"There's probably not much chance we'll find the gun either, is there?" he asked her.

"Oh, I don't think you've looked very hard yet."

Tibbitts glanced over at me. His eyebrows were raised. I shrugged.

"Tell me, Emmie," he asked. "If you were Lou Ling, what would you do with the gun?"

"Why don't we act it out?"

"Act it out?"

"Yes. We need to recreate the emotional state of Lou Ling that night." Then she proceeded to do just that. "He must know he's shot a man. He rushes back here, to his home, in a state of extreme excitement." She ran into the shack and we followed. "At last he breathes a sigh of relief." She did a reasonably good property sigh. "His palms are damp. He wipes them on his jacket and realizes he still has the gun." She looked agape at the imaginary gun. "He runs to the edge of the hillside...." Again we followed. "And flings it into the bramble below...."

Tibbitts walked to the edge of the hillside. It was a near-impenetrable mass of raspberry bushes and wild roses, with a good helping of poison ivy.

"Why don't you re-enact putting the gun wherever it

is now?" he suggested. "That might save us some trouble."

"I don't know what you're talking about, Sergeant. I'm merely presenting the most likely scenario. Perhaps if we start from the bottom and work up?"

We took the path around the bramble and down to the bottom of the hill. The growth wasn't quite as forbidding down here. We spread out, and all started kicking about. It was a big area, but it took just a few minutes before Emmie shouted to us that she'd found the gun.

While Tibbitts examined it, I took Emmie aside.

"What's the idea, Emmie?"

"Lou Ling didn't know exactly where it was."

"But why lead Tibbitts down here?"

"I have my objectives and you have yours, Harry."

She walked over to the sergeant and I followed.

"We're in luck," he announced. "There's an inscription. 'To Frank Rhodes, G.A.R.'"

"How's that make us lucky?" Jimmy asked.

"Well, we know Frank Rhodes is a veteran, in the Grand Army of the Republic. And if it was engraved at the Colt factory, they'll have a record."

"Sergeant, could it be the same gun that shot Mr. Twinem?" Emmie asked.

"Yeah, could be. A .45. And two empty shells in the cylinder."

Emmie smiled, but erased it as soon as Tibbitts noticed. We all caught the car back to Hunter's Point. Then I told Emmie I'd be going across the river with Tibbitts.

"All right, Harry. I'll see you later at home."

She went off to the Brooklyn car and we caught the ferry to 34th Street. Jimmy promptly drifted away from us, apparently having tired of police company.

"What do you have in mind?" Tibbitts asked.

"Well, Emmie and I are in a little rivalry. She's convinced the two shootings are linked. I think it's just coincidence."

"I'm not sure what I think anymore."

"Is Mrs. Twinem still at the Victoria?" I asked.

"No, she's at her mother's in New Jersey. You want to see her?"

"Not that badly. But I think I'll still head down to the Victoria to ask some questions."

"If you learn anything, I'll be at headquarters the rest of the afternoon."

I took the L down to the hotel and asked the clerk for Mrs. Twinem's forwarding address. After he'd given it to me, I asked when she'd checked out.

"Checked out last week." Then added under his breath, "Thank the Lord."

"You were happy to see her leave?" I asked.

He led me to the far corner of the counter.

"It isn't my place to complain about the guests. But even Mr. Cummings, the manager, became annoyed with her."

"How so? Very demanding?"

"Oh, yes. Of course, we're used to that. But that one was so... volatile."

"Got upset, did she? What about?"

"The first explosion occurred the night her husband was murdered, when she asked for her husband's papers from the safe. To be honest, it was partly Mr. Cummings' fault. I've cautioned him—you can't treat the modern woman like an appendage of her husband. This isn't 1870. The modern woman is much more complex than her mother. I'm sure you know what I mean."

"Yes, all too well. But in my case, complex doesn't begin to describe it. What exactly happened?"

"Well, I was filling in that evening for one of the night men. Mrs. Twinem came down to the desk and Mr. Cummings happened to attend to her. She said her husband had asked that she retrieve some papers he'd placed in our safe. Mr. Cummings demurred. 'Perhaps I might speak with Mr. Twinem,' he said."

"Mr. Cummings put his foot in it?"

"Yes, most decidedly."

"The lady was perturbed?"

"The lady was livid. In his defense, it *was* counter to Mr. Twinem's instructions. He had told Mr. Cummings specifically not to hand the papers over to anyone but himself."

"So the lady insisted and Mr. Cummings demurred. I suppose I can guess what happened next."

"Yes, Mr. Cummings' resolve crumbled."

"What time was it?"

"In the evening."

"Can you be more precise?"

"I'd just returned from a break, so about nine."

"Had you seen much of Mr. Twinem?"

"Yes, he inquired of us frequently. He seemed anxious to receive some correspondence."

"Did he receive it?"

"Them. Every afternoon."

"Do you remember anything about them?"

"No, just ordinary letters."

"How would you describe Twinem?"

"A brusque sort of person. Not particularly rude, just never friendly."

"What did he look like?"

"Fortyish. Dark hair, about your height and build."

"Were you surprised to hear he was killed at the Cosmopolitan?"

"Yes. Of all places. One doesn't like to speak poorly of the competition, but.... Let's just say its best days are behind it."

"Did you see them go out that evening?"

"I saw her leave. It was 9:20."

"How is it you remember so precisely?"

"She stopped to ask me the time. A little odd."

"Why's that?"

He pointed to the large clock above the desk.

"Was she carrying anything when she left?"

"Yes, the bundle of papers she'd retrieved from the safe."

"How can you be sure it was the same bundle?"

"It was tied up with a maroon ribbon."

"And after the shooting, she returned here?"

"Yes, that same night."

"Did she seem upset?"

"Yes, very upset."

I left him and went over to visit Tibbitts at the detective bureau.

"Did you see Ernie Joy before he was buried?"

"Yeah. And yes, he and Twinem looked a lot alike. You wouldn't mistake one for the other if they were standing beside you. But a stranger might confuse them."

"And, of course, Ernie Joy was an actor. That's the essence of Emmie's theory: Ernie impersonated Twinem and checked into the Cosmopolitan under that name. Then he and the Missus lured Twinem there in order to kill him."

"I told you, I tried that one. Even if the clerk made a

mistake, it still doesn't line up with the facts. You're going to kill a fellow, so you wear a jacket no one could help but remember? And what sort of plan was that for an escape?"

"Yes, there has to be a lot more to it," I agreed.

Emmie arrived home about an hour after I did.

"I'm afraid I have a confession, Emmie. I inadvertently substantiated your theory."

"How do you mean?"

"I went by the Victoria. I was hoping to verify that it was Twinem who took the manuscript to the Cosmopolitan. But it was his wife. So maybe her story about him meeting a man *was* just a ruse. And apparently Ernie wouldn't have had much trouble passing himself off as Twinem."

She gave me a smug smile. "I knew it. But I also have a confession to make. I was hoping to prove Carlotta never brought her prop pistol that night, so it wasn't a matter of someone having to switch them."

"How would you prove that?"

"Well, I thought perhaps that girl she was staying with, Eva, might have borrowed it. Or that it was just misplaced in her apartment. But she and I combed the place—it wasn't there."

"I suppose we could just call it a draw and leave it at that," I said.

"Drop the case when we're so close to solving it?"

"Are we close to solving it?"

"Closer than when we started, certainly."

"So in much the same way we're nearer to St. Petersburg whenever we enter the kitchen."

"That can't be right. Surely you mean St. Louis...."

But forget the mapmaking, Harry. We need to meet with this Mrs. Twinem."

"She's left town."

"To New Brunswick, New Jersey, I know. But that's just an hour away."

"Yes, but in which direction? I'm sorry, Emmie, but until we settle the orientation of the apartment, I don't think it would be safe to venture out of it."

Her reply consisted of a disparaging expletive, lobbed over her shoulder as she went off to bathe.

16

The next morning I woke breathing the inebriating atmosphere of Emmie-land. The chief inebriate was back to dripping ice water.

"We need to get ready, Harry."

"Get ready for what?"

"Visiting Mrs. Twinem."

"Why so early?"

"We'll need the time to prepare our costumes."

It was then that I first suspected the day would prove an eventful one. I began weighing various excuses for absenting myself when my thinking was interrupted by another dose of ice water.

"What costumes? What are you talking about, Emmie?"

"I came up with a foolproof way of proving she made up the story about seeing a Chinaman."

"What's that?"

"Well, say a policeman were to bring by Lou Ling and ask her, 'Is this the man you saw?' She would, of course, say yes. But if we're right that she made up the part about seeing a Chinaman, she has no idea what Lou Ling looks like. In which case she will have to assume whatever Chinaman she's presented with *is* Lou Ling."

"I suppose that makes some sense. You could suggest it to Tibbitts."

"We don't need Sergeant Tibbitts. It's simple, really. I dress up as a Chinaman, and you reprise your role as a policeman. You were very convincing back in Washington."

"That was a fancy dress ball."

"What about your work with the wife-beater?"

"I was playing to a crowd intoxicated with excitement and cheap beer. I'm unlikely to find Mrs. Twinem so gullible."

The telephone rang. Emmie refused to answer it, forcing me out of bed.

"It's Tibbitts. Remember asking me to send out a bulletin on Cliff Ainslie?"

"The one you never sent out?"

"Turns out I did. They picked him up out on Long Island. A little burg called St. James."

"Couldn't you just tell them to release him?"

"I tried that, but no go."

"What about the woman he was with? Nell Elwell?"

"What happened to her isn't exactly clear. I think she might be in some sort of custody."

"Some sort of custody? What the hell does that mean?"

"Not sure. I thought maybe I'd go out and see. You want to come along?"

"Yes, I'd prefer to rescue her before Emmie finds out what happened."

We agreed to meet at the Flatbush depot at nine. Then I went back to our room and told Emmie about Ainslie's arrest. She seemed surprised.

"Why was he arrested?"

"It might have something to do with the kidnapping report I gave Tibbitts."

"I thought you called that off?"

"So did I. I'm afraid I won't be able to perform an encore of my Officer MacDonald routine."

"Why can't Tibbitts handle it himself?"

"Complicating factors."

"What complicating factors?"

"Aunt Nell's current whereabouts."

"Where is she?"

"That's just it. But don't worry, chances are good we'll find her."

"Maybe I should go, too?"

"No, you go on to New Jersey."

"Who'll play the policeman?"

"Maybe Carlotta can suggest someone."

"I have a better idea. Why don't you go to New Jersey as the policeman? Xiang-Mei could play the Chinaman. Then I'll go rescue Aunt Nell."

"I don't think that would work, Emmie."

"Why not?"

"Well, for one thing, Xiang-Mei is pretty decidedly feminine. I don't think she could pull off posing as a man."

"But I could?"

"It was your plan, Emmie, not mine." Then I played my ace in the hole. "By the way, there's a canal over there in New Brunswick."

"What canal?"

"The Delaware and Raritan. It's curious Mrs. Twinem went there, with a canal so nearby...."

Of course, only a mind like Emmie's would find it curious. But at the moment, that was the mind I needed to convince.

"All right, Harry. You go find Aunt Nell. I'll take care of Mrs. Twinem."

To say I was relieved would be a gross understatement. No matter how thorny Nell's situation would prove to be, I expected it was unlikely to be anywhere near the one Emmie would be creating in New Jersey.

When we'd boarded the train, I asked Tibbitts about the lapse in his handling of the Ainslie affair.

"Oh, well, I've had some things on my mind lately."

"Another case?"

"Yeah, there's always that. But my wife has been a problem lately. She wants me to quit my job."

"She feels it's too dangerous?"

"Too dangerous? No, I think she's just embarrassed to be married to a cop."

"You married into the 400?"

"No, far from that. Let's skip it."

"All right," I agreed. "Emmie has a plan to present Mrs. Twinem with a Chinaman in order to trip her up."

"You mean show her some fellow she's never seen before and ask if he's the one who shot her husband?"

"Yes, that's it."

"I have the same plan. Jimmy Yuan's going out there with me tomorrow to play the Chinaman."

"It's a pity you couldn't have done it earlier."

"Why?"

"Because Emmie intends on executing her version today."

"How is she going to pull it off?"

"She'll play the Chinaman and get someone else to play the cop."

"Why's she have to make everything so complicated?"

"My diagnosis is that she generally starts out with something resembling a rational thought—for instance, present Mrs. Twinem with a Chinaman. Then the part of her brain that handles logic mentions the idea to the part where her imagination resides. Since the former is the size of a pea, and the latter reaches down to her ankles, the outcome is never in much doubt."

He stared at me for a while, then posed a question. "What do you think happened at the Cosmopolitan that night?"

"I can't say for sure. But Emmie can't be right they were lovers. If Ernie Joy was in on a plot to kill her husband, there was no reason for her to give his description. Unless...."

"Unless she *wanted* us to identify Joy as the killer. Then when we didn't do it fast enough, she links the two shootings by adding the Chinaman. So maybe her lover was someone else, and they just picked Joy to take the fall."

"That would explain a lot," I said.

"Yeah, but so far, nothing. I had the fellows up in Syracuse look into it, but they couldn't find anything. Not even a rumor. And the only times she traveled were with her husband or to her mother's place in New Jersey."

"But a lot of people are good at keeping that type of thing a secret."

"Sure. But what now? If the whole point was to kill Twinem so she could take up with the new boy full-time, they have to be itching to get together. When they scratch the itch, we'll have a name and can work backwards."

"You have someone watching her?"

"Not round the clock, but we're checking up on her. If she hops on a train, we'll know about it. In the meantime, I have a fellow trying to figure out who Frank Rhodes is."

"The inscription on the gun?"

"Yeah. All we know so far is he was in the G.A.R., and if he was in the war, he'd be at least fifty, probably closer to sixty."

"About the right age for her father."

"His name was Jacobson," he said.

"Had she been to the Cosmopolitan before?"

"Not according to the staff. But they said the fellow who checked in had."

"Under the name Twinem?"

"No, different names."

"That sounds like Ernie Joy. Apparently he toyed with women's hearts."

"So I've heard."

"But the night of the shooting, the fellow checked in as Twinem?"

"Yeah. That's the name on the card."

"Did you compare the signature to Twinem's?"

"Yeah, I have his card from the Victoria. It looks about right. But I have a handwriting expert looking at them."

We arrived in St. James about half past eleven. It was a tiny old-time village surrounded by a lot of newly constructed cottages. Tibbitts led me down a road that seemed to head out of town.

"Where exactly is the jail?" I asked.

"Ainslie's being held by a justice of the peace. Fellow named Pugh. Said he has a big house up the road here."

There was no mistaking Pugh's manse. It was a large, decrepit farmhouse, with a multi-colored sign announcing "Horace Pugh, Justice of the Peace for the Town of Smithtown, Magistrate and Chief Constable for the Hamlet of St. James, Chairman of the Citizens Vigilance Committee, and Plenipotentiary Inspector for the Greater New York Anti-Vice League."

"How do we address the fellow?" I asked.

Tibbitts shrugged.

Pugh was waiting for us on the veranda. He was an older fellow, over sixty certainly, and not taller than five-two. He had long grey hair and a shaggy grey beard. From his looks, and those of his house, I surmised he was one of the last relics of St. James's old guard.

"I suppose you're the fellow from New York."

"Yeah, Sergeant Tibbitts. This is Harry Reese. You still holding that Ainslie fellow?"

Pugh nodded over to an outbuilding.

"Didn't you understand? It was all a mistake," Tibbitts told him.

"Well, maybe your reason for wantin' him 'rested was a mistake. But *my* reason for 'restin' him was no mistake. No, sir."

"How so?" I asked.

"Sit down. I'll tell you."

We all sat down, but as soon as we had, he got up.

"You boys want a drink?"

"We're in kind of a hurry," Tibbitts said.

This, apparently, was a mistake. Pugh was the type of fellow who relished a captive audience. And once caught, resistance just drove the hook in deeper.

"That may be, Sergeant. But the wheels of justice turn in their own time."

In an effort to smooth the waters, I told him I'd favor a drink. He went off at a snail's pace, just to make clear whose hand was on the judicial throttle.

"I hope Nell isn't locked up in that chicken coop. Or there'll be hell to pay when I get home."

"What made you think Ainslie had kidnapped her?"

"Bad intelligence. I'd communicated with a couple of excited Celestials via a French mime who was in turn translated by my theatrically inclined cousin. It seems what they interpreted as an abduction was some sort of embrace."

"Huh."

Pugh came back with a bottle of cheap rye and three glasses. He made a ritual out of pouring it.

"Your health, gentlemen." He downed his and we followed suit.

"Can you tell us what became of the woman who was traveling with Ainslie? Nell Elwell?"

"Elwell! Ha! I knew it."

"Knew what exactly?" I asked.

"I knew they weren't married like they claimed. But I'll get to that in time."

He carefully poured us another round and offered another toast. This one to the stamping out of sin. When we'd all polished off our drinks, he leaned back and put up his feet on a stool.

"You see, yesterday morning I went down to Smithtown to see a fellow about...." There's no sense in repeating the whole of Pugh's desultory rambling. Suffice it to say he stopped by the police station and saw Tibbitts's bulletin about Ainslie and Nell.

"Well, as soon as I see he's an actor, I know where to look."

"Where?" I asked.

"Why, right here in St. James! They flock here every summer. It's Sodom and Gomorrah all over again."

He poured another drink and offered a toast to the damnation of actors.

"So I go by that Shore Inn. Full of those people. I look through the register and there he is! Ainslie! Didn't even bother to change his name. 'Mr. and Mrs. Clifton Ainslie' it says. Well, I round up a couple fellows from the committee and we wait 'til late and creep up to the balcony. They had the window wide open. We could hear everything went on in there. A good hour or more! I can't say any of us were surprised. Seen it all before up there. Some of them go on all night!"

His admission merely verified what I'd always suspected, that the chief qualification for membership in an anti-vice league was a prurient obsession with sex.

"Well, when they finally let up, we took 'em by surprise."

"Yes, I imagine so. And you brought them both here?"

"Tried to. We had him tied up pretty well, but she went a little crazy on us. Foamin' at the mouth crazy. Even wavin' a gun. And when I got that away from her, she nearly split the Reverend Simpson's head open with a ewer."

"But what's her current disposition?"

"The Misses Fowler were with us. Big women. They managed to subdue her. Then we brought them both here."

"You mean...." I nodded toward the coop.

"No, they have her upstairs. They're determined to teach her the error of her ways. Through readin' to her."

Nell had always seemed reasonably good humored, but I suspected when she learned it was due to my erroneous report that she'd been ambushed in bed, humiliated by vigilantes, and forced to listen to Bible lectures, her feelings toward me would sour.

Pugh led us upstairs. Fortunately, Nell and the two elderly Fowler sisters seemed to be getting on amiably.

"Hello, Harry. I was just telling the ladies about our excursion to Weedsport. Where's Cliff?"

"Waiting downstairs," I said.

We all went down and Pugh led the whole entourage to the chicken coop, where he removed a large chain securing the door. Ainslie was half dressed and tied to a chair. The stench of his cell was overpowering and he looked to be in a complete daze. We untied him and brought him out in the fresh air and he quickly recovered his wits.

Not too subtly, Pugh voiced his reluctance to release his prisoners.

"What will it cost to get the two of them out of here?" I asked.

"Well, *he'll* need to come back. But he can go now for twenty-five dollars bond, I suppose. Or the cost of the ceremony."

"What ceremony?"

"Wedding ceremony. See, if they *was* married, then there ain't a case."

"And if you perform the ceremony now, you'll be satisfied?"

"I reckon so."

"How much is that?"

"Twenty dollars."

There was a brief discussion and the decision was made to save the five dollars. For the first time that day, Pugh moved quickly. The whole thing took five minutes.

"Of course, it only does you good if you was married *before* last night. Say, yesterday afternoon."

Having the certificate backdated to the day before cost another twenty dollars. Nell asked him for the return of the prop gun, but he insisted on keeping it as a souvenir. Then the four of us caught a train back to Brooklyn.

Tibbitts, thankfully, kept quiet about my having gotten the couple arrested. They attributed it to the enthusiasm of local prudery. Nell even apologized again for having knocked me out in Albany.

"All's fair in love and war," Ainslie said with a smirk.

"I was just a civilian."

"War *is* hell, isn't it?"

I was beginning to dislike the fellow almost as much as he disliked me.

17

Simian howls greeted us as we entered the apartment that evening. Carlotta and Thibaut were rehearsing their zoo skit for the benefit of Xiang-Mei. Thibaut went from one make-believe cage to another. In one he was an elephant, and tickled Carlotta with his trunk, in another, he turned his jacket inside out and revealed the telltale stripes of a zebra. Carlotta simply acted amused, giving little squeals of delight. They had hit upon the ideal formula. One that made ample use of Thibaut's talents, without taxing Carlotta's. Even Ainslie was impressed.

When Xiang-Mei and Thibaut went into the kitchen to prepare dinner, Nell and Ainslie—who still carried the reminder of his recent incarceration in Justice Pugh's chicken coop—went off to bathe. Leaving me alone with Carlotta.

"I don't suppose there's any sign of Emmie?" I asked.

"NOT since **she** WOKE me UP AT the **crack** of DAWN!"

"Looking for someone to play a policeman?"

"Yeah. I gave her the name of Ernie's feeder. He could use the work."

"His feeder?"

"Yeah. You know, he sets up the joke. But without his funnyman, he has no act. Just like you with Emmie."

"How so?"

"Um, never mind."

A little later we had an excellent dinner of veal with a brown sauce and steamed vegetable dumplings. Xiang-

Mei was pretty fond of steamed dumplings. Either that or it was the only thing she knew how to cook.

About half past seven Carlotta rose from the table. "Come on, kiddo! We have to run!"

With that, she and Thibaut bolted out the door. And while Xiang-Mei went into the kitchen to clean up, Ainslie opened another bottle of our wine, graciously sharing it with Nell and me.

It did cross my mind about then to worry some about Emmie. The trip to New Brunswick and back wouldn't have taken more than a few hours. But worrying about what *might* have happened to Emmie would open a veritable cavern of anxiety. So I chose to divert my thoughts to something more pleasant.

"Would it be prying to ask how you two first met?" I asked Nell.

"Remember, back in Buffalo, I told you I'd been in a medicine show?"

"Oh, yes. But I'd always thought that might have been... apocryphal."

"That I made it up to make my dull past more interesting?"

"Well, you are Emmie's blood relation."

"In fact, it was all true. Cliff was the show's drummer."

"And that was when a drummer really pounded a drum," Ainslie added. "As soon as we arrived in town, we'd put on a little parade. I'd beat the drum, singing the praises of Doctor Glossheim's Authentic German Cure, Nellie just behind atop her pony, doing a pirouette."

"Did the Authentic German Cure ever actually cure anything?" I asked.

"It most certainly did!" Ainslie enthused. "Why,

what's the epidemic that runs rampant in every jay town, year in and year out? Smallpox comes and goes. So does scarlet fever. And sure, typhoid has its season. But what is it every man, woman, and child suffers from, day in and day out? Boredom. Ennui. Languor. Unrelenting tedium. And we cured it! And not just for the evening we were there, but for a week or two after."

"Were you two close then?"

"You might say so," Nell said. "After Cliff seduced me...."

"Wait a minute," Ainslie interjected. "That's not how I remember it. You got out the pony and did a Lady Godiva show for my personal benefit. What did you suppose would happen next?"

"What did you suppose would happen after breaking open half a case of cure with me?"

"I'd supposed lots of things, but not that midnight ride...."

"It must have been potent stuff," I said.

"In those days, you couldn't sell a patent medicine that was less than forty-five percent alcohol. People weren't as gullible as they are now."

"When was the last time you'd seen each other?"

"She abandoned me," he said with mock reproach.

"Cliff was arrested in Bowmansville, not far from Buffalo. A girl had accused him."

"It was all a lie. You should have had more faith, Nellie."

Nell started crying. I've always had a sort of visceral reaction to sentimental scenes and this one was starting to sound like a Thomas Hardy novel. I thought I'd shove it along a little.

"How did you arrange to meet in Syracuse?"

"That was pure chance. I was waiting to board the train when Nellie got off right in front of me."

"You had gone to Syracuse to see someone? About Ernie Joy's death?"

"Yes, a woman named Twinem. She'd gotten Ernie involved in some scheme."

"The scheme that ended with her husband getting shot?"

"I don't know that. But I know Ernie would never shoot anyone."

"What did Mrs. Twinem tell you?"

"She wasn't there."

"How'd you find out about her?"

"A fellow named Bauman. He worked with Ernie."

"As his feeder?"

"Yes."

"Had he seen Mrs. Twinem with Ernie?"

"No idea. But he knew Ernie was seeing her. Why?"

As if on cue, there was a knock on the door with the answer to his question. It was a telegram sent collect from the New Brunswick Police Department. Emmie was being held there. It suggested I could arrange bail in the morning.

I then told Ainslie and Nell about her scheme and how Carlotta had recommended Bauman for the part of policeman.

"If I were to conjecture, I would guess that Mrs. Twinem *was* familiar with Bauman. And that Emmie, who rarely confides her intentions to anyone, neglected to tell Bauman the true purpose of their masquerade. When he knocked on the door dressed as a policeman, he and Mrs. Twinem recognized each other. Then she called the real police."

When Xiang-Mei had finished in the kitchen, she came out and suggested a game of whist. Ainslie opened another bottle of wine and we had a very convivial evening. Ainslie cheated, of course. But Xiang-Mei, playing as my partner, was surprisingly good at it herself. I was beginning to have serious doubts about the effectiveness of American missionary work in China.

Once I'd gone to bed, it was hard not to think of Emmie, alone in a cold, damp cell. But a woman well-informed on the subject—a master jewel thief-cum-countess—had once suggested it would do Emmie good to put in some jail time. And here was the perfect opportunity to test that theory.

Scraping together bail money proved a bit of a problem the next morning. I'd already tapped out Nell, and Ainslie, who hadn't worked in a week, insisted he'd given the last of his savings freeing himself from the Plenipotentiary Inspector for the Greater New York Anti-Vice League.

I packed a change of clothes for Emmie and went off for the ferry to Jersey City. When I arrived at the New Brunswick police station, the desk sergeant informed me Emmie's bail had been set at two hundred dollars. I barely had half that.

"Might I see the prisoner just the same?"

They led me back to a little room and a while later a matron escorted Emmie in.

"Hello, Harry." She said it as if we'd run into each other in the park. "Is Aunt Nell all right?"

"Yes, she and Ainslie are back at the apartment. Married now."

"Married?"

"I'll let her tell you about that," I said. "I brought

you a change of clothes, Emmie. But I'm afraid I had some trouble getting the bail together."

"Oh, that's all right."

"It is?"

"Yes, my cellmate, Madame Sahlumie, and I have been having a wonderful time."

"You have?"

"Well, the food could certainly stand some improvement. But I've learned a lot from my new friend."

I could think of just one likely profession for a cellmate named Mme. Sahlumie and it wasn't schoolmarm. I only hoped the pointers she was passing on were at the artistic end of the trade and not the entrepreneurial.

"What exactly happened yesterday? Did Mrs. Twinem recognize Bauman?"

"What made you ask that?"

"Carlotta told me she gave you his name and that he worked with Ernie Joy. And Ainslie said Bauman had told him that Ernie was involved in some scheme of hers."

"I knew he was Ernie's feeder, but didn't realize he knew anything about the Twinems. However, it does explain what happened. I found him at Mrs. de Shine's boarding house in Manhattan. When I described my plan to him, he was very eager to join in. He even arranged his costume. When we got to her mother's house, Bauman knocked on the door and the girl went and fetched Mrs. Twinem. He may have recognized her, but she didn't seem to know him, at least in costume."

"Did she find your Chinaman convincing?"

"Oh, yes. 'Yes, that's the man,' she said. Then Mr. Bauman lost his head. 'What did you trick Ernie into?' he shouted. She tried to leave the room, but he grabbed her arm. Then she called for help and Mr. Bauman lost his nerve."

"He ran for it?"

"Not before shoving me into the arms of the cook, who'd come to the aid of her mistress."

"Gallant fellow."

"Yes. And that cook had an iron grip."

"From kneading bread, I'll bet. My aunt's cook had me in a headlock once. And they ate a lot of bread in that house."

"What are you talking about, Harry?"

"Sorry, just reminiscing," I said. "It seems odd Mrs. Twinem chose to involve the police."

"I don't think she did. The maid had gone out and flagged down an officer. When he came in, she made up a story about us trying to steal the silver."

"That explains the two-hundred-dollar bail," I said. "Well, I have to go see about raising more money."

"First, you must tell Tibbitts that she definitely made up the story about seeing the Chinaman. And when you return, make sure you have enough for Mme. Sahlumie's bail as well. Hers is just seventy-five."

"A bargain, no doubt."

At the depot I sent a wire to Tibbitts at the detective bureau: *Meet Thames noon.* Though cryptic, it's easily explained. Tibbitts's favorite rendezvous was a dark corner of a poorly-lit eatery on the shadier side of Thames Street, itself one of the gloomiest streets in Manhattan. It wasn't squalid like the dives you could find on the Lower East Side, but just as Dickensian in atmosphere. The sort of place where Mr. Guppy, the lowly law clerk in *Bleak House*, might dine. It was a grey day, and just as I rounded the last block it began to drizzle. I found

Tibbitts in his corner looking pretty gloomy himself.

"Rough night?" I asked.

"Yeah, but not the way you're thinking. What have you got to tell me?"

"Well, the first part of Emmie's plan worked like a charm. Mrs. Twinem identified her as the Chinaman who killed her husband."

"Must have been a good disguise."

"Oh, she's had some practice playing Chinamen."

"What was the part that didn't work?"

"The getaway. She's currently residing in the New Brunswick jail."

"You're not going to bail her out?"

"I went to do just that, but my means were insufficient. I don't suppose you could spare...?"

"Oh, leave her there. That was my big mistake. Not locking up my wife."

"I suppose having that prerogative provides policemen an advantage in family disputes."

"I wouldn't have needed to invent anything. I found her up to her neck in it."

It suddenly dawned on me just who Tibbitts's wife was. The clues were these: he had saved the woman from jail; she could readily interpret a Latin phrase; and, in a purely metaphoric sense, she was shrew enough to trouble a man through lunch. It had to be none other than Elizabeth Strout.

I first met Elizabeth when Tibbitts offered her as an informant during my investigation of a murder-for-insurance scheme. That was in the spring of 1901. Prior to that, she had twice been involved in shady schemes that had gone awry. And twice found herself pleading with a judge for her freedom, each time playing the part of the innocent led astray, teary-eyed and forlorn—but using different names. Tibbitts apparently was the only one to notice, but instead of exposing her subterfuge, he made use of his knowledge to enlist her as a stoolie.

A little later, and quite coincidentally, I learned that Elizabeth had attended college with Emmie, where she had a small business selling her classmates "ponies" (translations of classic texts) and choice bits of erotic literature. Her relationship with Emmie was hard to define—you might call it a bitter friendship. And over the previous year it had taken on many of the traits of a backwoods feud.

We'd both suspected things were a bit more complex between Tibbitts and Elizabeth than either let on. With Tibbitts, you might call it love-hate. With Elizabeth, who even for the closest of friends spared no venom, something closer to contempt-hate. However, I've probably given you a distorted view of her by dwelling too much on her negative traits. She could be very amusing—provided her witty jabs were aimed at someone other than oneself. But her most outstanding quality was her striking beauty. It may have been only skin deep, but it was real enough.

"How long have you and Elizabeth been together?" I asked smugly.

"You finally figured it out? Emmie did the other day. When we were talking about the manuscript."

"She didn't mention it to me."

"Remember I stayed on in Washington for a few days last December? And she supposedly went off to Hong Kong?"

"Bangkok, I believe. We did know she hadn't made the trip."

"She showed up at my hotel the next day. That was

that." Then he changed the subject abruptly. "What are you doing this afternoon?"

"Raising money for Emmie's bail."

"I got a lead on that gun. Frank Rhodes is a college professor in New Haven. I'm going up there to talk to him. Why don't you come along? Emmie can fend for herself."

"That's just what I'm afraid of. She's gotten a little chummy with her cellmate, a Madame So-and-so."

"Well, if you change your mind, I'll be catching the two o'clock express."

18

It was raining even harder when I approached our building. Then, just as I was crossing Vanderbilt Avenue, a closed carriage pulled in front of me and two fellows leapt out. They were Chinamen, one of whom I recognized as the fellow I dispatched with the pickled lambs' tongues back in Whitehall. From his expression, I took it he remembered the occasion as well and was hoping to find some way to commemorate it. They pushed me into the carriage and seated me between them. Opposite us was Jimmy Yuan and an older fellow.

"Good afternoon, Jimmy. Out for a ride in the park? Lovely day for it."

"Best not to joke with these fellows, Harry." Jimmy had lost his normal self-assurance. "This gentleman represents the Hip Sing Tong. They've lost... a certain cargo."

"Misplaced?"

"Stolen. It was a cargo of quite some value."

"Insured?"

"Unfortunately, no."

"Ah, well, there's the problem. Insurance isn't a luxury, it's a necessity. Unforeseen events are inevitable."

"Yes, but recovery is quite often possible. And in this case, the tong is very confident of recovery."

"Look, they can't think I have a gaggle of Chinese girls hanging about."

The older fellow then exchanged a few words with Jimmy.

"My associate suggests that by your insouciant attitude, you've already confirmed you know where the cargo has been hidden. He suggests that you may have some similar goods you value likewise."

"He's threatening me?"

"I would have thought that was obvious. But I suggest you not insist on proof of his sincerity in the matter. Of course, he is a businessman, and used to reaching accommodation."

"What is he offering?"

"He assumes you were acting as agent for others. The Chop Sing Tong, perhaps?"

"In fact, it's a particularly ruthless sect of religious fanatics."

"But you could provide the whereabouts of the six girls? Not without remuneration, of course. You could, in this way, have your cake and eat it too."

"How much cake are we talking about?"

The older fellow said something to Jimmy.

"Five hundred dollars."

"Doesn't sound like much."

"Ah, but you will also be assured of the safety of... your own cargo."

"Well, give me a few days to think about it."

"That may not be possible. This gentleman, though he may not look it, is of an impetuous nature."

"Those are my terms."

"Well, I can only give you some friendly advice. Be careful, Harry."

"Are we friends, Jimmy?"

"Of course. Any animosity I've projected is not my own. I am a mere conduit."

"That's reassuring," I smiled. "Tell me, you referred to six girls. I remember seven."

Jimmy said something to the other fellow. The old man stared at me.

Then for the first time he addressed me. "You know where Xiang-Mei can be found?"

"Not for certain. I was simply curious why she hadn't been included."

He smiled. The carriage stopped and I was freed.

I decided to leave my cargo safely jailed in New Jersey and go with Tibbitts to New Haven, if for no other reason than to distract anyone following me.

I'd already suspected Xiang-Mei was something other than a peasant girl sold to white slavers. My best guess was she'd been working the profession in some Chinese port and had been sent as a sort of chaperon to the other girls.

At Grand Central, I found Tibbitts already aboard. We exchanged grunts and then I sat down and took out a book.

"What's that?" he asked.

"*The Taming of the Shrew*. It crossed my mind this Frank Rhodes might be another English professor. Perhaps a mentor to Twinem. Maybe he can tell us what might have made that manuscript worth stealing, just in case it was really stolen. I thought I'd bone up on the subject so I can converse intelligently."

"It's not English he teaches. He's an expert on bugs."

"Bugs?"

"Something about insects."

"Not *insectivores*?"

"Yeah, that's it."

"Of course! *Rhodes on the Soricidae*. I should have recognized the name."

"What?"

"Shrews are of the family *Soricidae*."

"Sounds Italian."

"Frank Rhodes is the leading authority on shrews this side of Heidelberg. Twinem must have consulted Rhodes about the differing features of European shrews."

"You know, Elizabeth said the shrew thing was obviously just a clever metaphor and only a yap would take it literally."

I didn't answer Elizabeth's intended insult straight out. I just tossed my book to Tibbitts.

"You need this more than I do," I told him.

"Think it will work?"

"Can't hurt to try."

He apparently agreed, and spent the rest of the trip reading.

We arrived in New Haven just before four. Tibbitts hired a cab to take us to Rhodes' house, then left me to pay for it when we got there.

A housekeeper answered our knock.

"We've come to consult the eminent Professor Rhodes," I told her.

"You should have sent word first. He's with the circus."

"The circus? Is it in town?"

"*His* circus. Out back in the carriage house. But he's not to be disturbed."

"It's a police matter," Tibbitts told her.

"Be that as it may, he won't see you until rehearsal's over at six."

"I'm investigating a murder," Tibbitts insisted.

"Well, unless it was a shrew that was murdered, I doubt he'd be much interested."

"In truth, madam, it was not a shrew that was murdered," I confessed. "But shrews feature largely in the case. We wish to consult the professor vis à vis the distinguishing characteristics of the Etruscan shrew and its utility as a literary device."

"The tight-rope walkers?"

"Pardon?"

"The little tiny shrews...."

"Yes, the tight-rope walkers."

"You speak Latin?" she asked.

"Ah, amo *Crociduram etruscam*."

"All right, *you* can go around back. Your friend can wait here for you."

"Though my acolyte's manner is coarse, and his knowledge of the Insectivora limited, he strives to better himself. Show her the book, Sergeant."

He handed the play to her and she inspected it.

"A shrew tamer?"

"He aspires to be."

"All right then. Take the path 'round the house."

As we made our way, Tibbitts turned to me.

"You know, nine months of the year my cases are simple little murders. If it isn't a husband who killed his wife, or a wife who killed her husband, a fellow's either caught with a gun in his hand, or bragged about the killing, or starts spending the bundle he killed for. Then about the ninth month something comes up involving you and I find myself in New Haven trying to interview a nut who runs a shrew circus."

"There does seem to be a predictable regularity to it. I suppose it gives you something to look forward to during the otherwise dull routine of your work."

"Yeah. I suppose."

I knocked on the door of the carriage house. There

was no answer. Then Tibbitts gave it the patented police knock, which rarely fails to elicit a response.

This, however, was one of those rare cases. I opened the door gingerly and we stepped in.

"Close the door, you ass!"

When I did so, we were submerged in darkness. All the windows had been blocked, and the only light was afforded by three lanterns, each fitted with a deep red filter. My eyes had just begun to adjust when I was addressed.

"What d'yer want?"

This fellow was no college professor. He looked more like a circus roustabout. Another like fellow joined us.

"Youse spoilt the frail's cooch show!"

"Gentlemen, we apologize for the intrusion. But we've come to consult Professor Rhodes on a pressing shrew matter. The New York police are stymied, and have come to the conclusion that only an authority on *Soricidae* taxonomy can offer a way out of the impenetrable darkness."

"The kinkers like it dark!"

"Oh, we're all well aware of the nocturnal preferences of the kinkers. I was referring to the dark night of ignorance."

Another fellow stepped forward. He was dressed like the other two, but older, and clearly the man in charge.

"Dr. Rhodes, I presume?"

"Yes." He eyed me warily. "You'd better not be another pretender."

"Pretender? You do me wrong, sir. I only wish I'd thought to bring my copy of *Rhodes on the Soricidae* so as to have you inscribe it. I've unfortunately left it behind on my night stand."

"You have my book?"

"What other? The 1885 edition, with the small error on page 23. Printer's mistake, no doubt."

"Yes, the fools. I'm rather busy at the moment. We open tomorrow."

"An ingenious idea. Are they easy to train?"

"For God's sake, man. One doesn't train a shrew. One can only persuade it."

"Much like a cat?" I asked innocently.

"Cat!" he exclaimed. Both the big men began looking about the floor. "It's all right, gentlemen," he told them. Then turned back to me. "Can you imagine what havoc a damn feline would cause?"

"Yes, I see your point. I despise the creatures myself. As does Sergeant Tibbitts. The fact is, Professor, we've come to consult you about a fellow named Twinem."

"Twinem?"

"I believe he wanted to ascertain which species of shrew Shakespeare had been referring to."

"Him! The man's insane."

"Was, maybe," Tibbitts interjected. "He's dead now. Haven't you heard?"

"No, I haven't time to worry about him. I've the show."

"But he did consult you?"

"Yes, or tried to. Didn't know a damned thing about *Soricidae*. A pretender."

"You in the G.A.R.?" Tibbitts asked.

"Yes, I'm a veteran. I was there at Appomattox."

"Thank goodness you made it through the worst of it," I said.

"What's that? I'd just gotten out of training camp. Never actually saw any fighting."

"Not something you could have anticipated when you enlisted."

"Enlisted? Do I look like a fool? I was drafted."

Frank Rhodes was the first veteran I'd met who was honest about his service. The truth was that thousands of fellows had had to be dragged kicking and screaming into battle—not that I blamed them any. But I'd never met a veteran who'd owned up to it.

Tibbitts took out the gun we found on the farm and asked Rhodes if it was his.

"Yes—how'd you get it?"

"It was used to kill a man in New York," Tibbitts told him. "Where'd you last see it?"

"Upstairs, in my room."

"When was that?"

"When? It's been there since I was presented it."

"So you didn't give it to anyone?"

"Give away the gun my comrades presented me in gratitude? Of course not. I earned that gun. Do you imagine it's easy arranging a reunion dinner for six hundred, Sergeant? When you're given just four days' notice?"

"Could Twinem have taken the gun when he came to see you?"

"I don't see how. He was only in the house for ten or fifteen minutes. And never went upstairs. Can I have it back?"

"Not now, it's evidence."

The professor insisted on restarting the rehearsal and demanded that the door not be opened again until it was completed. We had missed the frail's cooch show, but the high-wire act the little Etruscans put on more than made up for it. A miniature red spotlight followed them scampering about, quarreling and chirping incessantly. The answer to Twinem's question seemed obvious. Kate was Etruscan.

Meanwhile, the Ferris wheel spun continuously on shrew power alone, and the aquatic members of the family took turns diving into a tank and devouring minnows.

When we were released, we had dinner in town and then caught an evening train back to New York. Tibbitts had been carrying a small valise during the trip, but hadn't made use of anything in it.

"Were you thinking of spending the night in New Haven?" I asked.

"No. I thought I mentioned it. I was going to ask you if I could stay at your place."

"Things that bad?"

"Yeah. Don't you have a couple spare rooms?"

"All full up, I'm afraid. But you can have the couch."

"That will do me."

We arrived at the apartment about half past ten, and a little while later, Nell, Ainslie, and Thibaut came in.

"Did you see the show this evening?" I asked Nell.

"See it? She was the star!" Ainslie boasted.

Nell blushed.

"You joined the act?" I asked.

"She jumped in like a trouper." Ainslie was talking like a proud father.

"Where's Carlotta?" I asked.

"I'm afraid she was arrested, Harry," Nell confessed.

"Arrested? For what?"

"Remember that policeman we met at the opium den, Sergeant...."

"Sergeant Eckel?"

"Yes, him. He came with two of his men. They took her just as they'd begun the zoo scene. Thibaut tried to stop them, but an angry baboon was no match for three policemen."

"It was a scream," Ainslie interjected. "We're thinking of incorporating it into the act."

"Don't worry, Harry. She should be back here soon. Cliff sent a man with the money to bail her out. You see, as she was being dragged away, Carlotta managed to instruct Thibaut to keep the act going so as not to lose their place in the show."

"So I nominated Nellie."

"Since I'd seen them rehearse so often. I thought I should help, if I could."

"She was an instant hit."

"I thought you were broke?" I said to Ainslie. "Who was it you sent?"

"Well, the truth is I wasn't able to follow through on that."

"But you swore to me you would!" Nell said angrily.

"I had to tell you that, or you wouldn't have gone on. Look, everything will be fine. Harry can go bail her out. She is his cousin, after all."

Thibaut had gone into the kitchen and came out eating a drumstick. He looked about and then queried Ainslie in French. Ainslie told him something that seemed to ease his mind and he sat down to his supper.

"You speak French?"

"I spent four years in Europe, back in the nineties, when things were dead here."

Tibbitts gave me an amused look.

"I thought this was your case now?"

He shrugged. "You know how it is."

I assumed he was referring to the byzantine hierarchy of the police force. It was a feudal system, with constantly shifting allegiances and endless power struggles over control of the booty. I filled him in on some of the details he wasn't aware of, such as Carlotta's pretend marriage to Ernie Joy. He just smiled, then asked where the telephone was.

He dialed a number, mentioned Carlotta's name, and then carried on a long, monosyllabic exchange. When it was over, he rejoined us.

"Eckel took her in on a second-degree murder charge, and indecency."

"He's decided to actually investigate the shooting? Why now?" I asked.

"Jimmy Yuan hasn't come through with his fine to the captain over there. They're putting the screws on. Eckel has your cousin down as the weak link."

"Get her to testify against Yuan?"

He shrugged again.

"Where is she now?"

"The Tombs. Any lawyer can get the murder charge dropped. You can probably get her out for a twenty-dollar fine."

"When?"

"There'll be a session of police court there tomorrow morning."

The only lawyer I knew who practiced criminal law was a fellow named Burleigh. I telephoned him and he agreed to meet me in the morning. Then I took up a collection. Ainslie contributed five dollars and I got ten from Tibbitts. Thibaut just turned out his empty pockets.

"I'll go with you in the morning, Harry," Nell told me. Then she went to their room and slammed the door.

Thibaut opened another bottle.

"You sure you don't have any more cash stashed away?" I asked Ainslie.

"I'm sure I can have all you need by next week."

"Next week?"

"Yes, no doubt about it. Why don't we just let Carlotta rest up for a few days?"

"Rest up? In the Tombs?"

"You see, Harry...." He put his arm around my shoulder. For the first time since we'd met he was acting friendly. "If Carlotta shows up tomorrow it's going to be awkward. Letting someone go is never pleasant."

"Especially when she's being let go from her own act."

"Yes, exactly. Now, if she were to spend another day or two... incapacitated, Nell will have the part down pat. And even Carlotta will appreciate it's a change for the better."

"I think that's rather unlikely."

"Well, then in a couple days we'll have devised another part for her."

"I'd suggest the usurped woman seeking bloody revenge."

"That's a thought." He stared up at the ceiling, considering it.

Xiang-Mei had hidden herself in the kitchen since our arrival, and I thought I should inform her of Tibbitts's presence.

She was baking little pies.

"Moon cakes," she told me.

I reached for one and she slapped my hand.

"*Wait* for the moon festival!" Then she nodded toward the door. "The policeman *staying* here?"

"Yes, I'm afraid so. Is Lou in yet?"

"Cricket hunt. He won't come *home* until very late!"

"Well, hopefully Tibbitts won't hear him. Lou should probably hide out here tomorrow. The police may be looking for him."

"But police *already* here!"

"Yes, but Tibbitts is relatively benign. The other policemen aren't so friendly."

"Ah. Father say, 'Better the devil *you* know.'"

"Yes, that's the idea. By the way, I saw Jimmy Yuan earlier today."

"Who is Jimmy Yuan?"

"Lou hasn't mentioned him? He ran the little show where Lou's accident occurred."

"Oh. *Lou* thinks of nothing *now* but crickets. He will *not* want to stay *inside* tomorrow."

"At least keep him in until sunset. There were some other men with Jimmy. From the Hip Sing Tong. Do you know them?"

She smiled and made a vague gesture.

"They seem anxious to find the other girls. The ones who crossed over from Canada with you. Apparently they've gone missing."

She shrugged her shoulders. "Oh, well. I must get *back* to work. You go now."

19

I woke the next morning to the smell of bacon. I found Nell preparing breakfast, but no one else was stirring.

"I suppose we should bring Thibaut along," she said.

"No, let's let him sleep. He doesn't even seem to realize what's happening. And he can be a little unpredictable—not the sort you want in your corner when you're trying to ingratiate yourself with a police magistrate."

As we left the apartment we passed Tibbitts sleeping on the couch. Ainslie was on the other side of the room, having lined up three chairs into a makeshift bed. Nell kicked out the middle chair, then rushed out the door ahead of me.

We met Burleigh outside the Tombs, not far from the Manhattan side of the bridge. I knew him from college and had stayed acquainted via various alumni events since. As soon as I'd thought of him, a vague feeling came over me, a sense that there was some reason I should hesitate before calling him.

He wasted no time in reminding me of the cause of my unease.

"I don't suppose you have that fifty dollars?" he said in a not very pleasant tone.

"Fifty dollars?"

"Remember, I lent you fifty dollars." He took out a slip of paper and read from it. "I.O.U. fifty dollars, to be paid within sixty days. Signed, Harry Reese. November 12th, 1900."

"I forgot all about it. You should have reminded me."

"I tried to, the next spring. You must have moved."

"What's fifty dollars between old friends?"

"Feels about the same as any other fifty dollars."

"Just add it to the bill when you send it."

"I will."

The Sunday morning session of the Tombs Police Court was a busy one. It was only after a small army of working girls, several pickpockets, and a wife-beater were disposed of that Carlotta was called.

As much as one might fault Burleigh for his over-attentive memory, there was no denying he handled the thing admirably. The judge agreed the murder charge was flimsy and levied a fine of twenty dollars for the act of indecency. It left me still holding a hundred dollars to put toward Emmie's bail. Until Burleigh became surly and insisted on immediate payment.

"I never knew you to be so petty, Tom."

"If you knew me at all, you'd know my name was Tim."

Well, there was no use disputing his point. He took my hundred dollars and went on his way.

"Where's THIBAUT?" Carlotta asked. It probably won't surprise you to learn that her mood wasn't a cheery one.

"I didn't bother to wake him. He was sleeping pretty soundly." My explanation seemed to strike her as inadequate. "You see, consoling himself required quite a bit of wine last night."

"Yeah? Cried himself to sleep, I'm sure." She sounded skeptical.

As we made our way toward Park Row, a brisk

breeze swept over us. Carlotta was shivering and I gave her my jacket. As I was helping her put it on, I saw one of the Chinese fellows I'd met the previous afternoon. He was spying on us from about a hundred feet away. When he noticed me looking in his direction, he ducked around a corner.

Nell and I tried to make conversation along the way, but Carlotta had worked herself into something very closely resembling a lather. I'd known her most of my life and I couldn't remember ever seeing her angry before. She was always the arch little girl who exasperated everyone else.

We entered the apartment to the sound of gay laughter. Thibaut was at the table amusing Tibbitts and Ainslie over their breakfast. I thought of intervening, but the look in Carlotta's eyes stopped me dead in my tracks.

"Et TU, Thi**baut**? ET TU?" she asked in a voice that would have pained the old bard a good deal had he been there to hear it.

Thibaut looked at her dumbly. She picked up the vase of flowers on the hall stand, swung it back behind her—sending the contents over yours truly—and then lofted it with great precision. The target was a good twenty feet away and yet it hit him squarely on the forehead. He seemed to have seen it coming but made no apparent effort to duck from it.

Whether his inaction was in fact due to cunning or mere inertia is impossible to say, but there's little doubt that in this case it was the correct course. Abject submission was the order of the day, and the sooner the punishment was executed the less prolonged it was likely to be. The vase ricocheted off his head, bounced off a plate of ham, and then hit his head again as he was collapsing onto the floor. (I don't see how he could claim authorship of the last bit of choreography, but he had certainly laid the groundwork.) Carlotta rushed over and knelt beside him. As she cradled his bloodied head, she began crying.

Unfortunately, Thibaut then made a strategic error. He regained consciousness. On realizing this, Carlotta shouted something in their patois, slapped him, and dropped his head back on the floor. Rising, she turned to me.

"Sorry about the flowers, Harry."

"That's okay, they needed changing anyway."

"I'm going to take a bath, if that's all right."

"Oh, yes. Quite all right."

While Nell took over ministering to Thibaut, Ainslie hovered about grinning. Tibbitts had spent the episode finishing his breakfast, every now and then looking up and shaking his head.

"I think we should call a doctor, Harry," Nell suggested.

"Ice water is what we need," Ainslie countered. Then he went into the kitchen to procure some.

"I need to be heading off," Tibbitts announced.

"Homeward bound?"

"Yeah. Your book's given me an idea."

"Well, I hope you have better luck with the enterprise than I did."

Ainslie returned with the ice water and his diagnosis was proven correct. Thibaut regained his senses. He seemed confused by Carlotta's greeting, and questioned Ainslie about it. While they had a short exchange in French, we set Thibaut on the couch and eventually managed to stop the bleeding, but not before staining a good portion of the table linen.

Xiang-Mei appeared about then, dressed in a silk robe. It flattered her.

"Poor *Thibaut*! Did he fall?"

"Yes, fell from grace," Ainslie told her.

"Look at all the *blood*. We must soak these *right* away."

She gathered the linen and went into the kitchen. I went and changed and came out just as Carlotta reappeared, carrying a small bag.

"I'll send for the rest of my things, Harry."

"Where will you go?" I asked.

"I've a few friends left. Did Thibaut pay you for the lawyer?"

"Ah, no. He seemed short of funds."

"Short of funds? What about our week's pay? We had seventy-five dollars coming. She then questioned Thibaut about it. He gestured toward Ainslie.

"Why do you have our money?" Carlotta asked him.

"To invest in the show, of course! I've got it all planned. Why don't you sit down and I'll explain everything."

Not surprisingly, Carlotta chose not to hear the plan, storming out of the apartment and slamming the door behind her. Thibaut was looking even more bewildered.

"Well, no time for sitting around here," Ainslie announced. "We have a show to do. Say, Harry, why don't you come and see it? What with Emmie away, I can introduce you to the Dainty Paree Burlesquers."

I took a pass and went into the kitchen to see about lunch.

A fellow I deduced to be Lou Ling was there. He looked to be about eighteen, a good decade younger than Xiang-Mei. He hopped up when I entered. Then, when

Xiang-Mei reassured him, he sat back down. He nodded at me agreeably and I said hello, but it was obvious he didn't know a word of English. He was eating steamed dumplings and Xiang-Mei insisted I sit down and have some, too. These were filled with spiced ground pork and various vegetables, and served with a sweetened vinegar.

"Very *busy* time for Lou Ling," she told me.

"Cricket season, you mean?"

"Yes, and now *moon* festival. Many *people* want crickets."

She said something to him in Chinese and he looked doubtful.

She seemed to admonish him and he looked appropriately abashed.

"I told him, he *must* show you how he catches *lady* crickets. But he's *afraid* you'll take his secret."

"You can assure him, my cricket-hunting days are over."

He led us into the little room they shared. There were dozens of gourd cages, each holding a light green cricket. There was a chirp now and then, but they were pretty quiet. I remarked on the fact, and Xiang-Mei smiled. She walked out of the room and came back with another gourd cage.

"Listen!"

She slowly brought the new gourd from cage to cage, placing the gridded openings together for a few seconds. Soon every cricket was chirping.

She held up the special gourd. "Very beautiful *lady* cricket!"

She handed the lady cricket to Lou. He put her in a sort of bird cage. Then he picked the male who seemed to be chirping the loudest and put him in with her. It took about fifteen seconds for them to get down to business.

"Well, at least no money's changed hands," I said to Xiang-Mei. She laughed, then translated for Lou. He smiled but held up a finger, signaling me to wait.

He shifted the female off the male's back without interrupting the business end of things. Then he took a toothpick and picked at something about the middle of the male's back, just between his wings. He held it up for me to see. It was a little white blob, like a bit of wax. Then he held it an inch in front of the female's head. She immediately disengaged from the male and seized the present.

"Love potion!" Xiang-Mei exclaimed. "*Better* than money."

She then explained the gist of Lou's business. Lots of Chinamen collected crickets in the fall. And the green tree crickets, being the rarer, were the most valuable. But to keep them chirping, you needed to have a female about. Otherwise, they got lethargic. So the silent females could fetch more than the males. The problem was to find them: how do you locate a cricket that doesn't chirp? It was Lou's novel idea to use the love potion the male provides to maintain the female's interest while he has his way with her.

By evening, Lou had prepared several glass vials, each holding a toothpick carrying a dab of love potion. We had another round of steamed dumplings for dinner and afterward he headed out the door.

Regrettably, Tibbitts came in just as Lou was leaving. They stared at each other, then Lou rushed out.

"Who's that?"

"That's the fellow who shot Ernie Joy."

"What was he doing here?"

"He's been staying in our maid's room. Did I neglect to mention it?"

"Yeah, must have slipped your mind. I suppose I should have a talk with him."

"You won't learn anything. He's just a farmer trying to earn some extra money."

Tibbitts stared at the door for a few seconds, then set down his valise and took a seat.

"I guess things didn't go well at home?"

"No. She gave me an ultimatum."

"I can easily imagine Elizabeth issuing edicts."

"But I was ready for her. I gave her my own ultimatum."

"Since you're here, I assume she didn't fold her tent."

"No, she sails for Europe Wednesday morning."

"That was her ultimatum? Sail to Europe with her?"

"Yeah. She even bought the ticket."

You might be finding it difficult to imagine anyone forgoing a free trip to Europe with a stunningly attractive blonde. If so, you haven't met Elizabeth.

"What was your ultimatum?"

"I took a job in Utica. Working in the district attorney's office."

"Doing what?"

"Same sort of thing. But I'll be the chief detective."

"Odds are, you'll be the only detective. I'm from Utica, you know."

"Yeah? What's it like living there?"

"There are worse places."

"Not much of a recommendation."

"Well, you'll be a celebrity. A real New York detective."

"'Big fish in a little pond,' Elizabeth says."

"She wasn't keen on making the move?"

"No, but she'll come around."

"What makes you so sure?"

He took Shakespeare's play from his pocket and waved it.

"Good luck."

I heard Xiang-Mei making noises behind me. She motioned me into the kitchen.

"How *much* will policeman take?"

"How much what?"

"Money, to *leave* Lou alone."

"Well, he hasn't mentioned it. He's got other things on his mind. I think he's already forgotten about Lou. But just how much do you have?"

"*Enough.*"

"I don't suppose you could lend me some to bail out Emmie?"

"Oh, yes. Very *glad* to."

She took me back to the maid's room again. All the boys were resting. She indicated I should turn around and a little later tapped me on the shoulder. She'd produced a little nest egg in yellow-backs. She counted out five twenties, but there were plenty left over.

"*More?*"

"Five more, I'm afraid, and maybe a couple extra for expenses."

She counted out seven more and then took out a little abacus.

"If you pay back *tomorrow*, no charge! Next week, just two dollars fifty cents *extra*. The week after that *five* extra dollars. Do you understand, Mr. Reese?"

I nodded. One doesn't need an abacus to calculate usury.

20

The next morning I found Tibbitts at the table finishing a cup of coffee.

"Thanks for the accommodations," he said. "I'll be staying at our place tonight. I think I have my strategy all worked out now."

"Strategy?"

He winked and waved Shakespeare's book at me again.

"Five will get you ten you're back here on the couch tonight."

He smiled, then picked up his bag and headed toward the door. Ainslie was once again sleeping on the three chairs. As he passed, Tibbitts kicked out the middle one and shot quietly out of the apartment. Ainslie woke spewing epithets and looking in my direction.

"Why the hell do you keep doing that?"

"Habit, I guess."

I finished my coffee and headed off to New Jersey. I'd decided whatever good would come from leaving Emmie in stir now had to be weighed against the interest our resident loan shark was charging.

As I approached the car stop, I found Jimmy Yuan walking beside me.

"Following me, Jimmy? Where are your friends?"

"They are about. They've asked me to give you a message. They know you sent your wife away. She's being followed, Harry. You must turn over the girls. There's no way to beat these fellows. They're utterly ruthless."

"You're sounding like King Brady, Jimmy."

He smiled. "I suppose I am. Well, let's say they are very determined."

"Is the offer of five hundred still good?"

"Oh, yes."

"What if I can include Xiang-Mei?"

He looked over his shoulder. "If you can do that, I imagine the price would go much higher. Do you really know where she is?"

"I might be able to locate her."

"Be very careful with her, Harry."

"Valuable cargo, or just dangerous?"

"Both. I suggest you make arrangements to hand over the girls very soon. Good-bye, Harry."

I found it hard to believe they knew where Emmie was, but just to be sure I didn't make it any easier for them, I took a car across to the Hamilton Avenue ferry terminal, then a boat to lower Manhattan, and then one from there to the depot in Jersey.

I had a new dilemma, and a novel one. If I paid Emmie's bail, I'd likely worry over her being abducted by a ruthless tong. But was the solution to leave her in the cooler, or just acclimate myself to yet another Emmie-inspired anxiety? By the time I'd posed the question, I felt acclimated enough.

The police clerk took my $200 and a little while later brought out Emmie.

"I'm afraid I don't have enough to bail out Mme. Salami, Emmie."

"Mme. *Sahlumie* was released yesterday."

"I hope it wasn't too terribly tedious without her."

"Oh, not tedious, certainly. Lizzie the Dipper joined me yesterday."

"Lizzie the Dipper?"

"She's the finest gonif in Jersey, matron says."

"Gonif?"

"You know, a fingersmith. Oh, and that reminds me. I need ten dollars."

"Funds are rather limited, Emmie. Don't you have any?"

"I contributed it all toward Molly's release Saturday. The bulls picked her up on her wedding day, so we paid her fine as a sort of wedding present."

"Very sisterly. What do you need ten dollars for just now?"

"To tip matron, of course."

"Is it customary to tip one's jailer?"

"It is if you expect her to remember you next time."

"Are you planning future stays here, Emmie?"

"One must be prepared for eventualities, Harry."

I gave her the ten dollars and she discreetly slipped it to the matron who'd been waiting off to the side. Then they exchanged a friendly little hug.

Emmie wasn't looking too bad, a little bedraggled maybe. But she had acquired a distinctive perfume. It was reminiscent of the one worn by waiter girls in Bowery concert saloons. A combination of perspiration and the cheap cologne used in lieu of bathing.

"I guess you're anxious to get home to a bath?" I said as tactfully as possible.

"I am, yes. But there's no reason to leave town with the job undone."

"Which job is that?"

"I'm certain Mrs. Twinem has the manuscript she alleges was stolen. If we can find it, it will prove her story is false."

"How can you be certain she has it? Maybe she tossed it into the river on the way to her mother's."

"If she disposed of it, no matter how carefully, there would always be the chance she'd be observed. No, the safest course would have been to hide it in her luggage and just carry it away."

"How do you expect to search her things?"

"It will be quite easy. You'll go up to the house and distract her. Then I'll sneak in the rear and up the back stairs."

"How can you be sure there are back stairs?"

"It's a large house, so it stands to reason."

"Then aren't there servants?"

"Yes, but I'm perfectly capable of evading them. Besides, when you mention how much money is at stake, they'll be eavesdropping."

"What money?"

"You've come as a representative of the Amalgamated Insurance Company of Oshkosh."

"Oshkosh?"

"Yes, definitely Oshkosh. It strikes just the right note. And it's in New Jersey."

"Wisconsin. How about Paterson?"

"Too pedestrian."

"All right. Oshkosh. I assume I've come to tell her Twinem left a huge legacy. Say, $25,000."

"I was thinking even more. Mrs. Twinem comes from a very wealthy family—the Jacobsons own the first-aid trust."

"I didn't know there was a first-aid trust."

"Oh, yes. They've cornered the market on bandages."

"Well, nevertheless, a college professor isn't worth

more than $25,000, Emmie. On this point, I stand firm. I won't be a party to making a mockery of the insurance industry."

"Oh, all right. $25,000. I suppose that will be enough to get the attention of the servants. But remember to stretch the thing out. I need to determine what room she's in and then find the manuscript. When I'm done, I'll go around to the front of the house and ring the bell. Then you bid her farewell and off we go. It's so simple it can't possibly go wrong."

So she said. But her insistence on tipping the matron led me to believe she wasn't as confident as she let on.

"I don't even have a notebook with me, Emmie."

"Here, you can use mine. But only as a prop, Harry. You must promise not to read it."

"Fear not, Emmie. I'll respect your privacy just as you would mine."

She replied with a weak smile, then led me to a house just a few blocks from the depot. While she went around to the rear, I rang the bell. A girl answered and I asked for Mrs. Twinem.

"She doesn't want to be disturbed just now."

"Well, I've come a long way. All the way from Oshkosh."

"Oshkosh?"

"Wisconsin. It involves a rather large sum of money. It's about the policy her husband had on his life."

"And your name?"

"Reese. Harry Reese. I seem to have left my calling cards at the hotel."

When she went off I perused Emmie's notes. I happened to have found the place where she'd recorded

Molly's lurid autobiography. I can only hope her betrothed knew what he was taking on. The girl returned—regrettably interrupting Molly's confession of her encounter with Father Dougherty in the vestry of St. Matthew's—and led me into the parlor. A minute later, a severe-looking woman of about thirty-five came in. She wasn't decisively unattractive. In fact, if you recorded her individual points—figure, facial features, dress, etc.—she'd score as reasonably good-looking. But she had a demeanor that could freeze water.

"What's this about an insurance policy? I've already made a claim on my husband's policy with the Metropolitan."

"Well, this was a recent acquisition. Dated just last month. Twenty-five thousand dollars in total."

She sat down. It would take a pretty tough constitution not to be affected by the news one was in line for $25,000. She almost became friendly. Then I spewed some nonsense about the procedures for making a claim, and she suggested coffee. Before I could decline, she got up and opened the door to call for it.

Just as Emmie predicted, both the maid and an older woman I presumed to be the vise-gripped cook had stationed themselves just outside and were making an abrupt getaway. But whatever censure would have befallen them for eavesdropping was put in abeyance when a cry of bloody murder came from somewhere upstairs. While the three of them froze, I ran toward the back of the house and was just in time to encounter Emmie charging down the back stairs.

"Run, Harry!"

We ran out the back of the house, nearly knocking down a fellow at the rear gate. I was sure I recognized him, but had scant time to mull the matter. We kept on running for several blocks, past a factory, and then down along the canal. But no one seemed to be following us.

"I have it, Harry." She flourished a sheaf of papers triumphantly.

"Who was it that screamed?"

"It must have been Mrs. Twinem's mother."

"Did you have to bludgeon her?"

"Of course not, Harry. What do you take me for?"

I didn't reply, just waved her notebook. She grabbed it and hid it away.

"Now we have confirmation that Mrs. Twinem's story was a complete fabrication," she said. Then she pulled an envelope from her pocket. "Unfortunately, this letter from Mr. Twinem's brother undermines my favorite theory."

She handed me a letter from a fellow named Arthur Twinem addressed to the widow. It was about funeral arrangements for her husband, Cyrus.

"What theory does this undermine?"

"Well, Arthur Twinem lives with his mother just a few blocks away. Mme. Sahlumie told me the two families are very close. My theory was that the widow was her brother-in-law's lover. And that they conspired to kill her husband. But if that were the case, he would never have written her such a formal-sounding letter."

"How would Mme. Salami know anything about the Twinems?"

"Arthur and his mother are regular clients."

"Really? Together or separately?"

"What? They're group sessions, usually."

"Very broad-minded for New Jersey," I said. "Let's just hope we don't encounter Mrs. Twinem again. Now she'll be able to identify us both."

"Oh, I wouldn't worry about that."

That much I was sure of.

After scanning the canal for floating bodies, we walked up to the depot and caught the 11:30 train.

"Tibbitts said you'd guessed he was married to Elizabeth. What was it that tipped you off?"

"It started when we were all in Washington that last afternoon. It was the first time I'd seen them together."

"The way I remember it, she was pretty cold to him."

"Oh, she *was* discomfited by seeing him. But it seemed like something more complicated than the loathing she claimed. Beneath it was some sort of mutual attraction."

"Not enough to keep her from making her exit."

"She did leave. But remember the next morning I told you I thought I saw her arriving back at the depot?"

"You said you saw someone who looked like her."

"Well, I realize now it must have been her. She took her train but then must have turned around and come back. And when I saw her this past spring, in the guise of the Marchioness of Karpolov, she told me she was married."

"And when Tibbitts told us his wife had been translating Latin for him...."

"Yes, I was planning on questioning him about his wife. But once he told us that, there was no need."

"Well, apparently being married to Elizabeth is much as you might expect. She's sailing for Europe Wednesday morning. And she gave Tibbitts an ultimatum, come along or else...."

"He's not acquiescing, is he?"

"No. He says he's taking a job in Utica. And he expects that she'll come around to the idea."

"Utica? It's difficult to imagine Elizabeth ever join-ing him there."

"He seems confident. He's been reading Shake-speare for tips."

"Speaking of Shakespeare, we should be looking this manuscript over."

She took it out and started reading. When she fin-ished a page, she'd hand it to me. After about ten pages, I suggested maybe they'd gotten out of order. But she insisted not.

"I can't make any sense out of it at all. Once he left shrews behind on page three, he seems to have lost his narrative thread."

"If I were you, Harry, I wouldn't be too critical on that score. But it is a bit dense. We'll need to call in an expert to find out if there's anything to it. As it happens, one of my college classmates married a Shakespeare scholar. And they're living just over in Manhattan."

"How serendipitous."

"Yes, isn't it? When we get back to the apartment, I'll look up her address."

In Jersey City nearly everyone leaving the train makes their way to the nearby ferry terminal. As they so often are, the ways to the Brooklyn boat were jammed and moving slowly. We were all forced up against one another and, as not infrequently happens, some men made an effort to gain proximity to young women. One such fellow had squeezed in ahead of Emmie. It was obvious he was proceeding more slowly than necessary just so she'd be pushed into him. Normally, I wouldn't have paid it much notice. Not that I'm indifferent. I just figure if Emmie is willing to ignore it, I'll let it go at that.

But right then I remembered Nell's suggestion that I

should prove my affection for Emmie through periodic displays of jealousy. Here was the perfect opportunity to demonstrate my feelings. As we left the ramp, I pulled the fellow aside.

"How dare you take advantage of my wife, sir!"

I punched him in the jaw as I had never punched a man before. He crumpled before me. It then came to my attention that the fellow had been traveling with a friend, who'd been directly behind me. And said friend was of an imposing stature.

Perhaps I neglected to mention that the fellow I knocked down was an older one, slight of build, and no more than five feet tall, all of which contributed a great deal to my choosing this occasion to exhibit my jealous rage.

Well, the giant took exception to my treatment of his comrade. Next thing I knew, Emmie was waking me up as I lay on a bench.

"Are you all right, Harry?"

"I've been better."

"The boat's docked—we need to hurry off now."

We got off and walked to the car stop.

"You were wonderful, Harry."

"Well, your honor was at stake."

"My honor? I was thinking of your wallet."

"My wallet?" I felt around. Sure enough, it was gone.

"Didn't you realize? They were gonifs."

"Fingersmiths?"

"Yes, of course. The first man made sure all those behind him were pressed together, giving the second man an opportunity to pick your pocket. We learned that gag back in Buffalo. Don't you remember?"

"Why didn't you say something?"

"Where'd be the challenge in that?" she asked sincerely. "Here's your wallet, Harry. And here's the wallet of the man you knocked down." She was making a survey of its contents.

"How'd you acquire that?"

"I helped him up as you distracted his accomplice. Then I got your wallet from the fellow who knocked you out. While he was gloating over you. They must have had a busy morning. There's nearly two hundred dollars here."

"Good. Then we can make a payment at Xiang-Mei's loan window."

"You borrowed money from poor Xiang-Mei?"

"I hate to destroy the literary illusion you created, Emmie. But there seem to be quite a few inconsistencies between Xiang-Mei and the story she fed you."

"What do you mean?"

"For one, she's a good deal older than Lou Ling."

"A few years, perhaps."

"And she doesn't speak the way one would expect a pious charge of missionaries to speak."

"What do you know about Chinese missionaries? Some lantern show you sat through in Sunday school?"

"One can infer."

"And what do you infer, Harry?"

"That she wasn't traveling as one of the girls, but as their escort. She's in the business herself."

"Are you implying she's a... chippie?"

"Yes, I am. And from the small fortune she carries, I think it's safe to say she is a madam chippie. Just like your Mme. Salami."

"Mme. *Sahlumie* is not a chippie, you gink. She's a priestess of the occult."

"A spook-compeller?"

"A spiritualist, yes."

"Well, I'm relieved to hear that."

"Why relieved?"

"Never mind."

"If you're right about Xiang-Mei, why would she go off with Lou and abandon what would have likely proved a lucrative business?"

"That I haven't figured out."

21

We arrived back at the apartment to find Thibaut, Nell, and Ainslie lingering over a late breakfast. From the remains, it looked as if they'd had yet another small feast. There are many disadvantages to running a refuge for penniless vaudevillians, but I can't say I fully appreciated their extent until our grocer began dunning proceedings a short while later.

After a brief exchange of greetings, Emmie and I went off to our room. There, she handed me her list of New York alumnae.

"You'll find her there—Lena Spire was her maiden name, class of '99. All I remember is she married a professor of English and they live near Washington Square."

Then she went into her bath. There were a good number of Smith graduates living in New York, but only one Lena—Lena Spire Rhodes. I joined Emmie and gave her the news.

"Of course. The name on the gun," she recalled. "What was it, Frank Rhodes?"

"Yes, but I've met the owner of the gun. He's a veteran living in New Haven. A well-known shrew authority... and circus impresario."

"Shrew authority and circus impresario?"

"Well, the combination may sound unlikely, but only until you learn the circus performers are themselves shrews. Rather ingenious. I'd never have thought the little fellows were actually tamable. But then I'm not Rhodes of *Rhodes on the Soricidae*. He's in a class by himself."

"Yes, I don't doubt it. What did he say about the gun?"

"Didn't know it was missing. But he did say Twinem had contacted him for information on shrews. I think the fact your friend married a man named Rhodes is probably just a coincidence."

"In a good mystery, Harry, coincidences always lead to consequences."

"Is this a good mystery?"

"You'd better hope it is, assuming you want to keep the franchise alive. And Lena Spire was not my friend. She considered me of the lower orders."

"Were you ever among the lower orders, Emmie?"

"I was an Irish Catholic. And my father was a mere merchant. Hers owned a buggy-whip factory."

"Are buggy whips made in factories?"

"They are in Westfield, Massachusetts. It's the center of the buggy-whip trade. I'm told that's why it's so prosperous."

"A sound economic footing," I agreed. "Well, I suppose we'll be able to tell at once if Professor Rhodes has anything to do with the case when we show him the manuscript."

"Yes, and until we learn more about that let's keep quiet about the gun."

She dressed and we went out and joined the others.

"Where's Carlotta?" Emmie asked.

"Stormed off," Ainslie told her. "What a temper that girl's got."

"Not entirely without cause, Cliff," Nell pointed out.

I then told Emmie the sordid story of Carlotta's arrest and betrayal.

"Thibaut, you went along with this?" Emmie asked him, first in English and then in his native tongue. She being the only one present other than Ainslie proficient enough to do so. He replied somewhat indignantly, then they went back and forth for a while, with Thibaut becoming visibly more upset.

When they'd finished, he walked over and assaulted Ainslie. Not particularly violently, but with a good deal of wrathful gesturing and Gallic opprobrium—and not a little Gallic expectoration. The combination unsettled Ainslie. Obviously remorseful, or at least fearful of losing the act's keystone, he pleaded, apologized, and finally promised to make things right.

"Rest assured, all of you," he announced. "Carlotta will return to her place in the company, and Thibaut will once again be the apple of her eye. Cliff Ainslie promises it, and Cliff Ainslie is a man of his word."

"You manage to picture the righting of the wrong you've done as some sort of noble deed," Emmie said.

"Thank you, Emmie. A fitting tribute to my humble oratorical skills."

"So you will set out at once to locate her?" she asked.

"Well, we can't just now. We have to get to the theatre—matinee's in twenty minutes."

He said something to Thibaut in French. It didn't work. Then Emmie told him something, and he went along with Nell and Ainslie.

"I assured Thibaut we would find Carlotta for him, Harry."

"It may be easier said than done. She was pretty hot when she went out."

"I'm certainly not surprised. It's difficult to understand what Aunt Nell sees in Ainslie."

"Yes, there do seem to be some notable flaws in his character. But he must have been handy to have around at a medicine show. I suppose Nell's infatuation can be marked down to a romanticized memory of her youth."

"I'd never suspected you capable of such drivel, Harry. It might have more to do with him being the father of her only child."

"He's Cousin Charlie's father? Did she tell you that?"

"No, certainly not. But the dates never quite made sense. I mean her marriage and Charlie's birth."

"Really?"

"Don't be so shocked. It's common enough. Take my own case...."

"Your mother?"

"She was young once, Harry."

A little later, Xiang-Mei came out of the kitchen to clean up the table.

"Thank goodness *you* are back, Emmie! We were all *so* worried."

"Thank you, Xiang-Mei. And thank you for lending Harry the money for my bail."

"Oh, *not* at all. What *are* friends for?"

I wanted to suggest a good source of profit, but it might have put a damper on the congenial atmosphere.

"Speaking of the loan, let's pay her back with what we have, Emmie."

"Then we'll be broke again. Besides, I earned this money. It's you who owe Xiang-Mei."

I knew, or at least felt reasonably sure I knew, that she was joking. But Xiang-Mei was clearly impressed by Emmie's accounting.

"In China, a *man* would be shamed if his *wife* paid his debts for him."

"Really? How strange your ways are.... Here, we look on it rather fondly."

When Xiang-Mei had gone back into the kitchen, Emmie suggested I telephone the Rhodes' residence, and that we only bring up her association after we met the professor. I was told he would be in his office that afternoon. Half an hour later, we arrived at a New York University building just off Washington Square.

The professor's third-floor space was a sizable one, but even though every inch of wall was covered with shelving, books spilled out everywhere. And wherever a bit of floor was free of books, there were knee-high stacks of paper. Which explained why it was so stuffy—one stray gust through an open window would mean a week of re-sorting.

Earl Rhodes was about thirty-five, normal-looking in most ways, clean-shaven, and of medium height. He didn't seem interested in Emmie's connection to his wife and made it clear he didn't like being disturbed.

"We do apologize for the intrusion," Emmie told him. "But a man has been murdered."

"What man?"

"Cyrus Twinem. He was an English professor at Syracuse."

"Yes, I read about that. But what does his murder have to do with me?"

"We wondered what you might be able to tell us about this." Emmie handed him the manuscript.

"Oh, yes. *What Species Kate?* I've read much of it before."

While he was fairly engrossed in his inspection, I managed to pocket a page of his writing. I looked to see if Emmie was watching me and noticed her performing her own petty burglary. She'd picked up one of those folding frames, where two photos can be displayed side by side, and very carefully slipped it into her bag.

"We were told it was nonsensical," she said to him.

"Nonsensical? Who told you that?"

"Apparently, that was the verdict of his own brother. He referred to it as *obscurum per obscurius*."

"What's nonsensical about that? It's an art, and the key to studying literature in any depth. This is a brilliant piece of work, at least what he allowed me to see."

"He consulted you?"

"Yes. I was flattered, of course. No one gets to the soul of Shakespeare as he did. He'd heard I was working on similar lines. With *A Midsummer Night's Dream*."

"What species ass?" I asked.

"How did you know that? I haven't told a soul— excluding Twinem."

"Just a guess."

"Well, in fact, it isn't the species that's in question. There's no disputing it was the common donkey. But which bloodline?"

"Do donkeys have bloodlines?" Emmie asked.

"Oh, yes. Dating back centuries. In this case, the clue comes from Bottom's comment in act four, scene one: '...methinks I am marvelous hairy about the face.'"

"Clue to what?" Emmie asked.

"Well, the average donkey *isn't* marvelously hairy. It has fairly short hair, particularly about the face."

"Yes, I suppose that's true."

"But the *Poitou donkey* is decidedly shaggy, *even* about the face!"

"I *see*. How inspired," Emmie jollied. "I never appreciated how useful a knowledge of zoology could be in interpreting Elizabethan drama."

"Few people do. Even experts in the field. The avenues it opens are limitless. But I trust you'll keep the nature of my work confidential. You wouldn't believe the depths academics will go to."

"Of course, Professor," Emmie assured him. "Would you happen to know if Professor Twinem consulted anyone about the shrew references?"

"Yes, he did. I was able to help there."

"How did you help him?"

"By directing him to my father. He's one of the leading authorities on the damn things."

"*The* leading authority," I corrected. "*Rhodes on the Soricidae* is the first and last word on the subject."

"You know his book? I'll be damned. Well, I don't think the old man was much help, after all. He's gone a little off, if you know what I mean. Spends too much time with his little friends.... But he did at least help Twinem with the nomenclature."

"Would Twinem's manuscript actually be worth anything?" I asked.

"Worth money? You must be joking."

"What about the ruthless academics you mentioned earlier?"

"You mean, trying to get the jump on him by stealing his research? There's certainly no shortage of low characters in the field, but Twinem guarded his work carefully."

"His wife says the manuscript was stolen by the man who shot him."

"Then how'd you get it?"

"She was lying," Emmie interjected.

"And now *you've* stolen it from her?"

"One could interpret the facts in that way," Emmie admitted. "But it's unlikely she'll be reporting the loss."

"What do you plan to do with it?"

"What would you suggest?"

"Leave it with me. I'll see it's published, alongside my own work."

"I suppose that would be a fitting tribute to Twinem," I agreed. "By the way, I understand your father was presented with a revolver by his comrades in the G.A.R."

"Yes, for gallantry while catering. What's that have to do with any of this?"

"Well, that's what we're trying to determine. Do you know what became of that gun?"

"How should I know what became of it? What does it matter?"

"The night Twinem was killed a second man was killed a few blocks away. He was shot with your father's gun."

"You can't think my father came into New York and shot a man? The old man must have misplaced it, or one of his circus cronies found it and sold it."

"When was the last time you saw it?"

"We spent a few days with him this summer. He had it out then."

"We?"

"My wife and I."

"But you never borrowed the gun yourself?"

"Why would I take his gun?"

"No reason, I just thought it might explain how it came into New York. Do you remember what you were doing that evening? It was the 2nd, the day after Labor Day."

"I was home, as I am most evenings."

"With your wife?"

"Yes, with my wife. But what business is that of yours?"

"What if we were to tell you...," Emmie started, but I interrupted.

"I doubt if Professor Rhodes is interested in Ernie Joy, Emmie."

"Who's Ernie Joy?"

"The man shot with your father's gun. A vaudevillian."

"Oh. You're correct—I'm not interested. Now, if you don't mind...."

"No, not at all."

We said our good-byes and Emmie and I went outside.

"Why'd you stop me, Harry?"

"You were going to suggest to him the same gun probably shot Twinem."

"Yes, I wanted to see how he would answer that."

"Well, if he is aware the shootings are linked, then he'd already have an answer prepared. But I don't think he is aware they're linked, and I couldn't see any reason to share the intelligence with him."

"That's ridiculous. Of course he's aware they're linked. The solution to the case is obvious, Harry."

"Is it?"

"Yes, Rhodes was having an affair with Mrs. Twinem. They plotted to kill her husband, and he supplied the gun."

"How did Ernie Joy end up with it?"

"I haven't worked that out exactly. Perhaps Mrs. Twinem charmed him into killing her husband. And he never realized he was just being used to protect her real lover, Earl Rhodes."

There was a certain logic to her theory, but I did think of one rather large flaw in it.

"Having met Mrs. Twinem, I find it difficult to believe it's within her abilities to charm a man into walking across a room, much less commit murder on her behalf."

"Beauty is in the eye of the beholder, Harry. Look how smitten Aunt Nell is with Ainslie, a man who oozes insincerity."

"Yes, but you must admit he manages to be charming even as he oozes. It's a talent some people have."

"People like P.T. Barnum. And Tammany ward healers."

"Yes, but not Mrs. Twinem."

"Perhaps she has hidden talents, as a lover. It's a gift that oftentimes runs counter to expectations."

"Are you speaking from experience, Emmie?"

"Yes, Harry, I am."

I at first took this as a compliment. But on reflection, I realized it had the ambiguous quality typical of Emmie's supposed flattery. Did she mean that my appearance, or manner, would lead to expectations that I was *not* a talented lover? I thought that a little harsh, but still preferable to the alternative: that the experience she spoke of was with someone other than myself. Or worse yet, *others*.

22

We left Washington Square and went off to look for Carlotta. Our first stop was at the boarding house we'd visited the week before. I knocked and the so-called slavey answered the door.

"Hello, I'm Carlotta Reese's cousin," I told her.

"Who's she?"

"Cissie Lightner."

"Oh, that one. Ain't seen her since she was tossed out." Then she turned to Emmie. "Say, weren't you Ernie's cousin last time?"

"Yes, that's right. Would Mr. Bauman happen to be in?"

"You his cousin too?"

"No. Just tell him his accomplice from Friday's caper wishes to speak with him."

The slavey raised her eyelids and then shouted over her shoulder, "Miisster Bauuumannn!"

A stocky older fellow came to the door wiping bits of something off his face. When he saw Emmie, he froze.

"It's all right, Mr. Bauman," Emmie assured him. "I didn't come seeking revenge for your having abandoned me. Though few would fault me if I did."

"I'm sorry, Miss. I lost my head. I'm not normally such a coward, but after what happened to Ernie...."

"Right now we're trying to locate Cissie Lightner. You wouldn't happen to know where she's staying?"

"Cissie—what a horrible name. Should've just used Carlotta. Ernie thought so, too."

"Yes, it was an unfortunate choice," Emmie agreed. "But we're willing to forgive her that and hoped you might know where she's staying."

"Last I knew, she was staying with another girl, Eva. Up on 27th Street."

"I spoke with Eva last week, and I had the impression she wasn't anxious to have Carlotta return."

"Fell out, did they? Probably over Ernie."

"Was Eva involved with him, too?"

"Oh, yeah. Let's see, that was last fall. Two before Carlotta. If you don't count a week in Jacksonville at Christmas."

"Few would, I imagine. But I believe their dispute was over nonpayment of rent."

"The love of money is the root of all evil."

"Yes," Emmie agreed. "And worse still, the source of a good many platitudes."

"Still, I'd talk with Eva. They were always pals, more or less."

We thanked him and then walked up to Eva's.

"It was Eva's rooms you searched for the missing gun?" I asked Emmie.

"Yes, she was very agreeable. But she didn't have any kind words for Carlotta."

Emmie led the way upstairs. A striking woman, not classically beautiful, but quite appealing—and who'd made only a perfunctory effort at modesty with a loose kimono—answered our summons. When she saw me ogling her, she put the curtain down by tying her belt. The women of vaudeville are not known for their beauty and Eva struck me as an anomaly. Until she opened her mouth.

"I thought youse was someone else. Ain't you Carlotta's cousin?" she said to Emmie.

"Yes, by marriage. My husband here is actually her cousin."

"I'm Harry Reese," I said.

"Are ya?" She seemed unimpressed.

"We were wondering if you've seen her," Emmie went on.

"Yeah, I let her back in yesterday. Came in all weepy. She said her friends left her high and dry. Stole her show.... Wasn't you two, was it?"

"Certainly not. She was the victim of a coup d'état perpetrated by a fellow thespian."

"How's that?"

"She was stabbed in the back by a ham named Ainslie," I clarified.

"Yeah, that's what she told me. Cliff Ainslie would stab his mother in the back if it'd get him a decent act."

"Yes, so we've gathered," Emmie said. "Carlotta wouldn't happen to be in?"

"Supposed to be. Said she'd have supper ready for me between shows."

"Are her things still here?"

"Yeah. Maybe she found work. Who knows?"

"Well, we wanted to ask her to return," Emmie told her. "Perhaps I could leave a note explaining."

"Sure." She let Emmie in, then closed the door in my face.

The air in the tenement smelled rather intensely of boiled cabbage. I walked down toward an open window at the end of the hall and noticed a van across the street bearing the name of Scanlan's Butcher Shop. Then it dawned on me. That was the surname of the fellow Emmie and I had encountered during our escape from the house in New Jersey.

Mike Scanlan was an operative for the Byrnes Detective Agency. I'd worked with him a few years earlier on an arson case. Then I remembered something else, something much more relevant. He was the one who had been watching us board Jimmy Yuan's electric wagon on Park Row, the night both Ernie and Twinem were shot. I'd recognized his face, but couldn't put a name to it.

I was a little leery of abandoning Emmie, especially since I'd neglected to mention the tong might be lying in wait for her. But since she only sometimes confided her plans to me, it only seemed fair I should do the same.

I took the L downtown and then walked along John Street to Broadway. The Byrnes office was in a building on the corner. I asked to see Andy Drummond, a supervisor I'd always been on good terms with. We exchanged small talk and then I got around to the matter at hand.

"I don't suppose you could tell me what your involvement with the Twinem case is?"

"Twinem?"

"Cyrus Twinem. The fellow who was shot at the Cosmopolitan Hotel two weeks ago."

"What made you think we were involved?"

"I saw Mike Scanlan watching the house where the widow is staying out in New Jersey."

He gave me a pained look. "When was this?"

"This morning, maybe eleven or so."

This time the pained look was accompanied by a guttural groan.

"All right," he said. "I can tell you this. We were hired, briefly, about a month ago. By whom, and for what, I can't divulge. We spent maybe four or five days on it."

"And that ended before the shooting?"

"At least a week before."

"Was Mike Scanlan working it?"

"Yes. But we gave him the boot soon after that."

"Because of how he handled it?"

"No, something else entirely. An embezzlement case. I can't go into details, but he was trying to make something on the side. We'd actually suspected him for a few months."

"So you have no idea what he was doing out there in New Jersey?"

"No."

"But you might have a good guess?"

"I might. But you've probably made the same guess."

He gave me Scanlan's address on West 34th Street. Then I went back uptown.

He wasn't in, but a neighbor volunteered that I stood a good chance of finding him in a saloon around the corner. He was at the bar.

"Hello, Mike!"

"Hey. Reese, isn't it?"

"Yes, Harry Reese. Quite a coincidence, seeing you twice in one day."

He smiled, then led me to a table off to the side.

"You working the Twinem case?" he asked me.

"No, ours was a sort of social call."

He smirked. "Yeah. Mine too."

"Actually, we're trying to solve the riddle of Ernie Joy's death. Would you happen to know anything about that?"

He shrugged. I passed him five dollars.

"Look, his name came up. But it has nothing to do with a Chinaman, or why he was shot."

"We know Mrs. Twinem lied about the Chinaman, and the manuscript being stolen. But not why she wanted

Ernie identified with it. Was the Byrnes Agency hired by Twinem to have his wife followed?"

"Something like that."

"A man doesn't get much for his five dollars."

"You'd need a lot more to get me to show my hand."

"I see. You know something about the widow you expect to profit from."

"Let's just say they were both too clever by half." He finished his beer and said he needed to go. We walked out together and then I headed back to Brooklyn.

I arrived home just before seven and found Emmie fixing us dinner. Xiang-Mei was also in the kitchen, preparing a meal for the ever-growing cricket population. It seemed to consist chiefly of overripe fruit, with a few insect corpses thrown in as seasoning.

"Boy crickets very *hungry*, but if they eat too much, they don't *sing*. Lou says I must be very careful."

"How about the lady crickets?" I asked.

"Oh, they can have *all* they want. Must *keep* the ladies happy."

I noted the parrot seemed to be missing, and Xiang-Mei explained she'd put it into our room.

"One of the ladies *escaped*. Bad bird *ate* it. If Lou finds out, parrot *not* safe."

It seemed odd to be going to such lengths to accommodate a nonpaying guest who'd given our maid's quarters over to a cricket ranch. But any proposal to do away with the damned bird could count on my endorsement.

Emmie and I took our dinner out to the table.

"Where are the rest of our guests?"

"Left for the theatre already. We need to hurry—I told Aunt Nell we'd see the show while she still has the part. Where'd you go off to earlier?"

"Oh, I just remembered I told a fellow I'd meet him for a drink."

"Hmph."

The only thing that bothers me more than the fact that I can never detect when Emmie is lying is that she can always tell when I am.

"I don't suppose Carlotta showed up while you were with Eva?"

"No, but Eva felt sure she was out looking for work."

We finished eating and then went off to Williamsburg and the Theatre Unique.

I'd seen most of the act during rehearsals at the apartment, so there wasn't a lot new. The American tourist, now played by Nell, visits Paris and hires a cabby to show her the sights. But when they get to the zoo, it's closed, so the cabby pantomimes a zoo. Then they find the wax museum, opera, and circus all closed.

The climax was a bit where Thibaut played a sharpshooter at the circus. He had Nell stand against a wall, picked up an apple from a table on the far side of the stage, placed it on her head, moved downstage, and started shooting. Each time he took a shot, an apple on the table would explode. This was much as I'd seen Carlotta and her old partner perform it a year or so earlier. But it had been improved by having an apple explode in the orchestra pit, and another while it was being eaten by a member of the audience—Ainslie himself.

The Dainty Paree Burlesquers came on next, revealing the requisite quota of feminine form with a good deal of vim and vigor, but not much else. No one cared if the girls were from Paris or Passaic, but they might have at least been able to kick in unison.

The finale had Mlle. Yvette, who weighed in at 200

pounds minimum, cavorting on a blancmange-like structure while various electric effects played upon her. The audience, which had been pretty vocal in expressing both pleasure and displeasure up until this point, went silent. Perhaps in reverence at the artistry, but more likely in stupefaction. I can only say it was a good thing small children weren't admitted, as it would have frightened them to death.

On the way back to the apartment, I asked about the sharpshooter bit.

"Carlotta and Thibaut had been using it since Weedsport," Ainslie said. "But rigging the apples offstage was my idea." The powder burns about his face in no way inhibited his boasting.

"Wait a minute," I said. "Did they include it in that Sunday matinee in Weedsport?"

Ainslie queried Thibaut, who, after a healthy amount of pondering, nodded in the affirmative.

"What difference does that make?" Emmie asked.

"It explains the mystery of the gun."

"What mystery?"

"The night of the shooting, what should have been a prop gun turned out to be real. Carlotta insisted she'd brought the prop gun and someone must have switched it. Then she borrowed another prop gun for the trip to Weedsport.

"But the night before the final show there, Nell borrowed one from Carlotta's trunk. The next afternoon, while she and Thibaut were using one on stage, the prop gun Nell had taken was in the custody of Deputy Sheriff Carson. Carlotta *must* have forgotten to bring it the night Ernie was shot and just never searched her trunk for it."

"Then I was right about the gun all along," Emmie

gloated. "Ernie brought it there himself. He wanted to get rid of it and only just happened to pick the spot where Lou expected to find the prop gun."

"The first piece of bad luck Ernie ever had," Ainslie added.

After leaving the car at Nostrand Avenue we made the slow walk home. Due to his short legs and desultory nature, Thibaut was a difficult person to hurry along. You couldn't pass a stray dog without him stopping to confer with it. Nell and Emmie had proceeded apace and were soon well ahead of Thibaut, Ainslie, and myself. At the plaza, I was again approached by Jimmy Yuan.

"You fellows go on up. I think Jimmy wishes to consult with me."

They left us.

"You were warned, Harry. Now you have twenty-four hours in which to produce the girls."

"Or?"

"Your wife, Harry. They have your wife. Didn't you notice she was missing?"

"I had her a minute ago."

Jimmy looked puzzled.

"Don't play games, Harry. They found where she was staying, on 27th Street. If you want to see her again, you must produce the girls by tomorrow night."

"When did this abduction occur?"

"This afternoon, I believe. The exchange will be made in the plaza here tomorrow at midnight. If you cooperate, your wife will be returned to you unharmed. And do not call in the police."

"I might need more time."

"You are out of time, Harry. Remember, these men are ruthless."

"Why do you always refer to them in the third person? Aren't you a party to this?"

"I'm only the messenger. I'm afraid I'm in much the same situation as you."

"They have your wife?"

"No. They have my dog, Harry."

With that, he wandered off. I went upstairs, where Ainslie was offering toasts with our wine and renewing his pledge to hasten the return of Carlotta.

"I'm afraid your undertaking will come up empty-handed."

"What makes you say that?"

"It would seem the tong has kidnapped her."

"Why would a tong kidnap Carlotta?" Nell asked.

"Because they thought she was Emmie."

"Why would a tong kidnap Emmie?"

"They've given me twenty-four hours to return some cargo that's been misplaced. Goods they were smuggling in from Canada."

"Oh...." Emmie said. "I suppose it was naïve to think they'd just forget about the... goods."

"Yes, apparently."

"What goods? What's it have to do with you?" Ainslie asked.

Before explaining, I made sure Xiang-Mei wasn't within earshot. Then Emmie and I gave Ainslie and Nell the general outline of our rescue and secreting away of the six girls.

"Where are they now?" Nell asked.

"It would be indiscreet to say," Emmie said. "But even if we were willing to give them up to a life of white slavery, it would be impossible to get them here within twenty-four hours."

"They warned me not to contact the police, but I don't see how we have any choice."

"Wait, I have a plan," Ainslie interjected.

"What sort of plan?" Emmie said suspiciously.

"Foolproof. You need a half dozen Chinese girls, and you will have them. But you'll have to trust me."

"That's a tall order," I told him.

"I guarantee Carlotta will be safely back home tomorrow night."

The market for Ainslie's assurances had soured appreciably in the last few days. But he did have one bidder.

"Give him a chance, Harry," Nell pleaded. "It's important you let him make amends."

"All right, but if you make a mess of this, there'll be hell to pay."

Of course, there was little doubt that I'd be the one doing the paying.

A while later, Emmie and I went off to bed, leaving Ainslie alone on the couch. Apparently Nell's backing only went so far.

"I'm not sure I can sleep not knowing what's happening to Carlotta," Emmie told me.

"She'll be all right. As long as they think they can get back the girls, they can't risk hurting her."

"Are you really going to trust Ainslie to come up with a solution?"

"No, I'll call Tibbitts in the morning," I told her. "I expected to find him here when we got home."

"Why would he be here?"

"He spent the last couple nights on our couch. Things got a little too hot at home. I guess they made up."

"Only if he backed down."

23

While Emmie was bathing the next morning, I made a search of her things for the money she'd relieved the pickpocket of the day before. I found it hidden in her lingerie drawer and slipped out a hundred dollars.

I also came across two pairs of folding frames. The first was the one she'd taken from Rhodes' office the previous afternoon. One side held a photograph of him, and the other side one of Mrs. Twinem, which had needed to be trimmed so as to fit a smaller frame. The other pair of frames contained a picture of a fellow I'd never seen and opposite it an empty frame. Then it occurred to me what Emmie had done. Sure enough, I found a photo of a second woman behind that of Mrs. Twinem. She must have taken the larger folding frame from Mrs. Twinem's bedroom at her mother's house in New Jersey—the fellow I didn't recognize must have been Twinem. Emmie had removed Mrs. Twinem's photo from that and paired it with Rhodes', covering up the photo of his own wife. Which was too bad, because Mrs. Rhodes was by far the better-looking of the two.

When I heard Emmie in the hall, I closed the drawer and went out to make my call to Tibbitts. Rather than immediately launch into the kidnapping of Carlotta by a vengeful tong, a circumstance that had resulted from a part of the story we'd neglected to tell Tibbitts, I told him I had information that might account for how Frank Rhodes' commemorative gun came to be involved in the shootings of September 2nd. He suggested I come over to

Manhattan, but I countered with an offer of a hearty breakfast.

A half hour later he was at our table looking hungry and tired. Emmie and I related what had transpired at the house in New Jersey and later at Earl Rhodes' office. When we finished, Emmie presented her theory that Earl Rhodes was Mrs. Twinem's lover.

"So, the way you have it, they were meeting at the Cosmopolitan and her husband surprised them?" he asked.

"No, not exactly. The shooting wasn't a result of Mr. Twinem's unexpected appearance, but a carefully laid plan. Suppose Mrs. Twinem and Rhodes met regularly at the Cosmopolitan and were planning to do so again that evening. Mrs. Twinem realizes her husband has been enlightened to her infidelity. Perhaps he hired a detective, and she saw his report. So on this evening, she and Rhodes lay a trap. She meets Rhodes at the Cosmopolitan, and he comes equipped with his father's gun. When Twinem, who she knows is following her, arrives, Rhodes shoots him, then flees. Meanwhile, Mrs. Twinem has seduced Ernie Joy...."

"Meanwhile?" Tibbitts asked.

"Well, over the preceding several weeks. She has arranged for him to meet her at the Cosmopolitan after the show that evening. He arrives just after Rhodes has fled. She tells Ernie she shot her husband and he must take the gun away for her. He does so, not so much out of devotion, but in panic.

"Fearing he's been followed, he joins Jimmy Yuan's tour. When we reach the opium den, he recognizes Carlotta and now is particularly anxious to rid himself of the gun. He hides it at the foot of the bunk as he's talking to her, not knowing that is the very spot Lou Ling expects to find Carlotta's prop pistol, which we now know she had left home in her trunk. Thus, Ernie Joy is the engineer of his own death.

"Mrs. Twinem then tells the police the fantastic tale about her husband expecting to meet someone at the Cosmopolitan, and that a thief shot him and took the manuscript. When she reads about Ernie's death and suspects he was shot with the very gun used to kill her husband, she calls you to make sure you'll make the connection, hoping Ernie's death, by its exotic nature, would buttress her own bizarre story and thus lead suspicion away from her."

There Emmie stopped, breathless, but with a self-satisfied smile.

"I suppose there could be something to it," Tibbitts said without much enthusiasm.

"Oh, most definitely. All we need to do is find the detective her husband hired."

"The detective you *imagine* her husband hired," he pointed out.

"Yes, that one."

Apparently, Tibbitts's acquaintance with Emmie had not been sufficient for him to fully appreciate how little it mattered to her whether any particular fact were real or imagined.

"Suppose there *is* a detective—how do you expect to find him?" Tibbitts asked.

"Sherlock Holmes would put ads in all the dailies," I suggested.

"We don't need to find him. In fact, it's not even important whether he exists at all. Perhaps better if he doesn't."

This left Tibbitts looking noticeably puzzled. I was puzzled as well, but it was such a frequent state for me I doubt it was evident from my expression.

"All we need to do is have someone pose as the detective, approach Mrs. Twinem, and offer to withhold what he knows for some remuneration. If she pays, we know she's guilty."

"Emmie, you've already tried twice to trick her with impersonations. Don't you think she may be a little leery the third time?" I asked.

"She may be suspicious, but if she's guilty, she couldn't dare not to pay."

"Remember, Emmie, you're only out on bail. If the New Brunswick police pick you up again, you can count on becoming much better acquainted with your chums there. And I will not be borrowing any more bail money."

"If Sergeant Tibbitts would help, we could do it very easily."

"Cops don't like cops from other jurisdictions playing games in their backyards."

"Yes, that's true. We need to entice her into New York. I'll work on that."

"All right," Tibbitts said noncommittally. "I'll leave that to you."

I still wasn't ready to bring up our little disagreement with the tong, so I asked him about affairs at home.

"I'm playing it like Shakespeare's shrew tamer."

"Is it working?"

"Not so as I can tell. She's still planning to take the boat tomorrow." He put down his napkin and was about to get up when I stopped him.

"There is one more trifle I wanted to bring up."

"Trifle?"

"Well, more of a predicament. Remember what we told you about the trip up north?"

"Not much of it."

"Well, that's just as well because there was one small bit of it we forgot to mention."

Interestingly, throughout our account of the girls' rescue and subsequent domiciling with the Corinthians, his blank expression never wavered.

"It's all true," Emmie assured him. Which, of course, had the opposite effect to what she intended. Still, there wasn't much choice but to soldier on.

"It seems the tong that arranged for the shipment of girls is harboring a grudge," I explained. "Thinking she was Emmie, they've kidnapped my cousin Carlotta."

I'd taken the thing forward a little too quickly. It took some time to illuminate the details, but finally he seemed to have the general picture.

"Maybe you should give them the girls," he suggested.

"Sergeant Tibbitts!" Emmie exclaimed.

"I thought perhaps you'd be willing to come along this evening, with some of your fellows."

"All right," he said. Then he turned to Emmie. "But if this is just something you *imagined* happened, some-one'll live to regret it."

"You needn't threaten me. Harry's the one in contact with the tong."

"Through their emissary, Jimmy Yuan."

"I'll have him picked up."

"I'd rather you didn't. At least as long as there seems a reasonable chance Carlotta will come out of this un-scathed."

After sharing the particulars of the appointed ren-dezvous, I walked him out to the street below.

"What was the name of the handwriting expert you mentioned earlier? The fellow who looked at the hotel registration cards."

"Mahar. Owen Mahar. He says he's reasonably sure that Twinem's card from the Cosmopolitan matches the card from the Victoria."

"Where does he work out of?"

"Has an office right in the Times Building. Why?"

"Oh, I just wanted to ask him something. Does he still have the cards from the two hotels?"

"Yeah."

I went back upstairs to find Emmie getting ready to go out.

"I probably won't be back until this evening, Harry."

"All right. But remember, no more bail."

She made a face and went out.

A moment later, Thibaut emerged and headed into the kitchen. I took the opportunity to search the room he'd been sharing with Carlotta for any evidence of Ernie Joy's handwriting, but found nothing.

At Mahar's office there was a note on the door saying he'd be out until two. From there I revisited the boarding house of Bauman, Ernie's feeder.

"I need a sample of Ernie's handwriting, and a photograph," I told him.

"What for? To tie him to that murder?"

"He's already tied to it—I'm trying to untie him from it."

It took a good amount of coaxing, but eventually he handed me a publicity photo and several notes Ernie had made earlier that summer. Apparently he'd played Puck in a production of *A Midsummer Night's Dream* over at Manhattan Beach.

It was still before noon, so I went up to Madison Square and visited a fellow in the fraud department of the Metropolitan Life Insurance Company. I told him I might be able to save them some money on Mrs. Twinem's claim on her husband's life policy. The normal arrangement was for an investigator to reap ten percent of whatever he saved the company. If he had had a $50,000 policy, I could pay my debts and still live for a year on what I'd net.

Unfortunately, it was a boilerplate through the university for just $5,000. Still, the five hundred he agreed to would be enough to free me from the clutches of my usurious house guest, and maybe even send something on account to the rest of our creditors. Between that and Emmie's new career as pickpocket, we might be able to live all right for a while.

I was now just a few blocks below the Victoria Hotel and decided to see if I could find out a little more from the loquacious desk clerk. I found him sorting the mid-day mail.

"Do you remember mentioning how Twinem was always asking about his mail?"

"Yes."

"How about the day he was shot?"

"Yes. He received one letter in the early afternoon mail, I believe. Then another arrived that evening."

"What time that evening?"

"Not long before he went out."

"Was that before or after Mrs. Twinem asked for the manuscript from the safe?"

"Before. I was just leaving for my break, so about half past eight."

"And that was just another letter?"

"No, there was something in it. Something metal, maybe a key."

"A key?"

"Well, that's just a guess. A key with a tab, like ours."

He held up one of the room keys, with the room number inscribed on an attached metal tab.

"And it came in the mail?"

"No, I don't believe so. There was just the name on the envelope. And actually, it was Mrs. Twinem's name."

"*Her* name?"

"Yes, Isabel Twinem. I'm almost certain of it."

"Did you see who left the envelope?"

"No, I found it on the desk, with her name on it, so I naturally put it in their box."

I thanked him and left. After lunch at a chop house a few blocks to the east, I went back to Mahar's office in the Times Building and found him reading the newspaper. I asked him about the hotel cards Tibbitts had given him.

"As I told the sergeant, they are very likely by the same hand. The average person is fairly inconsistent, so no two signatures are ever exactly the same."

"But it's possible the second signature was made by someone else. Someone who'd studied the first?"

"Yes. I would have to say the other samples of Twinem's handwriting more closely match the first card."

"Would it help if you had some samples from the potential forger?"

"It would make all the difference."

I handed him Ernie's notes. He spent some time looking back and forth.

"This is an excellent case. I'd like to have all these

photographed, if you don't mind. I could use this in my book."

"You see a match?"

"There's no question, the card from the Cosmopolitan is by this hand."

Business must have been slow. Ten dollars was enough to convince him to accompany me to the Cosmopolitan Hotel. As we were going up the front steps, Emmie came running down.

"You're wasting your time, Harry. Those fools won't tell you anything." She continued on her way, but then called over her shoulder. "I'm missing some money, Harry."

"Are you? I'll keep an eye out for it."

"Yes, do. By the way, I won't be home for dinner."

"But you plan to be there for the entertainments later?"

"Oh, yes."

We went in and I asked to speak to the manager.

"We'd like to look through the registration cards."

"Only the cops are allowed to see those."

"I'm working with Detective Sergeant Tibbitts. If you'd like, I can call him over. But I'll tell you right now, he'll be annoyed."

The Cosmopolitan had once been a fine hotel, but like myriad others in their dotage its attention to propriety had slackened. It was now a place of assignation, with many guests never spending a night. And among the ones that did, more than a few were likely to be known to the police. In short, it couldn't afford to annoy detective sergeants. He took us to the desk and handed us a box of about a hundred registration cards, the oldest being about sixty days.

"I'd like you to look through these and see if you find any other matches to either Twinem or Joy," I told Mahar.

He sat down on a stool and got to work while I spoke with the clerk.

"The woman who left just before we came in, she showed you some photos?"

I handed him a dollar.

"Yeah, a man and a woman."

"Did you recognize them?"

Another dollar.

"No, never saw either."

"The night of the shooting here, didn't you see the woman?"

Another dollar.

"Which shooting?"

"The night of the Tuesday after Labor Day, the 2nd. A fellow named Twinem was shot dead. Did you see his wife?"

"I leave at seven. That was the night man on then."

"Does he stay here?"

"Yeah, he's upstairs. Room 612."

"Here's one," Mahar announced. He handed me the card. It was from Tuesday, July 23rd. Mr. and Mrs. Peaseblossom, of Athens, Georgia.

"This matches Ernie Joy's?"

"No, Twinem's."

"Do you remember a Mr. and Mrs. Peaseblossom?" I asked the clerk.

This was two dollars.

"Who could forget a name like that? Mostly we get Browns. And Smiths. And Joneses."

"Had you seen them before?"

Another two.

"Three or four times, I'd bet. Check the older cards. Afternoon guests."

He gave Mahar another box of cards to look through.

"So the night man wouldn't have seen them?"

"I'd reckon he saw them leaving now and then. They weren't as quick about it as some. She wasn't a working girl."

"So you saw Mrs. Peaseblossom?"

"Oh, yes. I wouldn't forget her."

I showed him Ernie's photo.

"Ever seen him before?"

"Not to remember, but that doesn't mean much."

I went up to 612 to find the night clerk getting dressed. I showed him Ernie's photograph.

"Is this the fellow who checked in the night of the shooting, under the name Twinem?"

"The dead fellow?"

"No, that really was Twinem. You told the police that you recognized Twinem as having checked in."

"I'm sure I recognized him. He'd been here before."

"Perhaps under the name Peaseblossom?"

"Yeah, that's right. Who the hell would call themselves that?"

"Could the fellow in this photo be the man who checked in as Twinem?"

"Impersonating him, you mean?"

"Yes, exactly."

"Could be, I suppose."

"Did you mention to the police you'd seen the dead man before?"

"They didn't ask."

"You didn't think it might be pertinent?"

"How should I know? Listen, if we started telling the cops half of what goes on around here, we'd all be looking for work tomorrow."

"Yes, I can see how your clientele might be sensitive on the subject," I agreed. "How about Mrs. Twinem—had you seen her before that night?"

"No. She came to the desk, maybe a half hour before the shooting. Asked for the room Mr. Twinem was in."

"Was she carrying anything?"

He thought a minute. "Yeah, a bundle. She dropped it right as she came up to the desk."

"Did it look like a stack of papers bundled up?"

"Could have been."

I went downstairs, where Mahar had found several more Peaseblossom cards dating back to the spring.

24

About five I arrived home to find Xiang-Mei busily making more moon cakes. When the thespians arrived, Thibaut headed into the kitchen to prepare dinner, Nell went off for a bath, and Ainslie helped himself to another bottle of our wine.

"How are preparations coming for tonight's rendez-vous?" I asked.

"It's a cinch. All I need from you is $150."

"I can spare twenty."

"Now listen, Harry. You want me to produce a half dozen Chinese girls in the middle of Brooklyn for twenty dollars!"

"Forty."

"These girls are perfect—almond eyes, tiny feet...."

"Fifty. And that's final." I gave it to him.

"All right, but don't blame me if they come up short."

"They should be short."

"They'll *be* short, don't worry."

We had dinner, sans Emmie, and then at about half past seven I went around to Mrs. de Shine's boarding house and asked for Bauman. The matron of the house answered and informed me he'd joined another fellow in a "rube and Hebrew" act at Hyde & Behman's, a vaudeville house back in Brooklyn.

I got to the show just as they were coming offstage. Bauman recognized me and came over.

"Could Ernie have been seeing another woman without you knowing? Recently, I mean."

"He'd been seeing that Twinem dame the last week or so."

"But you never saw her?"

"Sure I did, in New Jersey."

"But never with Ernie?"

"No, just caught the name," he said. "Wait. I did see him talking to a woman, outside the stage door. That might have been her."

"Might have been?"

"I was talking to the doorman, on the inside. They were in the alley. I just caught a glimpse of her as she was leaving. But I'd say it was her all right."

"When was that?"

"During the matinee, that last day."

"Did they part as lovers would?"

"What?"

"I mean, did they embrace, or did one kiss the other?"

"No. No, I guess not."

"Did she look to you like the type of woman Ernie'd go for?"

"No, but I definitely saw her name on a letter that told all."

"When was that?"

"About a week before he was shot. He let me read it and then burned it. He didn't want his girl at the boarding house to see it."

"And it was signed 'Isabel'?"

"'Isabel Twinem.' And how many Isabel Twinems are there?"

Even rarer is the married woman who'd sign a note to her lover with her full name.

I got back to the apartment about ten. An hour later, Emmie arrived.

"Where have you been?" I asked.

"Preparations for tomorrow evening."

"What sort of preparations?"

"Mme. Sahlumie has agreed to conduct a séance."

"Where?"

"She has a new studio in Manhattan. All the Twinems will be there."

"They're going along with this?"

"Oh, yes. I told you old Mrs. Twinem was already a client. All that was necessary was to have Mme. Sahlumie contact her saying she'd heard from her son. Then she explained that the rest of the family would need to be there as well. And Professor Rhodes, whom the late Mr. Twinem requested specifically."

"So, Twinem is going to confront his widow and her lover, Rhodes?"

"Yes. Mme. Sahlumie has a man very adept at playing these roles, but he's taken to his sick bed. I was thinking you could take on the part, Harry."

"Your undying faith in my talents at impersonation is gratifying, Emmie."

At half past eleven, she and I went downstairs to await the rendezvous on the plaza. Jimmy Yuan was already there, standing before a carriage.

"Where are the girls, Harry?"

"Should be here soon. You said midnight."

"My associates are rather anxious."

It was then he realized Emmie was standing beside me.

"It seems the tong mistook my cousin Carlotta for Emmie," I explained.

"I see," he said. "But you're still willing to bargain?"

"Oh, yes. Where is Carlotta?"

He motioned toward a second carriage.

"I don't suppose I still get the five hundred, too?"

"I suggest you not broach the matter."

Just then, a train of three cabs arrived. Ainslie, Thibaut, and Nell hopped out of the first.

"Here they are, Harry. And they're beauts!"

I should probably have guessed his source for young girls would be the Dainty Paree Burlesquers. He'd taped their eyes into almond shapes and dressed them in kimonos. Given the dim lighting, there might have been some chance of pulling the thing off. Provided they'd been anything remotely like dainty. In fact, they had the physique of wrestlers, and any one of them would have outweighed three of the Chinese girls we'd liberated.

Jimmy inspected them and then looked at me quizzically.

"Don't you realize these people are very serious, Harry?" Then he started back to his carriage.

It was still well before midnight. I needed to stall until Tibbitts arrived.

"Wait," I called after him. "I have Xiang-Mei."

Jimmy turned about.

"It better not be another stunt, Harry."

"No, she's the real McCoy."

He looked at me warily for a moment or two, then went over and consulted with the fellow in the carriage.

"Bring her, but you have just five minutes."

Emmie stopped me. "Harry, you can't be thinking of turning over Xiang-Mei. No matter who she is, she clearly doesn't want to be found by these people."

"We don't have a choice, Emmie. Besides, Tibbitts should be here any minute."

I went on my way and she followed. Upstairs, Xiang-

Mei was just taking another pan of moon cakes out of the oven. I explained the situation to her. Instead of acting frightened, she scolded me.

"Silly man. Why *did* you not *tell* me they took Carlotta?"

"I assumed your sympathies were with them."

"Silly man."

She put on a jacket and preceded us downstairs. I pointed out Jimmy Yuan. She approached him and then shouted something in Chinese. Jimmy looked decidedly discomfited. Then the tong boss fellow I'd met the other day came out of the carriage, gave Xiang-Mei a little half bow, and was shouted at in his turn. He gave a command to someone in the second carriage and Carlotta emerged.

"HarRY, thank GOD! I **was** kidNAPPED by **a** TONG!"

"Yes, I heard a rumor to that effect. But you're safe now. Why don't you go on up to the apartment? Emmie will explain everything."

As Emmie and Thibaut led her away, the tong fellow got in his carriage and drove off. Xiang-Mei smiled at me and then went upstairs with Nell.

"What was that all about, Jimmy?"

"Xiang-Mei is the daughter of the very big boss, in Hong Kong. She left home without his permission and he sent out word there would be a big reward for finding her. But that if any harm came to her, well.... Where has she been?"

"Staying with us. When's your show reopen?"

"Never. Not here, at least. I have a better idea. I can create a Chinatown where there isn't one. In Paris, say. Or Berlin."

"That ought to cut down on the competition."

"Yes, exactly. We'll tour Europe, just like Buffalo Bill. Good night, Harry."

Before I could respond, an ugly mutt of a dog bounded up and leapt into Jimmy's arms. It was obvious they wanted to be alone.

I turned to see Ainslie surrounded by six not at all dainty burlesquers and three angry cabbies, all insisting on payment. He shouted to me, but I pretended not to hear. Just then, Tibbitts arrived with a couple other fellows and they were all drawn into the melee.

Upstairs, I found Carlotta collapsed on the couch. Thibaut was very wisely weeping at her feet, while Nell and Emmie attended to the petting and cooing. She seemed to be recovering from her ordeal, and to help things along I mixed her a whiskey sour, her favorite cocktail. Then she and Thibaut had a little exchange in patois.

"Thibaut and I are getting married tomorrow," she announced.

About five minutes later Ainslie staggered in. I handed Carlotta the bottle of Old Harper No. 4 and she once again demonstrated her skill as glassware markswoman. Then she went off for a bath.

Ainslie was out cold. The mob below had given him a pretty adequate beating but Carlotta's handiwork with the bottle drew the most blood. It took a while for even Nell to voice any concern. But eventually she had me drag him off to their room so she could minister to him.

I went back out to find Tibbitts pouring himself a drink. We sat down with Emmie.

"You were late, Sergeant," Emmie told him.

"We were here at ten to. You must've got started

early. Besides, your cousin got home all right. How'd you get them to give her up?"

"It's a long story," I said. "Let's save it for later."

"All right," he agreed. "Hey, what are you two doing in the morning?"

"I had feared we'd be attending Carlotta's funeral, but now it seems it may be her wedding. Why?"

"I'm taking the bull by the horns. Elizabeth still expects me to show up on the boat tomorrow morning."

"But you have other plans."

"No, I'll be there, all right. I'm throwing a little party before the boat sets sail. I've got a couple dozen people coming. It should be fun. See, I told everyone I *ordered* her to go to Europe."

"Very clever," Emmie said. "But certain to elicit a wrathful response."

"Yeah. But not while everyone's there. And I even arranged a cabin-mate for her. The wife of a fellow I work with was heading over next week on a second-class ticket. Bridget. Wait 'til you meet her."

When he finished his drink, he went off to make last-minute arrangements for his affair on the boat. Now that we were alone, I told Emmie what Jimmy had told me about Xiang-Mei.

"I suppose that explains the money."

Xiang-Mei, having overheard us, came out of the kitchen and offered us each a moon cake.

"Does Lou know who you are?" Emmie asked her.

"Lou is a *farm* boy. He wouldn't understand. But *you* won't tell?"

"No, of course not. So you plan to stay with him?"

"Oh, yes. But now *we* can't stay here. *Sorry*, but you need to find a *new* maid."

"That's all right. Where will you go?"

"Buy a *farm*. Special *cricket* farm. Lou has a plan."

"To corner the cricket market?"

"Yes. But *must* be away from New York *now*. My *father* will come looking."

"I know a farm upstate that needs some help."

"*Far* from New York?"

"Hours away. No one would think to look there."

"That's a wonderful idea, Harry. You could help with the girls, too, Xiang-Mei."

"You left the *Chinese* girls at this farm?"

"Yes. We were thinking we could find suitable husbands for them."

"Would have to wait *long* time. Tong would hear about it. But they can *help* on the farm. They are all good *peasant* girls."

When we came into the hall the next morning, Ainslie was on the phone with Nell at his side. He finished his call and hung up.

"It's on for today, at noon," he told her.

"Cliff has arranged for Carlotta and Thibaut to be married this morning. And luncheon afterward," Nell told us.

"Who's footing the bill?"

"We are, Harry. Cliffie insisted. You just need to be at the church at noon."

"Which church?"

"Church of the Transfiguration. On 29th Street, just off Fifth Avenue," Ainslie added. "Then on to Sherry's!"

We had some coffee and a quick bite, then headed off to the car stop.

"Where'd he get the money for that?" I asked Emmie.

"Aunt Nell was wired some yesterday from home."

"She could have used some of it to save him a beating last night."

"I think she has a plan to reform him."

"A plan that incorporates periodic beatings?"

"Yes, I imagine so. But only at the hands of others. Aunt Nell has always stood firmly against any form of violence."

It was half past nine when we found Elizabeth's cabin. Tibbitts was there with a dozen others, and he was uncorking bottles of champagne with a liberality one appreciates in a host. Elizabeth herself was in a corner giving everyone a sort of frozen smile. Beside her sat Bridget, her traveling companion, reading from a brochure that extolled all the exciting attractions the ship had to offer. When she saw us, Elizabeth hopped up and led us into the passageway.

"Was this your doing, Emmie? I don't believe Tibbitts came up with it himself."

"It was Harry who lent him Shakespeare's shrew-taming manual."

"And was it Harry who had me in a harem in Bangkok?"

This obscure reference needs explanation. Earlier that year, Emmie had tried to resurrect a defunct literary journal. And for want of content, she had included a "Letter from Bangkok" purported to have been written by Elizabeth, who had led us to believe she was going to that city. It was a colorful little tale describing Elizabeth's abandonment by the fiancé she'd gone to meet and her subsequent sale into the king's harem. Emmie then distributed the few copies she'd managed to print to former classmates of hers and Elizabeth's.

"That was your own fault," Emmie answered. "I'd have had no need to turn to the magazine if you hadn't foiled the publication of my biography of the countess."

Well, I could stop to explain that reference as well, but it would just lead to another. Suffice it to say, a series of recriminations were exchanged until Tibbitts came around with the champagne. While Emmie led him off, I changed the topic to something that could allow Elizabeth to exhibit her superior knowledge of all things literary.

"Where's the name Peaseblossom come from?" I asked her.

"Are you quizzing me, Harry?"

"Certainly not. It came up in this case. I'm sure it's from something I've read, but can't place it."

"Peaseblossom is one of the fairies in *A Midsummer Night's Dream*."

The ship's whistle sounded and a steward came along ringing a chime. We made to leave with all the rest of the guests so as to give Tibbitts and his colleague a chance to say good-bye to their wives.

"Have a delightful crossing, Elizabeth," Emmie cooed sweetly.

"Thank you, dear Emmie," Elizabeth answered likewise. "And do make sure you read Kitty Graham's next newsletter. Tibbitts told me all about your escapade upstate."

Emmie wanted to find out what she meant, but we barely had time to leave the boat.

"Who's Kitty Graham?" I asked.

"A former classmate. She puts together a letter with all the gossip on everyone and sends it out. She provided an amplification to my rendition of Elizabeth's trip to

Bangkok. I hope she doesn't compromise the location of the girls."

"I doubt there are many members of the tong among Kitty Graham's readers."

"No, I suppose that's true. But she does manage to find some very interesting bits of news."

"I'm going to head back to the apartment before the ceremony, Emmie."

"There isn't time. We need to shop for a present."

"I'll be quick, and you can pick something out. I'll see you at the church at noon."

I rushed home and went into our bedroom, where I located both of the folding frames. I removed the photo I presumed to be of Mrs. Rhodes from behind Mrs. Twinem's and placed it in the empty frame beside Mr. Twinem. Then I put this in my pocket.

A minute later, Carlotta emerged in a gown Ainslie had arranged for from a prop man. Unfortunately, that's exactly what it looked like. Thibaut looked even sillier in a top hat and tails. But then Thibaut looked pretty silly however he dressed.

Ainslie had hired a carriage, and during the ride over the bridge, I showed the photo of Mrs. Rhodes to Carlotta.

"That's HER!" she exclaimed, as only she could. "That's the **swell** I was TELLING you **about**. The one ERnie WAS with **just** a WEEK before **he** was SHOT."

We arrived at the church just a little before the hour. Emmie was there waiting. All six of us went up to the altar and the whole thing lasted about ten minutes. There was no organist, so it was a quiet ceremony. At least until Carlotta's "I DO!" sent a pair of twins waiting to be baptized into hysterics.

25

Like a lot of men, Ainslie could be very generous when he was spending his wife's money. We had a sumptuous, five-course luncheon at Sherry's. Then the four artistes hurried off to the Theatre Unique for their matinee.

"I need to go back to Mme. Sahlumie's, Harry," Emmie told me. "And I won't be home for dinner. There's much to be done before tonight."

"What time's the show?"

"Eight, but you need to arrive by half past seven to get into position. Also, we need a second man, to act as Mme. Sahlumie's assistant. Do you think you could convince Ainslie to come along?"

"I think I might be able to do that."

"Good."

She wrote down an address on West 43rd Street, and then hurried off.

I took the 6th Avenue L down to the Cosmopolitan and found the day clerk I'd spoken with the day before. I showed him the frame with the photos of Twinem and Mrs. Rhodes.

"Know them?" I asked.

"Maybe...."

Five dollars.

"That's them."

"Which them?"

"Peaseblossom, and the woman he said was his wife."

"Is the night man up in his room?"

"Yeah, he's up there, sleeping. But don't knock, it'll never wake him up. Just go right in."

I could think of only one reason he'd give me such specific instructions, especially when they came accompanied by a playful expression. I knocked, heard voices inside, then knocked again. A second later, a chambermaid rushed out of the room. I went in and found the fellow washing his face.

"It's only you? You put the fear of God in that girl, and it took me two weeks to get her in here."

"My apologies."

"That's not enough, is it?"

"Well, I could talk to the manager...."

"Him? He wouldn't dare. I know all about his night rounds."

"This is a busy place. Keeping the hinges oiled must be a full-time job."

"What do you want, anyway?"

I showed him Mrs. Rhodes' photo alone first.

"Know her?"

"There you go—that's Mrs. Peaseblossom."

"And Mr. Peaseblossom?" I brought out the other photo.

"Yeah. But the cops said he was Twinem."

"He *was* Twinem. But was he the one who checked in that night as Twinem?"

"I told you, I can't be sure. Looked the same when they showed me the corpse in his room."

"But when he came to the desk that evening, and signed in as Twinem, did you recognize him as Peaseblossom?"

"No, I guess I didn't."

I left him and then went up to Washington Square, where I found Professor Rhodes leaving his office.

"I suppose you've heard of the séance Twinem's mother is putting on this evening?"

"Yes. It's silly, but I suppose there's no harm in humoring an old woman."

"Well, I'm glad that's your attitude. You see, I've been cast as Twinem's voice."

"Is this a regular part of your business?"

"No, this is a novelty. My wife's idea. The problem is, I never met the fellow. What sort of voice did he have?"

"Deep, kind of gravelly."

I gave it a try.

"No, that's not it at all."

"Well, I suppose I can plead the effects of decomposition," I said. "Will Mrs. Rhodes be attending as well?"

"Yes, she's rather keen on it. Why do you ask?"

"Just want to make sure the seating works out correctly. By the way, did you happen to see the production of a *Midsummer Night's Dream* at Manhattan Beach this summer?"

"Yes, a very adequate production."

"The ass's mask appropriately shaggy?"

"Well, not shaggy enough, but closer than most."

When I got home, I found Xiang-Mei making yet another batch of moon cakes. There were now stacks of them covering every inch of space in the kitchen.

"Tonight is the *big* festival," she told me. "You must *come*."

"Where is it?"

"At the farm, *on* the bay. Lou's farm."

"We have an engagement at eight."

"Come *later*, it will be a very *big* party."

Just then the parrot squawked something in Chinese.

"I thought you exiled him," I said.

"He was just *too* hungry. You never feed him *enough*."

"What's he saying?"

"Chinese girls *very* beautiful. So Lou remembers."

A while later the vaudevillians returned from their matinee. Carlotta had regained her place in the act, with Nell moved to a supporting role as her mother. When the others wandered off to their rooms, Ainslie opened our last bottle of wine.

"The act's better than ever," he told me.

"Do you think it can spare you tonight? There's a little performance I need you for."

"Sorry, I have to be there to keep the whole thing paced."

"I was rather depending on you."

"That was foolish. Even my mother never made that mistake."

After he'd had a good laugh at his joke, I told him I knew he'd pawned some of Nell's things.

"How would you know if I had?"

"Doesn't matter, really. But I'd hate to have to embarrass you."

"God, you're a low bastard," he said. "All right, what do I have to do?"

"It's simple, really. You play Ernie at a séance. Do you think you could do his voice convincingly?"

"Sure. And a reasonable likeness."

"This will just involve the voice. Maybe some rapping and whatnot."

"Who's paying?"

"Twinem's mother is putting on the show, but you'll have to be satisfied with identifying those responsible for Ernie's death."

"Who's that?"

"You'll need to wait and see."

Not liking my answer, he sulked off to his room with my bottle of wine under his arm. I went to the phone and called Tibbitts's office.

"What'd you think of my little party?"

"I'd say your shrew isn't entirely tamed just yet."

"Yeah, it's slow work."

"Seems like poor Bridget will be bearing the brunt of it. Six days in a tiny cabin with an annoyed Elizabeth. That's a tough sentence. I'd lay odds she's either done in or jumps overboard before the ship reaches Cherbourg."

"Oh, I wouldn't worry about Bridget. From what I've heard about her, she'll hold her own. That fellow with the black eye was her husband."

"Did Emmie invite you to tonight's entertainment?"

"Yeah, said I'd be able to make an arrest. She's still thinking Rhodes and Twinem's wife, isn't she?"

"Yes, I think so."

"She's wrong there. I've checked on them both."

"Still, you might want to be ready for an arrest."

"Yeah? Care to add a name?"

"I can give you one. Ever hear of Mike Scanlan? He used to work for the Byrnes Agency."

"No. You think he shot Twinem?"

"No, but odds are he knows who did." I gave Tibbitts Scanlan's address on West 34th Street. "Can you have him brought around to the show tonight?"

"Sure. But I have to have a reason."

252

"You'll have plenty on him when it's over. Accessory after the fact, extortion, etc."

"So you have it all figured out?"

"Well, there's a healthy amount of conjecture involved. But Scanlan should help clear that up. Just keep him out of sight until we're ready for him."

He agreed to and we hung up. Ainslie and I left the apartment just before seven and took a car to Park Row. I handed him a little script of just a few lines.

"Think you can memorize these?"

"Sure, that's my job. Just to satisfy my curiosity, how'd you know about Nell's bracelet?"

"Just a guess. Seemed a safe one."

"Elwell had given it to her. It was inscribed."

"He was her husband for twenty-odd years."

"And someone else's at the same time. It made me sick that she kept it. I thought I'd free her from the memory."

"Very selfless. Of course, there's that other reminder of her marriage to Elwell, married and living in Buffalo."

"Oh, I don't mind the boy. Sounds like a good kid. You've met him, haven't you?"

"Yes. Nice fellow."

"Nell told me he married the daughter of his father's killer. So he can't have been too attached to him."

"No. But to be fair, he didn't marry her *because* she was the daughter of his father's killer."

He laughed. It seemed odd that he hadn't figured out he was Charlie's father. Or that Nell hadn't told him. But it certainly wasn't my place to reveal the family secret.

We arrived at Mme. Sahlumie's about twenty to eight. While Emmie was admonishing me for being late,

Madame herself appeared. She was quite a sight, all done up in flowing robes. And a ruby the size of a goose egg attached to her turban.

"How do you do?" she said in a kind of indistinguishable European accent.

We replied in kind. Then she smiled, and from then until the arrival of the guests, she lapsed into the voice of a Hoboken dockhand.

"Who's playing the corpse?" she asked.

I nodded toward Ainslie. When Emmie objected, I pointed out he had more experience.

Madame showed him the chamber where he was to perform, a little closet with two chairs. Coming out of the ceiling was a speaking tube of the sort you see on ships.

"You talk into that, and it comes out there."

She pointed to the chandelier and told Ainslie to try it.

"I am the voice of Ernie Joy, coming from the great beyond." Then he added a sinister laugh.

"A little too much, dearie," Madame informed him. "Say as little as possible."

"And you aren't Ernie Joy, you're Cyrus Twinem," Emmie added. "You just say what I tell you to. I'll be right next to you."

Mme. Sahlumie took me aside to explain my duties and give me my lines. Then she had me help her rig up some pyrotechnic displays and, for five dollars, allowed me to rig up one of my own.

I asked Ainslie to come over and assist me in assembling my costume.

"Which is it?" he asked. "Am I Twinem or Ernie?"

"Go ahead and play along with Emmie to begin with,

but when you hear me bang that gong over there, deliver the lines I gave you as Ernie."

Just as I finished positioning my turban, Tibbitts arrived.

"Scanlan's just down the hall," he told me.

"Good. Have him sent in, alone, when the gong strikes twice."

"Are you serious?"

"I'm trying to keep with the spirit of the affair."

He gave his men the instructions and then sat down. A moment later there was a knock on the door. Emmie and Ainslie got into the chamber and I greeted the Twinems: old Mrs., the mother; the brother; and the widow.

"L'chaim." I gave each of them a little bow. "Please take your seats. Madame Salami will join us shortly."

Then Professor Rhodes and his wife came in. The photograph of Lena didn't do her justice.

Once everyone was seated, I dimmed the lights. There was a flash and a poof of smoke at the end of the table. When it cleared, Mme. Sahlumie was in position.

"We must join hands." Her words dripped with solemnity.

Then she went into a trance, chanting, "Katmandu and Kalamazoo..., Timbuktu..., Tippecanoe and Tyler, too! Spirits, arise!"

There was another flash and poof of smoke, this time in the middle of the table. Then the groaning started—the dead man's tormented soul, no doubt. "Mother..., Mother, are you there?"

"I'm here, Cyrus! I'm here!"

"Has my death yet been avenged? Have my killers been brought to justice?"

"No, my son. Who was it? Who shot you, Cyrus?"

"My own wife, mother! It was she who shot me! But she did not act alone."

The dead man's widow broke the circle. "I won't stand for this nonsense. Mother, you can't believe this. The woman is a charlatan."

"Let's hear it through, just for laughs," Tibbitts suggested. He pushed her back in her chair. "Okay, spirit, who else was in on it?"

I decided it was time to bang the gong.

"This is the spirit of Ernie Joy...."

"Who are you?" the old woman asked. "Get my son back on the line, this instant!"

Emmie's muffled voice could now be heard coming through the pipe, "*What are you doing?*"

"I am Ernie Joy, and I've come to accuse those responsible for my death. Two women...."

"*You're Cyrus Twinem!*" Emmie was becoming heated.

"No, really I'm not...." Ainslie's voice had temporarily lost its ethereal timbre. But then he got it back. "I'm accusing two women. Mrs. Twinem did shoot her husband, and tried to lay the blame on me. But it was the other harpy who drew me into it first. And she sits in this very room.... *Ouch! Cut that out, Emmie.*"

"Okay, who is it?" Tibbitts insisted.

"Mrs. Rhodes! She and her lover, Cyrus Twinem, wanted to use me in their scheme to kill Mrs. Twinem.... *Jeez, Emmie. I'm bleeding.*"

The door of the closet flew open and Emmie and Ainslie rolled out, locked in some sort of wrestling hold. She seemed to be trying to separate his head from his neck. I went over and helped Ainslie to extricate himself.

"You're behind this, Harry," Emmie seethed. "You've ruined everything."

Now Mrs. Rhodes had risen. "Take me home, Earl."

"Not so fast." Tibbitts was blocking the door. "All right, Reese. The show's over. Now tell us what you know."

"Well, to begin with, Cyrus Twinem was having an affair with Mrs. Rhodes, the young wife of his esteemed colleague. They met at the Cosmopolitan Hotel a dozen or so times over the last year. Using the name Peaseblossom."

"Peaseblossom?" Tibbitts asked.

"Yes, it was a sort of joke. It's the name of a fairy in *A Midsummer Night's Dream*. A play Mrs. Rhodes' husband is obsessed with. The desk clerks at the Cosmopolitan identified photos of her and Twinem as the couple known to them as Mr. and Mrs. Peaseblossom.

"At some point, they decided to do away with Mrs. Twinem. Perhaps she wouldn't agree to a divorce. Or her husband feared being left without her fortune if she did. But if she were to die, he'd have his cake and could eat it too.

"While visiting her father-in-law, Lena Rhodes took a commemorative gun of his, probably not realizing it had been inscribed. She gave this to Twinem. Then they set up an elaborate scheme to make it look as if *Mrs.* Twinem is carrying on an affair. And that when her husband catches wind of it, he follows her to the Cosmopolitan, surprising her in bed with her lover. A gun is produced by the lover, there's a struggle, and Mrs. Twinem would lie dead.

"But they needed a dupe, someone to play the lover. That's where Ernie Joy came in. Somehow he and Mrs.

Rhodes became acquainted. He'd played Puck in a production of *A Midsummer Night's Dream* she and her husband attended this summer. It was possibly there that she first noticed him.

"Ernie fell easily for an attractive woman, and she no doubt found it a simple matter to string him along. They were seen out together by at least one witness. But she told Ernie her name was Isabel Twinem.

"This is where something went wrong. The real Mrs. Twinem had become suspicious of her husband's frequent trips to New York. She hired private detectives who confirmed he did meet a woman in New York. Then she somehow learned the details of the plan he'd hatched with Mrs. Rhodes. To find out how exactly, we need to make another call on the spirit world...."

I banged the gong twice, and just as the door began to open set off another flash. Mike Scanlan emerged from the smoky haze.

26

Or, more accurately, stumbled from the smoky haze. The flash had gone off just in front of him and it was some time before he regained his sight. During the interim, he serenaded the company with a succession of oaths catalogued during what must have been a colorful life. When at long last he exhausted his repertoire, I suggested he sit down.

"We were just considering the question of how Mrs. Twinem learned of her husband's plan for her, Mike."

He took out a handkerchief, dunked it in a carafe of water, and gave his face a thorough cleaning.

"I don't know what you're talking about."

"You don't? And yet you followed Ernie Joy to Park Row the night Twinem was killed."

He shrugged, then smirked at me.

"You're not taking a murder charge very seriously, Mike."

"Murder? You're just fishing."

He was right, of course. But I did get a nibble from Mrs. Twinem.

"It's true!" she shouted. "He shot Cyrus. Then he blackmailed me into keeping it a secret."

By now, Emmie had her notebook out and was taking everything down.

"If he shot your husband, what did he have to blackmail you with?" Tibbitts asked.

"He threatened to expose Cyrus's infidelity. It's all true about the Rhodes woman and him. It would have

ruined Cyrus's chances of getting his manuscript published. And that meant so much to him."

The story was ridiculous, and the delivery lacked
anything approaching sincerity. Still, you did have to
admire her for thinking on her feet. Even if all it achieved
was to set Scanlan on his own hind legs.

"Why, you scheming little...." Tibbitts pushed him
back down in his seat and he adopted a more cooperative
attitude. "I was following her husband—what she hired
us to do. I found out all about the Rhodes woman and
filed my report. That was supposed to be the end of it."

"But you had found out something more?" I asked.

"To identify the woman, I had to follow her. So one
afternoon, after she left Twinem, I trailed her over to
another little rendezvous. This time with that vaudeville
clown, Ernie Joy. And she seems just as cozy with him.
Then I find out she's married to this college professor...."

"And you smelled money?"

He shrugged. "I lost my job a few days later. I figured I'd learn what I could and offer my services."

"You'd refrain from telling her husband about her
infidelities for a fee?"

"Something like that," he said. "But then I found out
things went a lot deeper. I was looking for something in
writing, something she couldn't deny. I got hold of a note
she'd left for Twinem at his hotel. It was sort of vague,
but I guessed what they had in mind."

"To do away with his wife?"

"Yeah. But there was more to it than that. The
Rhodes woman had told Ernie Joy *she* was Isabel
Twinem."

"And that put you in a quandary. If you turn them in
to the police for conspiracy to murder, there's no chance

for blackmail. So why didn't you just blackmail the two of them to keep quiet about their plot?"

"I thought about it. But I found out Twinem didn't have much of his own—it was all in a trust in his wife's name."

"So you went after the big money and approached Mrs. Twinem?"

"Yeah. I told her I had something much more interesting on her husband. And that I had enough evidence she could take it to the cops. She liked that a lot."

"How much did she pay you?"

"Plenty. But it was nothing to her."

"So you gave her the note you'd intercepted?"

"Yeah. She said she'd take care of it and I was to forget all about it."

"But you didn't forget about it."

"She didn't do anything with it. Not that I saw, anyways. So I started to wonder what she was up to."

"Where was she staying then?"

"At her mother's, in New Jersey. But she was coming into town every day. Then, on the last Saturday in August, she joins her husband at the Victoria Hotel. I followed her around, but didn't see anything of interest until the next Tuesday afternoon, the day after Labor Day. She went around to Proctor's, on 23rd Street, and waited at the stage door. When Ernie Joy came out, I heard her tell him she was a friend of Isabel's."

"But *she* was Isabel Twinem."

"Yeah, but the Rhodes woman had told him that was her name."

"What else did Mrs. Twinem tell him?"

"There'd been a change of plans. He should register at the Cosmopolitan that evening, just before his show, as

Cyrus Twinem and wife. He thought that was a queer idea, but she told him there was a reason for it. Then they walked off too far for me to hear."

"But you heard enough to think it worthwhile to keep an eye out at the Cosmopolitan Hotel that evening?"

"Sure. I found a comfortable place to watch the front and camped out. About ten of eight, Ernie Joy shows up. He goes in and ten minutes later comes out."

"That's when he took the room as Twinem."

"Sure. Then a little before nine, Twinem shows up."

"Did he have anything with him? Something like a bundle of papers?"

"Not that I saw. But she did."

"She?"

"His wife. She came about 9:45."

"Was she carrying anything besides the bundle?"

"Not that I saw."

"Then Ernie came back to the Cosmopolitan. When was that?"

"Ten. I didn't recognize him at first—he was wearing some ridiculous outfit."

"A red and yellow plaid jacket. He left the theatre after his act without changing."

"That's right. He went in and two minutes later I hear the shot. Thirty seconds after that, he's running out from the alley."

"He'd come down the fire escape. And you followed?"

"Sure. He was in on it somehow."

"Why'd you give up the chase?"

"I knew who he was, and where to find him."

"And turning him in to the cops would have eliminated any chance of blackmailing him?"

He shrugged again.

"So you didn't know exactly what went on that night upstairs in the Cosmopolitan?"

"I knew enough to know she'd arranged for her husband to be shot. And probably pulled the trigger."

"But it's all circumstantial. You couldn't prove it."

"I could prove enough to make it unpleasant for her. I wasn't trying to get her hanged for it."

"I suppose the only one who could have told us more was Ernie Joy."

"I can tell you more," Mrs. Rhodes said quietly. "I thought the police would have enough sense to accuse her, but evidently they're too incompetent."

"Let's say preoccupied," I said. "You admit you and Twinem plotted to kill his wife?"

"Yes, there's no use lying about that now. I left an anonymous note for his wife, saying her husband would be meeting a woman that evening, and that she should go to the Cosmopolitan Hotel and ask for Mustardseed. Meanwhile, Ernie Joy was supposed to check into the Cosmopolitan under that name, and then bring the key to the Victoria and leave it in the name of Mrs. Twinem."

"But Ernie thought he was meeting you?"

"Yes, but he knew me as Isabel Twinem. Cy would then ask at the desk of the Victoria for messages at 8:30 and take the one for his wife, the one with the key in it."

"How was the shooting to have taken place?"

"Once his wife arrived, Cy would hold her in the room under some pretext, or at gunpoint, if necessary."

"Then Ernie Joy would show up, thinking he was meeting you. Was it part of the plan that he be dressed in his outfit from the act?"

"Yes, I'd sat through one of his performances and

saw it. I told him we'd be pressed for time, that he should come without changing."

"He wasn't suspicious of that?"

"Not suspicious. I believe he thought it was some sort of fetish of mine."

"But it was to make him more conspicuous?"

"Yes."

"When Ernie arrived, Twinem would let him into the room and shoot his wife?"

"Yes. Of course Ernie would run off, like a scared rabbit. Then when the police arrived, Cy would tell them he'd surprised his wife with another man. The man pulled a gun and in the struggle she was shot. Then the man ran off...."

"And since he was wearing such a colorful outfit, there'd likely be witnesses who saw him running off."

"Yes. We didn't intend for anything to happen to him. Honestly."

"I'm sure. So you had it all worked out. But somehow Mrs. Twinem got wind of it. By intercepting another note?"

"No. After that first one was lost, we never put anything in writing. She must have listened to a conversation we had out on a ferry."

"So then she met with Ernie, telling him she had a message from you. That he was to register as Twinem, not Mustardseed. She also must have given him a sample of Cyrus Twinem's signature so he could imitate it. That would fit in with her story that she and her husband were at the Cosmopolitan simply to meet a man about his manuscript."

"Apparently. And she knew Cy had the gun hidden somewhere. She must have gotten to it first."

"Was it your plan to get Ernie to take the gun?"

"It never occurred to us he'd be that much of a fool. Cy was simply to say he dropped it on leaving."

"That's where Isabel Twinem made her big mistake," I said.

"What mistake?" the woman herself asked.

"To make your own use of the plan formulated by your husband and his lover, you only needed to change three things. First, have Ernie register at the Cosmopolitan as Twinem and wife. That was a simple matter of telling him it was the wish of the woman he hoped to bed. Second, make it appear that your husband was a party to the trip to the Cosmopolitan. That you did by getting his manuscript from the safe at the Victoria. Then you made sure the clerk there saw you leaving with it, and the clerk at the Cosmopolitan saw it when you arrived. And third, you needed to gain control of the gun. I imagine that was the most difficult."

"Not so very. When I entered, I could see he was holding the gun in the pocket of his jacket. He told me to sit down, but I showed him what he thought was his precious manuscript. He reached for it, but I tossed it onto the fire escape. I knew he would go after it. As he was climbing out the window, I grabbed the gun from his pocket. He turned around and I shot him."

"But it wasn't the manuscript you had?"

"No, just blank pages tied up in the same ribbon. After I'd shot him I flung it out into the alley. But what was the mistake you spoke of?"

"After the shooting, you thought it a clever idea to plant the gun on Joy."

"I slipped it into his pocket without him even noticing. He was in such a panic. 'Run!' I told him, and he ran."

"Yes, but it would have been better for you if he'd been left out of the story. It was your linking him to it, and then the Chinese fellow who shot him, that made it obvious you were lying. If Ernie hadn't had the gun, he never would have been shot. And it's unlikely he would ever have mentioned what had happened at the Cosmopolitan that night. Mike was right. You were all too clever by half."

Tibbitts called out to his men in the hall. Two fellows came in and gathered up Scanlan, Mrs. Rhodes, and Mrs. Twinem. Then he walked over and seized Emmie's notebook.

"What are you doing!" she protested.

"Thanks. I forgot mine," he told her.

She insisted I stop him, and not having finished Molly's narrative, I would have been happy to do so. But he left with his prisoners before I had a chance.

"What a show!" Mme. Salami pronounced. "D'you think you could do that on a regular basis?"

"Absolutely!" Ainslie assured her. "I can have the thing cast by tomorrow afternoon."

While they discussed logistics, I led Emmie toward the 34th Street ferry terminal.

"Where are we going?"

"We've been invited to a Chinese festival out at Bowery Bay."

"That's what all Xiang-Mei's baking was for?"

"Yes. Apparently moon cakes are an essential part of the holiday," I told her. "Sorry about turning in your classmate, Emmie."

"Lena? Oh, I despised her. She was the worst sort of snob. Remember I showed you that page devoted to the Ancient Order of Hibernians in my yearbook?"

"The parody, where the girls gave themselves comical Irish names."

"She was part of that crowd. And it was no parody, with those requisite caricatures of inbred Irishmen. It was just another assertion of superiority." Then her mood lightened. "Will they send her to Sing-Sing? I hope so."

"Unlikely, I'm afraid. But maybe a few rough months on Blackwell's Island."

"Well, I suppose that will have to do," she said. "But I feel bad about Mrs. Twinem."

"Emmie, she *shot* her husband."

"Not without good cause. If she were given a true jury of her peers—twelve women—she'd never be convicted."

Then she pulled a wallet out of her bag.

"Whose is that?"

"Ainslie's. I took it from him while we were in the closet together."

"Things must have gotten intimate."

"That was your doing," she reminded me. "Look, he had seventy dollars." She deftly slipped it into her own wallet. "And a pawn ticket."

"That will be for Aunt Nell's bracelet."

"He pawned her bracelet?"

"Yes, to free her from the memory of the husband who'd given it to her."

"What a snake."

"Reptilian, certainly. And not as bright as I might have thought."

"Why do you say that?"

"He seems unaware that Charlie is his son. Do you think Nell will tell him?"

"Oh, yes. In time."

It was past eleven when we got to Bowery Bay. There was a full moon, and out on the bay colored lanterns hanging from moored boats reflected across the water.

Lou was doing a brisk business in crickets, the ladies netting him five dollars each. And the farmers had tables of food laid out, most prominently the moon cakes prepared by Xiang-Mei—the only Chinese woman present.

About midnight the fireworks started. The show went on for a good hour or two. Then Bowery Bay reverted to its usual nocturnal tranquility.

27

We rose pretty late the next morning and were greeted first thing by the parrot, which now had the capacity to vex in three languages.

A little later Xiang-Mei emerged from the kitchen bearing warmed-over dumplings and unsold moon cakes.

"Crickets more *liked* than my cakes!" she announced with mock chagrin.

Then Nell and Ainslie appeared, followed soon after by the happy couple, whose patois had degenerated into a cloyingly precious amalgam of patter and petting.

"*Mon **petit** chouCHOU*," Carlotta squealed as she nestled Thibaut in between her "tétons."

"*Ma féesante!*" he mumbled back.

"Does it have to go on while we're eating?" Ainslie asked.

Nell, though looking a little nauseated herself, shushed him.

Then the parrot chimed in, "*Ne mords pas si fort, Har-ree!*"

"Oh! *Silly* bird! You *forget* your Chinese!"

There was a good bit more of the same, but the taste I've given you should provide sufficient explanation for why we so readily abandoned our guests. I handed Emmie her jacket and we discreetly made our way out of the apartment. Outside, we encountered Mrs. Harwood, one of our neighbors. She was pacing back and forth in front of the building trying to soothe her baby.

"I don't understand," she told us. "All of a sudden

she's become troublesome. Doctor says it's too early for teething."

"Did it begin about a fortnight ago?" Emmie asked.

"Yes, and all at once."

"I suspect it's ephemeral and will have run its course by next week."

"Oh, I hope you're right."

It was a cool, overcast day, so we hopped on a car to Coney Island and took a quiet walk along the shore.

Emmie was being uncharacteristically introspective.

"Well, you got just what you wanted, Emmie. A real murder."

"Yes, but I was sure I had solved it as well. Of course, it was hardly fair. You keeping Mike Scanlan a secret until the very end like that."

"Whereas you tell me everything?"

"Everything you need to know, certainly."

"Well, cheer up. If it hadn't been for your setting the whole thing up, three happy couples would never have gotten together. Carlotta would never have met Thibaut, Lou would never have been thrown into Xiang-Mei's clutches, and Aunt Nell would never have been reunited with Ainslie."

"Yes, but it's hardly the same, is it? I mean it's just not nearly as exhilarating as solving a murder."

"Well, if they follow the course of most marriages, there's a good chance one of the three will end in a homicide."

"What a horrible thing to say, Harry."

"I'm offering nine to two it's Ainslie who's first to go."

"I'd buy the bullet if it wouldn't upset Aunt Nell so. She's very attached to him. But your arithmetic is off."

"How so?"

"I deserve credit for bringing Elizabeth and Tibbitts together, as well. If I hadn't engineered your job in Washington, they never would have encountered each other there and become reacquainted."

"Are you sure that should be credited as a success? Their marriage seems to be in a precarious state. She may not have gone to Bangkok, but she is on her way to Europe."

"Oh, she'll be back," Emmie assured me.

"You think Tibbitts has mastered the art of taming her?"

"That's not very likely. But I think Elizabeth derives some satisfaction from an adversarial relationship."

"Even when she doesn't always come out on top?"

"Especially then."

Kitty Graham's next alumnae letter alluded to Mrs. Rhodes' predicament:

> *Lena (Spire) Rhodes ('99) will be spending the autumn season on a nearby island resort, recuperating from a recent encounter with the Molly Maguires. Erin go bragh.*

It also contained the piece on Emmie and me that Elizabeth had mentioned:

> *Emmie (McGinnis) Reese ('99) and her husband, Harrison, have taken it upon themselves to resurrect the old Brooklyn branch of the Oneida Community and are looking for converts. They assure us that their sect will remain true to the guiding principles on which the orig-*

inal community was founded. Ergo, applicants need be of a forthcoming disposition and possess an appropriate appetite for the good work to be done. Semper Libidinosae.

That elicited a good deal of correspondence from Emmie's fellow alumnae, their spouses, their friends and relatives, and even their servants. Most of them were merely playing it for fun, but more than a few were in earnest. Including a comely parlor maid who helpfully included a photo. I still have it tucked away.

The next week, Carlotta and Thibaut left us for the road, and in the months to come their act became a staple of the second-tier vaudeville houses. With her baby's colic having cleared up just as Emmie had predicted, Mrs. Harwood began regularly consulting her for pediatric advice.

Meanwhile, Ainslie and Aunt Nell began touring with Mme. Sahlumie, scalping rich mothers and widows. It seemed out of character for Nell, but perhaps it was her life in Buffalo that had never fit right.

Xiang-Mei sent us regular briefings from the farm, where the Corinthians and Chinese lived in harmony for some time. Then, gradually, the girls married, and the old folks went to their maker, leaving her and Lou alone with their growing broods of children and crickets.

Emmie's interest in murder seemed to wane in the months that followed. She now devoted almost all her time to literary pursuits. But not until that summer did she share the fruit of her efforts with me. It would be unfair for me to reveal more about that here, but rest assured, the tit for tat with Elizabeth is still running hot.